FLAUNT

(F-WORD #1)

E. DAVIES

Publisher's Note: This is a work of fiction. Names, characters, places, and incidents are a product of the author's imagination. Locales and public names are sometimes used for atmospheric purposes. Any resemblance to actual people, living or dead, or to businesses, companies, events, institutions, or locales is completely coincidental.

Flaunt / E. Davies. – 2nd ed.
ISBN: 978-1-912245-19-2

FLAUNT

1

NIC

"Don't be such a fucking man about this."

Nic bumped his head against the window as he stared at the red light. Then, he craned his neck to look at his surroundings.

Nope. Still no clue.

He'd left the office ten minutes early to make sure he had time to find Grace Road. And now here he was, stranded in some little suburb of L.A., still clueless.

Nic swore under his breath when he glanced at his dashboard clock. From what he remembered his boss telling him, he was just a couple minutes away now. Yet he'd circled this block twice and couldn't figure out where the damn intersection was supposed to be.

He really should have paid more attention to writing down directions. Felt a bit like his life at the moment.

It wasn't like they were hidden away in an industrial park. The turnoff should be obvious. He'd spotted several other charities, a union office, and two coffee shops. Nic had made a mental note of them both as promising spots to work if he needed a spot out of the charity's office but close by. Assuming he ever found the office.

They also weren't on the main stretch, from his quick Google Maps search earlier. Another thrill of nervous anticipation went through him at the thought about why they didn't want to be front and center in this suburb.

He was on assignment with his company, Synergy, to work with an HIV charity. Not just any charity—one dedicated to gay men's health. Nic drew a deep breath and let it out rather than think about that conversation with his new boss.

He'd finally come out and told Greg that he'd do the job if it would make people at their new client more comfortable to have another gay man around. He'd hinted at it in the hiring interview, so he'd already known Greg was fine with it.

Then there was the other thing—the one nobody knew, and he liked it that way. Nic had only been read as male without fail for the last couple of years. He still had visceral memories of walking into gay bars and having men give him quizzical stares, or worse, having lesbians hit on him.

Now and then, he still had a moment where he felt like an impostor among gay men. He imagined they might, at any moment, see through him to something else entirely—a part of him that never existed.

"Fucking thank you," Nic breathed out when he spotted a gas station, giving him a place to pull off.

He parked around the side and squinted at his notes.

Turn to Grace Road.

Then there was a splotchy bit, washed out by the minor incident with his morning coffee and a curb. And then... what the fuck did that say? It was a good thing his job involved much more typing than handwriting. He couldn't even read it himself.

His phone GPS told him where the turnoff to Grace Road was, but not the charity. He hadn't thought to sign into Google Maps and save the damn place—and his phone was doing that *thing* where it couldn't figure out where he was.

All the anxious thoughts racing around his head made his chest tighten until he took a deep breath and released it.

Fuck this shit. I'm going to be an adult about it.

Nic slammed the car door and strode inside, swallowing his pride. Avoiding interaction with people wasn't worth being late to his first day with a new client, earning Greg's disappointment.

"Excuse me," he said as he approached the counter, jerking his chin up in a friendly nod at the attendant. "I'm a little lost."

"You're not the only one. You hit the 4G black hole around here?" The guy was young, reddened pock marks dotting his cheeks, and his hair was pulled back in a... man-bun, did they call them? Had to be in his early twenties.

He eyed Nic up and down, and not in a friendly way— maybe taking in his business clothes. He looked slightly more friendly when he looked up again. No wonder. Gas stations were dangerous places to work.

"Yeah, man. My phone just won't help," Nic shrugged. "I'm looking for Plus."

The attendant squinted and leaned on the counter. "The what?"

"The..." Nic tried not to let his cheeks redden. Nothing to be ashamed of. "Gay men's HIV foundation. The charity nearby."

"You want to find that, you wanna be down south of State." The attendant smirked at him, turning to his register. He reached out for something and Nic flinched, tensing up instinctively and checking the exit.

3

The guy was only grabbing his water bottle. He crinkled it obnoxiously, popping his lips and chugging a few sips.

Fucking relax, Nic told himself, squaring his shoulders again. "South of—?"

"That's where the street kids curb-crawl. You'll get it fast enough there. I hear they give them free shit so they don't get the rest of us normals sick."

Nic's jaw dropped. *Did he just...?*

The attendant leaned on the counter and quirked a brow, his face and eyes hard. He didn't look away from Nic. Nic had been hanging out with mostly guys long enough to know instinctively what that meant.

He wasn't going to punch out some idiot behind a register for being ignorant. He had to remind himself of that fact a few times before it sank in, though.

"I'll take that as a no," Nic muttered and stepped for the door. His attention was still sideways, keeping the other guy safely in his peripheral vision until he shouldered through the door, out of the gas station.

His hand shook on the car door handle, but he gripped it tight and almost flung it open.

As he dropped into the seat, he shook his head and yanked his phone out of his pocket again. He opened the GPS with a glare. "You better be fucking ready to help now."

There it was—the blue dot showing him squarely at this gas station. He pressed the directions button, filled in Plus in the "to" box, and held his breath.

"Please drive to highlighted route."

Finally. Nic buckled up, pulled out of the lot, and spared one more glare at the gas station in his rearview mirror.

He was back on track, however hard the world tried to keep him in the woods.

2

KYLE

"I got a feeling..." Kyle shimmied in his seat, one hand on top of his steering wheel. He leaned forward to flip over his parking permit and pull into his spot all at once. "Hm-hm-hmm, da-da-da, do-do-do."

The lot was small, tucked around the side of his charity's building. He kept clicking his tongue along with the music as he craned his neck to make sure he didn't ding Denver's car. It wasn't like Denver drove a Beemer—he wouldn't be pissed off, but Kyle wasn't sure his own car would survive the impact.

Once he was sure he left enough room for visitor parking, he shut off the car and shimmied once more.

Kyle was in a damn good mood. This morning's work had been rewarding. Although most of his work was, it was easy to forget that fact in the face of the more annoying aspects of his job.

Working for a charity had its benefits: getting hit on by the cute university guys, which always left Kyle flustered. Apparently he looked like one still, probably from his trademark green hair dye and unconventional clothing choices.

It helped him connect with kids who wouldn't talk to an older guy or a woman—especially MSM, the board's favorite term for men who had sex with men. That was their focus and their mandate, but educating the student body as a whole paid off.

The charity, Plus, had a partnership with several universities and colleges nearby to provide sexual education. One of Kyle's favorite parts of the job was setting up booths at events to run quizzes, pass out condoms and pamphlets, answer questions, and sneakily educate students.

He'd long ago learned that people didn't like being preached to, and they didn't like to think of any of their choices as having long-term consequences. Some believed HIV was a death sentence, or a punishment, or a weapon of fear to wield over them, and they would rather stick their heads in the sand.

Kyle's message was that it *wasn't* a life-threatening disease anymore, but it did have the potential to cause life complications, and it made dating harder, among other things. Prevention was important, but so was early diagnosis and treatment, and regular testing.

He focused with these students on regular condom use, PrEP when possible and suitable, and frequent testing. He wrapped it in a message about overall sexual and physical and emotional health as being important things to begin focusing on in this stage of life, as students took control over their own lives and health.

And young people—not that he, at twenty-six, was ancient, but fresh-faced nineteen-year-olds always made him feel that way—had great questions when someone was willing to hear them.

Kyle's appearance itself told people he was open to hearing basically anything, and that did wonders. Today's outfit choice was a plaid skirt over skinny jeans, bright red suspenders, and a black ruffled blouse. He'd worked long enough at building up his wardrobe that basically any of his staple clothing items could be mixed and matched.

After checking his hair in the mirror, Kyle grabbed the first box of leftover pamphlets, condoms, and table banners. He had the fair kit down to three boxes, but he couldn't quite squeeze them into two so he could stack and carry them in one trip.

He scanned his card at the door and backed through the front door, whistling under his breath at how light the box felt in his arms. That meant it had been a good day.

Once Kyle made it through the front hall, he scanned the card again to get into the staircase, then twice more—to get onto their floor and into their office. It was an awkward, wrist-bending affair when he had a box in his arms, but he had figured out the trick to it long ago.

"Hey, good-looking. What's cooking?"

Kyle grinned and rolled his eyes at his boss. "Takes one to know one, darling. It was a grrrreat morning!"

"Oh, you flatter me. The *new* gray hairs I found this morning don't agree," Denver mournfully sighed, spinning in his office chair to take in Kyle. "All at my temples still, but I'm wise beyond my years now." Denver was a couple years older than him, only barely out of his twenties, but already graying.

Kyle snorted and slid the box onto his desk, propping his hip against it. He gestured with a finger for Denver to spin in his desk chair. When he did, Kyle solemnly shook his head. "Nope. Still no whining allowed. It's a handsome look on you."

"You always say that." Denver clicked his tongue and propped up his heels on his desk, flipping through the booklet on his lap. "But I don't see the men knocking down my door."

"It's all the damn security. They're lining up outside. They

7

just can't get in," Kyle assured him, straight-faced. "I'll go grab a couple of them to schlep the other boxes inside."

"Good idea. I'll pull the blinds down. Get me a tall blond," Denver's voice followed Kyle back out to the hall, and Kyle laughed.

When he was back inside the building, he set down the boxes and dropped into his chair, beaming at Denver. "Passed out two-thirds of what I brought."

Denver raised his brows and turned to Kyle again, his finger marking his place in his reading material. "That's more than usual. Did you promise them kisses?"

"You make me sound like a siren." Kyle bit back his grin and slid the boxes under this desk—one of his two workspaces in the office. The boxes would live here until the next fair, a few days away.

"I suspect that as the root cause of your green hair. Get it? Root cause."

Kyle burst out laughing. "Have you been saving that up all morning? 'Cause I'll tell you what *I've* been saving all morning..."

"Oh!" Denver pretended to be scandalized. "Lusting after the handsome young things?"

"Never." Kyle meant it, too—it was just a little weird to be hitting on guys *that* side of twenty-five when he was, if barely, on *this* side. "Anyway, it went great. Got some smart questions, only a few pearl-clutchers and bigots."

"Great." Denver smiled at him. "Good job. I send my best guy for a reason."

"Good thing I'm a sucker for your puppy eyes," Kyle sighed dramatically, spinning in his chair and kicking out his legs. "I have to finish rewriting that pamphlet on the testing centers, though. Did they announce what they're doing about the State mobile clinic?"

"Yep. It's caught up in red tape. Something about licensing for the parking."

"The fuckers." Kyle glowered to himself. To him and to Denver, human lives were never worth red tape. They often disagreed with doctors, pharmacists, pharmaceutical companies, city councillors, lawmakers, and other "special interest groups" on that point.

Denver snorted. "Yeah. I know. You ready for the meeting?"

Meeting... meeting... Kyle skimmed through the agenda in his brain, but he drew a blank and raised his eyebrows.

"With the tech company liaison."

"Shit! I mean, um. Yes. Obviously." Kyle pulled open his desk drawers all at once, rifling through the paperwork in them to grab his notes before the guy from Synergy arrived.

Denver laughed and left him to it, going back to his reading.

Kyle had written the user manual for their existing software, although he hadn't even been a teen in the late nineties when it was developed. He grabbed a copy of that and his notes on their requirements for the new programs. He'd printed screenshots of the glitches in their existing software, too. What else was he missing?

The phone on the desk rang and Denver gestured Kyle toward it. "That's probably your man there."

Oh, damn it. Now I'll look disorganized. Kyle was keenly aware of how charities often came across—unprofessional and inefficient compared to tightly controlled corporations. He didn't often get along with upper management types.

Hopefully this guy would be easygoing.

Kyle kicked across the floor to wheel to the little table between their desks, where the reception phone sat. "Hello?"

"Uh, hey. This is Nic, from Synergy. I'm looking for... Kyle?"

"That's me. I'll be right down. Sorry to keep you waiting."

"Oh, um, yes. No problem. I was going to say the same."

Kyle glanced at the clock. Five after the hour. That worked out perfectly, then—at least he'd look *somewhat* put-together if the other guy was late, too.

"No problem." Kyle pushed himself to his feet. "Be right there, two secs."

"You gotta choose one, you know," Denver called after Kyle as he strode for the door.

"What?"

"A sec, or two seconds." He still wasn't getting it, so Denver called out, "Say it slower."

Kyle was in the stairwell before it hit him, and his cheeks flushed. "To sex. Yeah, right." Nic was probably some fifty-something, straight, married guy who'd been sent here for bad behavior.

But the guy waiting outside the glass front door of the building was young, with neat stubble and gelled hair. He was well-dressed, too. The usual moment of surprise crossed his face at the sight of Kyle—and Kyle was used to it, since his appearance inspired that in most people. But then Nic smiled warmly at him before Kyle even had the front door open.

Kyle's cheeks, heart, and dick all clamored to get the first word in.

Oh, I'm in so much trouble.

3

NIC

He *knew* he shouldn't have worn a suit and tie.

"Welcome to our headquarters! Er, not that we have other locations. Not full-time, anyway. Don't worry about being late. I'm not even ready. I'm so sorry." This had to be Kyle—the voice on the intercom matched this peppy yet sibilant, rapid-fire speech.

"I—that's fine," Nic assured Kyle with a quiet laugh. He was relieved not to be in trouble for showing up late, nor for showing up in formalwear when everyone else was probably going casual. "GPS pointed me the wrong way."

"Oh, they do that! Right this way, please." Kyle scanned his card against a reader near the staircase door. When he twirled to hold the staircase door open, his skirt flared out a little.

Kyle was wearing a *skirt*, over men's skinny jeans and boots, and a blouse, and chest hair peeked out from the top of the blouse, his biceps unmistakeable. And his suspenders reached under the skirt, presumably to his jeans waistband. It made Nic wonder if he was wearing garters, which was a *wholly* inappropriate thought for their first meeting.

He awkwardly stepped through the doorway and Kyle brushed past him to trot upstairs at top speed, already talking again.

"I'm so glad you showed up. Well, I mean. Of course you would. Just, we've been waiting for this new software since before I was *born*. I mean, I'm only twenty-six, but I'm fairly sure the program lectures me on *those damn millennials* every time I open it."

All Nic could do was laugh, his cheeks flushing as he kept up with Kyle for this flight of stairs, then waited next to it for Kyle to scan them into the second floor. "I... I've run into some programs like that. I'm the same age."

But he wears it better than me. Kyle was a whirlwind in dress, speech, and personality, whereas Nic... well, Nic was all layers of moodiness and caution. Nic's first impression was that what you saw was what you got with Kyle. It was... overwhelming, but not in a bad way.

In fact, in quite a *good* way. He was exactly the kind of guy to fluster Nic, but this was strictly professional.

He went with the first thing he could think to say. "Um. Have you been working here long?"

"A few years now! I got the job almost straight out of school. Lucky bastard, I know," Kyle beamed. "I didn't think anyone would hire me wearing platform heels and blue eyeshadow straight after a night out, but Denver—that's my boss—told me I'd better not stop being *me*."

"Wow. That's cool." Nic didn't exactly have room to connect with him over that, given that he was dressed in the safest, most boring suit there was. So instead, Nic just felt awkward over not having more to say or more flashy clothing, even if Kyle didn't seem to notice or mind.

A guy maybe five or ten years older, a little grey-haired but with a roguish smile on his lips, was holding the final door for them.

"Leaving me so soon?" Kyle gasped, pressing his hand to his heart.

Denver waved a hand. "There's a donor... thing."

"A thing," Kyle repeated teasingly.

"I'll explain later," Denver tutted, then smiled warmly at Nic and reached out for a handshake. "Nic? I'm Denver. Kyle will take care of you. Kyle, remind Ben and Ash to take their lunch break, not spend lunch hour making out and complain they're hungry later. *Again.*"

Even Nic had to laugh under his breath as Kyle chortled. "Right, boss. Catch you later." Kyle clapped Denver's shoulder on the way by, then ushered Nic inside.

The office was small but cute—room for maybe eight or ten people to work comfortably, or more if the desks were crammed together, plus a few side offices and meeting rooms. Nic had been to smaller charities.

Everyone Nic spotted nodded or raised a hand before getting back to what they were doing. In the corner, there were two guys squinting at a computer screen, designing a poster. They were squeezed onto the same roomy office chair. Ben and Ash, he assumed, unless everyone here was gay and dating a coworker.

Just being around gay men now, after so many years in his tiny Idaho hometown, was a thrill. Nic had to try not to stare at them and give the wrong impression.

They were all, to a man, dressed down. *A sweater and tie next time,* Nic decided.

"Okay, let's head in here," Kyle gestured toward one of the side rooms, scooping a pile of papers off a desk on his way by.

Wherever he walked, he did it with a strut, like the world was his catwalk. Nic decided he liked this guy already.

"Phew. All right." Kyle closed the door behind them. There was a small round table there with eight chairs set up around it. "Before they start flirting with you and keeping us busy all morning."

Nic grinned. "I see why my boss wanted the token gay guy to work this job." Then, his cheeks flushed. Had that been a totally inappropriate thing to say about Greg? "Not in a, like, *discriminating* way..."

"No, no," Kyle laughed and winked. "I know what you mean. I used to tell my ex-boyfriend to wear his ugliest sweater to visit me at work."

Nic couldn't help a laugh. Kyle was so attentive and welcoming that he was starting to unwind. He liked the vibe here already. Flirting and all, it sure beat the white cubicles at his office.

"So, here's what we have right now. I'll show you all the documentation we have on it, and the gaps, and then... I guess it's up to you what you need to see."

"Great. I studied the specs already," Nic nodded. "From what you sent over, it shouldn't be too hard." He was back on his home turf: computers, and what made them tick. It was a stereotype, but it was true—a lot of shy guys liked them because they were a shitload easier than people.

Kyle pulled up a chair next to him and scooted so close their knees bumped, opening up his pile of paperwork to start showing Nic what they had. Kyle's proximity distracted him, but Nic tried his hardest to stay focused on Kyle's points, not the ways he made them.

If he hadn't gotten laid in too long, that wasn't Kyle's problem to deal with.

But after they reviewed the papers and Kyle grabbed his laptop to show Nic use cases live, it got harder to ignore those tingles running up and down his spine.

Nic took over before long, clicking around the software to figure out the main functions and how they compared with what the charity needed. And though he kept his eyes firmly on the screen, Nic could swear he felt Kyle studying him from the side as he clicked around.

The whole time, Kyle maintained a conversation that was entertaining, but not distracting. How the hell he did it, Nic had no idea.

"You just moved here? Oh, my gosh." Kyle drummed his fingers on the table. "Welcome! What do you think so far? Where were you before?"

"Pretty... big." Nic took notes on his phone as he observed the number of identical outbox emails. They had no way to pull resources from the database directly into email templates, so they copied and pasted often. A function could do that a lot faster, and automatically. "Um, I lived in Idaho, then Minneapolis before. A little smaller, a little colder."

"Oof," Kyle breathed out. "So cold. I'd turn into a Kylecicle instantly. I'd never make it through November."

Nic laughed. "Yeah, I've barely worn a sweater since getting here. I like that." He nodded at the screen. "You literally copy and paste?"

"Let me show you."

Nic wasn't quick enough to pull his hand away from the nipple in the middle of the keyboard that served as a mouse, and Kyle's hand blanketed his for a second.

Their hands were about the same size, but Kyle's fingers

E. DAVIES

were thinner and longer, the nails chipped and showing the remnants of clear polish. More importantly, the palm brushing against the back of his hand made Nic's body shiver to attention again.

Down, boy. Nic took a breath and slid his hand across the keyboard and away, nodding in apology.

Kyle definitely didn't mind. He just winked sideways at Nic and turned his attention to the screen, pursing his lips and clicking around. "Mmmm."

Nic did his best not to look at Kyle's pretty pink lips. He *really* needed to work on finding a boyfriend now that he was living in the big city.

But not this guy. Christ, he wasn't going to be the one to break what professional distance there was between them. He had the feeling if he did, Kyle was the kind of guy who would be in his lap and think nothing of it. That would be one hell of a mixed signal. Where he came from, standing a little too close and looking once too often was bold.

Not that he'd fit in with Kyle, however gorgeous he looked. His chest ached. He wished he were bold enough to catch Kyle's attention for more than a polite yet fun business meeting. Whoever the lucky guy was going to be, or already was, Nic already envied him.

"There."

Nic nodded dumbly and took notes, then squinted at his phone. "Yeah, that'll be easy."

"Really? Oh, my God, you'd save us *so much* copying and pasting," Kyle enthused. "You're my new favorite superhero."

Nic's cheeks flushed as he reminded himself Kyle wasn't the kind of guy who meant that for real. He just offered an easygoing smile. "Yeah, that database structure's simple. I'll

16

have a markup of all the stuff we discussed by the next meeting."

"Really? It's that easy? Well, for me. I hope you don't have late nights for this," Kyle breathed out, his eyes wide.

It did feel nice to be a superhero, if for a few weeks. "Not too many." Nic couldn't resist exaggerating slightly. He had a cushy job—not in the support side, where midnight escalated calls could wake him up, but the nine-to-five division. Unless a project were running late, but nothing could come up to derail him that badly from a simple project like this.

And simple meant cheap for the charity, which he was sure Kyle would appreciate.

Kyle was beaming at him, saying something about having pizza for their next meeting.

Nic smiled and stood, his senses on overload. His elbow brushed along the table and knocked the stack of papers off the table before he even noticed. "Oh, shit." He bent instantly to start gathering them up.

Never make yourself a nuisance on a client's turf, he scolded himself. It was a rule that had helped him score a job here at Synergy, a prestigious firm even within the L.A. market.

"No, no, it's okay! I'm a klutz. I've dropped laptops—oh, I'm not supposed to say that to techies," Kyle breathed out, crouching by the papers to help Nic gather them up.

Oh. They were *close*, just inches and a few booklets and papers separating them now. He could smell something sweet —shampoo, maybe—and a touch of something that made his skin crawl with desire.

Burning chemistry pricked Nic's thighs and stomach and hands and every *inch* of his skin the second he looked up into

17

Kyle's eyes from so close. It made him rock back on his heels, suddenly dizzy.

Kyle smiled brightly at him and took the papers he was holding to shuffle them into his own stack, his fingers trailing along the backs of Nic's hands.

If Nic didn't know better, he'd have said it was deliberate, but Kyle was standing up now and setting everything back on the table. Nic pushed himself to his feet quickly and patted the papers. "Sorry about that. Um, okay. So, until our next meeting."

"Until next time. Take it easy. I can't wait to see what you make for us," Kyle beamed at him, pulling open the door.

Nic barely remembered anything between the meeting room door and the parking lot as he followed Kyle back out to the front door of the building. He made conversation about something—the drive over. He admitted again that he'd gotten lost and played it up to make Kyle laugh, but of course, he didn't tell him about the homophobic asshole at the gas station.

Nic's cheeks flushed as he raised his hand in a quick wave and got into his car.

With that, he'd survived his first encounter with the force of nature that was Kyle Everett.

Nic let out a breath once he was in the car. It took him a second to even remember that he needed to find his car keys, let alone remember where they were.

I'm so fucked.

4

KYLE

"Did you breathe wrong on it?"

"I called it a bad name." Kyle pouted at River as he pushed away from the front of the building. What a hell of a day he'd had, and he was grateful for about the millionth time that River was both a great human being and the owner of a great car.

River gave him a sympathetic look and leaned over to open the passenger door of his gorgeous little red Mazda. "It died at the university?"

"No, no. It made it back from that." Kyle mournfully flopped in the passenger seat and buckled up, then tugged his skirt down. "It decided to die when Denver and I went out for lunch."

"Nice. Leaving you stranded—"

"—at Subway. The less stabby Subway, though!" Kyle informed River, beaming. "Not the one around the corner from Alex's. Or I might have been worried for my bodily integrity. And not in traffic! It was much safer than it could have been."

"You gotta squint to see that silver lining, baby." River laughed and pulled away from the charity parking lot, flicking the turn signal. He braced his elbow on the sideboard of the car and ran his fingers across the close-cropped sides of his platinum hair. Even without a wig, he still frequently played with the air around his head like he was wearing one. It always fascinated Kyle to watch.

"My eyesight is better than perfect, thanks," Kyle smiled brightly. "Chinese?"

"Sold. I could use about eight tons of sweet and sour chicken."

"Aww. That bad a day, huh?" Kyle pouted. River was such a sweetheart, but he was just as hopeless in love and had bounced between several jobs in the last year, which put him one step behind even Kyle. He was working at a beauty counter in the mall now and hoping to land a job in an actual storefront for one of the big makeup brands. Some brands hired more men than others, so jobs were scarcer for him than they otherwise should have been given his talent.

"Well, first of all, when did the mechanic say your car will be ready this time?"

"Tonight!" Kyle smiled brightly. "Should be a simple fix this time. Something something wiring... I don't know. I wasn't listening."

River eyed him but snorted with unmistakably fond laughter. "It's a good thing you're pretty, hon."

"I know. And it's cheap this time! I'm sure he gave me a discount for fluttering my lashes." Kyle propped his chin on his fist.

"Or you've reached the top tier of their frequent customer program."

Kyle laughed richly but elbowed River. "Ouch. Don't diss my baby."

He let River get away without answering the question until they got to their favorite cheap Chinese buffet and got their usual plates of food, then found a table in the corner.

"So, your day," he prompted River, eyeing him over his glass of Coke. He knew River was supposed to have had some makeup lessons to give, plus a date.

River sighed and raised his shoulders. "That date ditched me and ghosted me."

"Oh, no," Kyle crooned, scowling deeply. Anyone who put that look on River's face—trying to hide the moments of insecurity that afflicted them both occasionally, but River more often—was a fucking scumbag, in his opinion. "I'll go kick him in the balls for you."

"Would you?"

"Twice. Was he pretty?"

"A lot less than his photo," River muttered, and Kyle grinned. Cattiness was better than moping.

"Maybe just once, then. Being ugly was God's advance punishment for him being a dick to you."

"To me specifically?" River was laughing as he pushed his fork through the fried rice to dig out the bits of egg.

"Yep," Kyle confirmed brightly. *I bet Nic wouldn't do that. Ditch someone. He's a solid kind of guy. Sincere. He'll do great work for us, I know it.*

River eyed him. "What's that look for?"

"Oh. I had the first meeting with the, er... with the liaison for the tech company." Kyle waved his fork and dug into his veggies.

His attempt to underplay it wasn't working, though. River

had his eyebrow raised. When that didn't work, River put down his fork and folded his arms, staying silent.

"Fine," Kyle relented. "He might be... *really* cute. *And* gay. *And* single." He bent his wrist, gesturing in a circle with his fork. "*And* new to the area."

"Get *on* that before the gold rush," River breathed out, leaning in over the table. "Go on!"

"No, no," Kyle waved him off. "It's not *going* anywhere. A relationship with him would never work. But he was adorable. Dorky adorable. Adorkable?" River giggled and he went on. "Kind of an otter, I think... scruffy, probably a little chest hair, that kind of look. Awkward and shy. Smart as hell."

"All I hear is *exactly your type*, Kyle," River informed him. "So, why wouldn't it work?"

Kyle didn't have a very good answer. "Just... wouldn't be good. Business with pleasure and all that." River didn't look impressed, so he added, "And you know I'm not looking for someone to spend my life with."

"Maybe he isn't, either," River pointed out.

"He looked like the commitment type. And one-night stands are obviously the way forward for me these days," Kyle stated firmly.

River snorted. He tossed his head and swept his hand over his shoulder to rub his scalp behind his ear, a little gesture he did when he was out of drag but automatically moved like he had hair to push back, then realized there was none there. "I'd be more impressed with that if we didn't know you have that little tendency of running from your past."

River knew him well. Way too well. He was godfather and practically uncle to Kyle's son, and he could pick a dude, dress, or dinner for him correctly every time.

Kyle glanced down at his plate and pushed his fork

through his rice to arrange it into a pile, then started working on his veggies again. "True. I know. But..."

River nudged his foot with his own to make him look up. "Was he flirting with you?"

It was hard for Kyle to judge that. If it weren't, he probably wouldn't accidentally flirt with everyone he talked to. "I think so. Maybe. Maybe not."

"You deserve it, baby." River gave him an affectionate smile. "I'll kick *him* in the balls if he hurts you, so take the risk."

Kyle drew a breath. It was enough to get him thinking, but he wasn't going to encourage River to plan their wedding yet. "Maybe," he conceded. "After the project."

"You're going to be spending a lot of time together. At least enjoy that," River told him.

Kyle groaned. "Well, I don't have much choice. Not that I'd *want* to avoid him."

"You're so cute when you're crushing," River said matter-of-factly and grabbed his plate, pushing himself to his feet. "Spring rolls?"

Kyle closed his mouth when he realized it was open. "Uh. Yes."

"And the blush is *very* fetching," River teased him.

"Hey." Kyle couldn't quite slap River on the ass before he scooted by, grinning broadly at him.

It was a nice thought to distract him, but not much more than that. However much River teased him, Kyle couldn't rush into anything, and they both knew it.

Strictly business, then... with a bit of fun.

5

NIC

"I figure it'll take me the week to get the prototype operational for them, but it'll be just in time for the next progress meeting." Nic eyed his computer screen as he pushed himself back to stare around his home office. The phone propped between his ear and shoulder seemed archaic compared to his dual-monitor flatscreen setup and coding keyboard.

"Damn. Your work is fast, Nic." Greg, his boss, sounded impressed. That was always a good sign after starting a new job.

"I was playing around with a few options earlier. I think I've pinned down the one that will work fastest." Nic clicked his fingers. "Right. I forgot to send those over. I'll email you, if you want to see."

"Oh. No, I trust your judgment. As long as it fits their specs. But you're coming up with options first? Great thinking," Greg praised. "I'm impressed by the good work you do. You should keep it up."

Naturally, Nic wondered what the catch was. Was this project going to require overtime? Or was Greg hoping the opposite—that inducing him to work faster on it would keep him on hours? Either way, he was letting him work from home more days than not on this project, so he couldn't complain.

Since he couldn't question it, all he went with was, "Thanks. Will do." He saved and backed up on autopilot. "So I'll call tomorrow after I squash my way through the eighty million bugs I've just created." Thank God he was on his own and not trying to coordinate with someone from the charity. That was the route to real disaster.

"Sounds great."

After they hung up, Nic frowned, pressing his phone to his lips for a few long moments as he stared at his empty desktop.

Then he launched his internet browser and opened Facebook on impulse, only half-aware of what he was doing, and that he probably shouldn't be doing it.

There was no point in even doing it, but he was going to check on Jake, his ex. Jake messaged every now and then, every few months. The first few times, it had been under the pretense of checking that he hadn't left anything at Nic's place. After Nic moved, it was to wish him a good life after the move.

Nic had kept his thank-you message short and to the point, and after a month of near-daily messages, had removed Jake on Facebook. He didn't take back cheaters. As far as he was concerned, that was a one-way trip.

Didn't stop Jake messaging him, but Nic had ignored them ever since deleting him on Facebook.

Jake's Facebook wall was the usual mix of sad lyrics, inspirational quotes on pretty nature photos, half-naked men, and Facebook quiz memes. No sign of a new boyfriend, judging especially by the lyrics.

God. Nic hoped he found someone, so he'd stop bugging him.

Nic sighed and closed the tab, spinning in his office chair before he slowly walked to the kitchen. His voice felt rusty from disuse, since he'd spent the whole afternoon coding since coming back from Plus.

Just for company, he talked aloud as he approached the fridge.

"Should get something to eat."

He opened the fridge.

"Ugh. Nothing I actually *want*, though. Ohhh. Wait. I have a can of SpaghettiO's." He usually saved them for when he was sick, but what the hell. "That sounds exactly up my alley right now."

He hummed under his breath, pouring them into a bowl.

"Wonder how fast the bug-squashing will go tomorrow. Now's when I find out how cleanly I worked today, huh?"

While he waited for the microwave, Nic headed for the television and turned it on. It was time to distract himself with something or another and stop talking to himself like a total loser all night.

And it was time to take his mind off Jake. He didn't think of him much these days, and when he did, he didn't care much. That was probably a good sign. But in his weak moments, once in a long while, he thought about answering him.

Nic never did. He wasn't *that* lonely.

But he missed being half of a whole, and he missed having a family. It hadn't been his fault they'd broken up—Jake had been utterly unready for a relationship—but his family had been sweet, and had welcomed Nic in with open arms.

More than anything, leaving that had broken his heart.

But again... one-way trip. He'd rather be alone here than

with a cheater out of desperation. He checked on Jake much less frequently these days. It felt like Jake was naturally fading out of his life, which was as it should be.

Nic just wished there were someone to replace him.

The microwave dinged and he jumped. Staring at the channel menu, lost in his thoughts, had distracted him completely from what he was doing.

Nic chose the first movie that came on and headed to the kitchen to grab his bowl and fork. Healthy food could wait for tomorrow. Tonight was a junk food night.

As he settled on the couch, pulling the blanket around his shoulders, Nic smiled to himself. A nature documentary. Perfect.

He fell asleep to the lulling tones of the narrator describing jellyfish species and the backdrop of gentle music over lapping waves. Aside from the drone of the television, the house was utterly soundless and still.

6

KYLE

Kyle didn't think of himself as a paranoid person, but he refused to sit in his car in parking lots. There was always the lingering possibility at the back of his mind that, liberal state or not, someone who didn't like the way he existed or moved through the world could follow him back here. It had happened before.

Still, he was breaking his own rule as he opened the white paper bag in his lap and shoved the contents of the other bag inside, then neatly rolled the top down.

"Done. Ready to go."

Kyle coaxed his car to life, patting the wheel and praising her new wiring circuitry spark thingy blah blah. The pretty mechanic had told him something about that, only minus the "blah blah" part, while flexing his shoulder muscles distractingly.

It was a quick drive from the store to Evie's house. The mother of his son had texted earlier that day to say Kevin was sick. And she'd had a request:

I know it's not your custody day but could you come over?

Kyle had said yes, of course. He adored Kevin, and although their parenting arrangement was far from traditional, fatherhood was as important as work in his life.

That was one major reason—the biggest, really—that dating was out for him.

"Kyle. Oh, you came." Evie looked desperately relieved to see him: no makeup, sweatpants, and bags under her eyes like she hadn't had a good night's sleep in days.

"Oh, Evie. You should have texted sooner!" Kyle chided her as he stepped inside.

"I know, I know. I didn't want to bother you at work."

"I can blow off work for my favorite girl." Kyle hugged her around the shoulders and kissed the side of her head, then handed over his white paper bag. When Evie opened it and spotted the Aero bar for her, coloring book for Kevin, and extra children's cold medicine, she looked like she could cry, then leaned into him.

"You didn't have to."

"Of course I did. Grab some food and a shower for yourself, hon. I'll take care of Kevin." She handed the bag back to him and headed for the bathroom.

Evie was a total sweetheart, and he loved her dearly. They'd been friends since middle school, and they had a lifetime of inside jokes and affection for each other to prove it. With him being tremendously gay, they'd never been romantically interested, so he'd gotten himself a close friend for life.

Kyle would never have believed he'd wind up coparenting with her, but life was funny that way. All the adoption agencies Evie had visited had interviewed her, done home visits, and found convenient excuses to turn her down. She was "too young," one said, at twenty-three. Another said she "didn't make enough money," which was ridiculous, because she had run an online clothing boutique since she was fifteen, graduated in computer science at the top of her class, and landed a job at Synergy, the tech company that Plus had hired for their coding project. Yeah, she was doing fine financially. Worst of all, the last agency told her she "didn't have a stable male partner in her life."

She'd only had to ask Kyle to lend his sperm to the cause and he'd agreed.

Being a parent was something he hadn't envisioned of himself so soon, but Evie had talked him through the first few months and what to expect, and they'd made it here already—a bouncing, healthy four-year-old whose vocabulary was frankly scary.

Kyle's one condition of the deal: that he got to retain partial custody and be in the baby's life as a father, not just a family friend. He'd always wanted a kid of his own, and he figured he wouldn't get another chance.

It meant a lot to him that Evie had suggested the name Kevin from blending their names. The other, subtler, option was Levi, but they'd agreed Kevin was cuter. And it turned out it suited him.

"Hey, big fellow," he greeted Kevin, pushing open his son's bedroom door and peeking inside.

Kevin's broad, gap-toothed grin was always, *always* worth the drive or the time off work. "Daddy! I'm siiiick."

"I know, buddy." Kyle frowned as he closed the door, carrying his bag of supplies. "And being sick sucks." His son nodded gloomily. "So I brought you some medicine, and we're gonna do something fun, okay?"

"Okay!" Kevin scooted over so Kyle could sit on the edge of the bed and kick out his legs. Kyle was wearing a pretty, knee-length gray skirt and patterned tights today with his dress shirt and tie, and Kevin took a moment to look at him before he looked up. "Daddy?"

"Yes?"

"Do you have nice legs?"

Kyle burst out laughing. "I... I've been told I do. I think all legs are nice legs."

Kevin stretched his own out, and Kyle saw that he had already kicked off the covers. He took the chance to rest the back of his hand against the kid's forehead. Yeah, he was running a fever. "Are my legs nice?" Kevin asked.

"You have excellent legs," Kyle nodded without missing a beat, opening his mouth in mock-shock. "Ten out of ten. Full marks on their legginess." He reached for the bedside table to eye the notepad and pen there. Evie always kept track of which medications Kevin had been given, and he checked his watch to make sure it was safe for him to have another dose.

Once Kevin took some more medicine and Kyle had made a note of it, his son lay back, then giggled. "Daddy?"

"Mmhmm?"

"I wore a dress last—last week... and everyone liked it except one kid."

Kyle put his arm around his son's shoulders. Evie hadn't mentioned it, but they hadn't exactly had a chance to catch up. "Yeah?"

"He said it was for girls, but *I* told *him* that my daddy wears dresses, and—an'—and that anyone can wear anything they want."

Kyle's chest swelled with pride. He glanced at the door so Kevin didn't see the tears that formed in his eyes before he blinked them away. Then, he beamed at his kid. "Way to go. And what did he say?"

"He thought about it for a few... few minutes," Kevin carefully said. "And then he said it was okay if I wore one. And when... Mom and Dana picked me up, Dana said I did the right thing."

"Hah. You don't need his permission to wear one," Kyle grinned, ruffling Kevin's hair. "But she's right." He didn't know a lot about Dana yet, except that she and Evie had recently gotten together for real, and that she was out of town a lot. "I'm glad he understood you when you explained it to him. And Dana liked your dress, didn't she?"

Kevin frowned to himself and nodded. He rarely wanted to talk about her, but Kyle guessed he'd been sneakily trying to work up to it. Kyle decided to put that on the back burner.

"What color was the dress?"

"Purple!"

Of course. Kevin's favorite color, and it had been all year. "When you're better, you should wear something purple on one of your days with me. I'll get something purple and we'll match."

Kevin looked overjoyed at the idea. "Yes." He was getting curious about the bag on Kyle's lap, though, and he crawled closer, leaning into Kyle's chest to try to peek into it. "What's that?"

"Uh uh," Kyle scolded, grinning at him. "What do you say?"

"May I... see what's that?"

Kyle chuckled gently. "Yes, you can." He took the medicine bottle out of the bag and handed it over.

"Coloring! And it's cool. Spaceships!"

Kyle grinned. "Yeah. Space is awesome. I bet you can use lots of purple in space."

"Space is black, silly," Kevin corrected him. "That's why you can't see through it, except for—for... the stars on it."

We can revisit this in a few years. Kyle bit his tongue, then laughed. "You must be almost ready for first grade by now."

"I read a book every week," Kevin informed him, flipping through the book to look for a picture to color.

Kyle settled in with his son to talk about the books he'd read and help him color in the planets and stars in the picture.

It didn't take long before Kevin was nodding off, but he didn't let Kyle go. "A story," he murmured, giving him the familiar wide-eyed gaze Kyle had only seen in the mirror. "Please?"

Kyle couldn't resist that look. "Of course. Which one?"

"The cowboy one. I hate being sick."

"I know, hon." Kyle kissed Kevin's forehead. "You'll be better soon. The cowboys will help, you'll see."

He sat next to the bed as he read the cowboy story—only for the hundredth time that year—and did all the silly voices Kevin wanted him to do. Well, strictly speaking, Kevin didn't ask, but he took it upon himself to do them.

Kyle noticed near the end of the story that Kevin was asleep and that Evie was leaning in the doorway, smiling fondly at him.

"He'll be out like a light," Evie murmured.

Kyle took a moment to gaze at his son, pulling the covers up more firmly around him before standing up. "Yeah."

"Thanks so much for coming over, Kyle." Evie pulled away from the doorway to let him through, then tugged the door shut. She'd showered and she looked a little brighter already as she padded through the house, pajama-clad and in bare feet, to the living room.

"Of course. Text me anytime, you know that," Kyle scolded her. "And I'm staying tonight to check on him so you can sleep."

"I will, I will," Evie chuckled, dropping onto the couch and breathing out a sigh as she pushed her hands back through her damp hair. "I thought Dana could come over to help, but she got called away."

"Again?" Kyle frowned sympathetically. He couldn't judge, but it had to be hard on Evie not to have someone around.

"I know, I know."

"Darling, I'm not judging. I've only met her a few times, but she seems sweet. And you're good for each other," Kyle told her gently, sitting on the arm of the sofa next to her and wrapping his arm around her. "But it has to be hard. That's all."

"It is." Evie sighed, pressing the side of her head against Kyle's shoulder for a moment before she pulled back. "And what about you?"

"What about me?" Kyle evaded the question, patting his pockets down. He'd squirreled away the Aero bar somewhere while taking charge of the pharmacy bag. Aha, there it was— and in his breast pocket, so not even melted.

Evie took the chocolate bar but laughed. "I see you trying to distract me."

"There's nobody, Evie." Kyle met her gaze and sank onto the couch next to her, sitting properly this time. "Even coparenting is a lot of work, and you know how much my job means to me. I'm okay with that."

Evie hesitated, biting her lip, then lowered her voice. "Are you really, *really* okay with that?"

Kyle couldn't lie to her. Not after knowing her for this long. He glanced away for a second to compose his thoughts. "Not in the long term. Someday, yes, I need—want someone.

But especially with Kevin around, I'm not rushing anyone. I want *him* to be the right person to be around Kevin, too."

"That sounds a lot like forever-love talk," Evie teased him, crinkling the wrapper and throwing it at him.

Kyle laughed and caught it. "Oh, shut up. I'm not... not yet."

"Is there someone?"

"Not yet." Kyle was getting way, *way* ahead of himself if he thought he had a shot with Nic. Not with all this baggage of his.

No, not baggage. Kevin wasn't baggage, and his wardrobe wasn't baggage, and his family life in the past wasn't baggage. They were important parts of him. But any one of those things might be enough to scare off a new lover, and had been before.

"But on a much *more* fun note, the new guy your company sent is great. He's going to revolutionize our work flow."

Evie sensed not to pry, and accepted the change of subject to work. Strictly speaking, less of a change of subject than it seemed, but that was beside the point. She just patted his knee. "Good. I hoped Greg would send one of our best. Well, keep me posted. I need to get some beauty sleep."

Kyle clicked his tongue. "I keep telling you, you'd be fine with an hour a week."

Evie blushed and swatted him as she stood up to grab the blanket and pillow from the cupboard. "And I keep telling you it means a little less coming from the gayest man I've ever known. The only man who *hasn't* taken an interest in this," she gestured at her chest, "even when I was nursing."

"Ah, what can I say?" Kyle dramatically flopped onto the couch. "I gave up on that when I stopped nursing. I'm sure I tried my best before then, though."

Evie shook out the blanket over him and, like he'd leaned down to kiss Kevin goodnight, kissed his forehead. She perched on the side of the couch for a moment and handed him the pillow. "You always do, Kyle. Thank you. For everything."

Kyle crunched his ab muscles to sit up, then pulled her in for a good, tight hug. "Go get some sleep. Absolutely no leaving your room until it's daylight tomorrow. I'll check on him in the night."

As he settled down in the familiar living room, Kyle turned onto his side to find the perfect, cozy spot in the couch.

Ah, there it is.

Yeah, Evie was right—he wasn't happy *forever* without a man by his side for longer than a night at a time, but for now, it would do. His life was pretty damn good.

NIC

Heading into the office after a couple days working at home was still strange. Nic had only been working at Synergy for three weeks, and attending the weekly Friday meetings was optional, depending on everyone's project load.

This was his second meeting, and he already spotted a few new faces. Nic slid into the same chair he'd chosen last time, because everyone else had left it empty. The last thing he wanted was to choose someone's traditional chair. That had the unfortunate effect of leaving him in the corner of the room, but only for a few moments.

A dark-haired woman approached and plopped into the seat next to him, then offered her handshake and a friendly smile. "Hello! You must be the new guy. The one who got sent out to the Plus project, right?"

"Hi. Yes." Nic nodded and shook hands. "I'm Nic."

"Evie. Good to meet you! Enjoying work so far?"

"Er, yes. I can't complain," Nic agreed, relaxing and smiling back at her. It didn't seem like she had some office politics agenda underlying her friendly approach. "I've been head-down in coding this week, building the framework. I need a roughly functional prototype by next week."

"Big piece of work for one guy," Evie whistled. "Nice. Oh." Greg had come in and rapped the table. She offered another smile, so Nic smiled back before pulling his notepad close. He hadn't actually needed to take notes last week, but one never knew—this week could be important. It paid to be prepared. Evie had a notebook, too, so at least he wasn't the only one.

"Good to see you all at the end of another week," Greg greeted them. "So, let's talk workloads and what projects are on the go right now."

Nic tried to keep track of them. They had four major clients right now, and it sounded like his project was actually one of the smaller ones.

It was kind of exciting in a nerdy way to know that he was working somewhere he'd be forced to improve his skills in order to keep up. In fact, that was one of the reasons he'd taken the job, apart from being ready for a bigger city and more money.

"And we have Nic on the... um... who are they?"

"Plus," Nic supplied with a smile.

"Yes. That, thanks," Greg chuckled.

"What's that?" someone—Nic wasn't sure her name yet —asked.

"Gay men's HIV charity," Nic supplied. "I can give you the rundown on it now. Founded '77 under another name, lots of amalgamations and splits and mandate changes. This iteration of the charity has been running for about a decade. Their software is from the *last* iteration, though, which was... '98."

"Before Y2K," Hank whistled. He was one of the guys

from another team—working on some kind of pharmaceutical chain project, if Nic remembered right. "Did you catch any bugs?" He smirked.

Nic felt Evie stiffen beside him. After a second, he realized why and caught his breath.

What an asshole.

It was just vague enough that he couldn't ask for clarification—especially as the new guy. And Hank knew it. His expression was self-satisfied.

Fuck's sake. I had no idea things were that *bad.* Well, in reality, Nic knew the stigma—some of it perpetuated by well-meaning people, some by assholes. He'd just never faced it directly himself. After facing transphobia and homophobia for this long, it was weird to find a whole new facet of hatred aimed at him... and he wasn't even personally involved.

"Millennium bugs, I assume you meant," Greg addressed Hank, with the edge of a reprimand in his voice. Hank nodded and glanced at Nic.

"Nah," Nic said simply. "None of those."

The conversation moved on, but Nic's mind stayed on that comment—and Evie's reaction, which had been as quick as his own. Others like Greg had taken longer, and many hadn't seemed to catch it at all.

Once the meeting closed, Evie leaned back in the chair. "So, they picked a heck of a first project for you."

"Yeah. I guess I had the right... aptitude," Nic half-smiled.

Evie smiled. "Yeah, I heard you were a coding whiz kid. Word gets around. And willing to take on a charity project. Those are always trickier."

Nic felt himself turning red. "I... thanks, I think?" he laughed. "A little late to be a whiz kid now, though."

"I know," Evie mournfully sighed. "I miss my participation trophies. My partner threatens to give me participation trophies for cooking, it's that bad."

The comment and word choice—partner—was *just* disjointed enough that it sounded like a deliberate attempt to throw the word out and read him. Nic played along.

"Yeah? Mine and I never really cooked. I *do* cook, but we ended up just ordering takeout all the time. God knows how —" *don't say* he *yet* "—any of my exes survived, really. At least I can, you know?" Nic gathered his notebook and flipped it shut, pocketing his pen.

"Oh, yeah. I can burn rice as well as the next person." Evie grinned at him. "So, you doing anything tonight?"

Nic's heart soared. *Oh, let this be a social invitation.* It sounded sad, but he really was missing a friendship group. He'd at least known some people, even if some of them weren't exactly the best people back in Minneapolis. "No, nothing fixed. Maybe going out somewhere."

"You want to come along with us? There's a group of us— my friends and me, not coworkers—who go to the Woody's downtown most weeks," Evie invited him, just as he'd hoped. Then, she dropped her voice. "Gotta stick together."

And Woody's was a gay bar. She was practically confirmed as *one of us*, then. "Yeah. I'd love that." Nic glanced across the room at Hank, who was chatting with Greg, then back at her. "Thanks."

"Thank you. Can't wait to see you. We meet there around ten." Evie looked satisfied with herself, but not in the same nasty way Hank had, as she pushed herself to her feet. "That all right?"

"I'll try not to turn into a pumpkin," Nic joked, heading

out of the conference room and over to his desk to back up the work he'd done from home.

"Can't wait!" Evie waved and headed across the office to her desk.

There we go. Friendship. You can do this, Nic.

8

KYLE

As Kyle tapped his pen on the page, he furrowed his brow. He hated working in the space that was technically his office, one of the few side-rooms off the main space of the charity office. Every time he did, he missed the contact and the casual back-and-forth he had with the other paid employees and volunteers there.

He preferred the desk he kept out in the main office, next to Denver's. Luckily, there was room here for both of them to keep two workspaces. If the charity kept growing, there wouldn't be, but that would be a great problem to have.

Argh. There went his train of thought again. There was no question he needed to focus. The paperwork in front of him was one of the aspects of the job he liked less. He had to prepare a review for the board about the efficacy of their educational programming.

It was dry language, but the content was critically important. It was Kyle's job to show what was working and what wasn't, which would help guide which programs were allocated more funding, where they'd direct their fundraising efforts, how much they consequently received from donors and grants... basically everything.

The exact time and date of his presentation wasn't scheduled yet, because the board meeting wasn't. But as soon as they nailed down the date of that next board meeting—a few important board members' schedules were hard to resolve—he'd have a deadline. He hated deadlines looming over his head, making it impossible to focus on anything else.

Kyle spun in his chair and sighed, casting his mind back over that year's university outreach programming. It felt like he was getting more effective every year, but it never seemed enough for the board.

And this was a milestone year for several of their educational programs. The PrEP outreach was starting to take hold, and there was backlash to deal with, too. They had to be absolutely sure they weren't having negative effects on the community health, as some put it.

Kyle would fight tooth and nail for access to prophylactic antiretrovirals for anyone who felt he needed it, but there was only so much they could do up against the big pharmaceutical companies. The right of access was a huge bone of contention. They'd had to fight more than one battle with insurance companies on their clients' behalf last year. Luckily, many had come around to seeing the financial benefits.

It all came down to money.

There was a knock on the door, and Kyle stopped spinning and turned toward it. "Yeah?"

Denver poked his head in. "Hey. Your monk-style retreat helping?"

"Not really," Kyle admitted. "I want to bounce these numbers off other people. There's low uptake on two measurable results of the PrEP program, and I don't want the board to think..."

"Right," Denver nodded. He knew and shared Kyle's passion for that particular program. "Do you have a few minutes?"

"Oh, dear. Of course." Kyle folded his hands on his chest and gazed up at Denver as Denver closed the door.

"Do you have the dates you agreed on with Nic for the progress on the database... software... stuff? And any progress reports?"

Kyle winced. "Um. Let me check. Why?" Denver hadn't seemed deadline-motivated about that particular ball he was trying to keep in the air before now.

"One of the board members..."

"It's that..." Kyle searched his memory. "Cal Whitesmith dude, isn't it?"

Denver rolled his eyes in silent acknowledgment. "He's breathing down my neck."

"Oh, God. Doesn't he have anything better to do with his time?" Kyle wadded up his scratch paper and tossed it in the trash, then searched through his stack of papers for that particular section of stuff. "Must be on my desk out there. I wanna move out there anyway."

He grabbed his laptop and tucked it under his arm, then followed Denver out. The thought of the mortification that Nic had quickly tried to hide when he mentioned dropping the laptop made him grin as he led the way out to the main room.

"Do you need anything else for your report?"

Kyle groaned. "How about you write my report, I write yours?"

"Somehow, that seems... ineffective. Can't think how," Denver chuckled.

"What?" Kyle winked. "But then, it's not like *real* work we do here." An allusion to a comment Cal had made a few board meetings ago.

A full-body shiver of annoyance rippled through Denver. He was hard to get worked up so fast. Kyle was momentarily proud of himself. "Hey. Don't remind me," Denver laughed

Kyle dropped his voice and stage-whispered, "And it's all for our *own* benefit, so we may as well be volunteering."

"What gets me," Denver huffed, dropping into his chair, "is how he thinks it's right to assume anyone's HIV status just because they're working—or volunteering—here."

"I'm not going to tell him I'm negative. I'd rather he thinks I'm one of *those* guys if it means he doesn't treat me like a golden boy... savior... saint, something," Kyle snorted. He didn't want the guy acting like he was doing Denver and the other poz guys here some kind of massive *favor* by working to advocate for them.

Besides, he'd rather be thought of as a man like Denver than one like Cal any day.

Denver clapped his shoulder. "I know. Those dates?"

"Oh. Right." Kyle had gotten so worked up he'd momentarily forgotten what he was here for. "Here." He yanked out his notes and handed them over, then flopped down at his desk to keep working on the impact report.

It didn't take him long before he was smiling again, though. If he let every little twerp get under his skin, he'd be much less happy. He'd once had nothing else in life but his sunny persona, and he wasn't ever going to let someone blot that out.

9

NIC

For only the second time since moving to L.A., Nic was standing at his mirror trying to look at himself as a potential love interest might.

No, a one-night stand. That was all he needed right now. *One step at a time, Nic,* he scolded himself. *A lot easier to find one of those who's willing to take a chance on me.*

Even in a smaller town, he'd been the awkward wallflower for the first few years of clubbing. Formative experiences of not being quite sure how other guys saw him had left him shy, even if he was different now.

He got a lot more attention with a full face of scruff, chest hair he had to constantly keep shaved, and something in his pants that he could feel guys grab. He was smaller than they expected post-meta, but there were definitely balls to feel.

Nic suppressed a shiver and adjusted himself. He really wouldn't mind finding someone handsy tonight.

The taxi honked and he nearly slipped on the bathroom floor in his haste to rush to the door. He didn't want them leaving before they even picked him up.

The momentary nervousness he felt at giving the club name dissipated when the taxi driver had no real reaction to it. They must see everything anyway, Nic figured. One more gay guy heading to the club was nothing.

You're just one more gay guy tonight, he reminded himself, drawing a deep breath as he watched the lights of the suburbs pass. Evie had spotted him and zeroed in on him, just as he'd suspected with her. It was a little harder to tell who was who here, with more straight people dressing... well, gay... than back home. Still, his instincts were still solid, it seemed.

He paid and hopped out, checking his watch. A couple minutes early. Perfect. That gave him time to stand in the lineup outside, shifting from foot to foot until he got to the door. Thank God this part wasn't a problem anymore.

Once he was inside, Nic unzipped the light sweater he'd chosen and headed straight for the bar for a drink to unwind his nerves.

There was something familiar—safer—about a gay bar than a straight bar. At least he knew only half of his identity was in question and potentially dangerous at any given time, and these days, he was barely even read as trans. Sometimes even in bed, guys didn't figure it out. He was almost wholly in his element. He couldn't complain.

He still didn't *feel* in his element as he found a spot by the bar, against the wall, to watch people dance. Early it might be, but other people had started earlier.

The harsh taste of whiskey against his palate kept him grounded. No sickly-sweet coolers or bland beers for him. High-ABV drinks were a leftover habit from when he had to make sure he didn't need to pee more often than strictly necessary.

He got casual look-overs from a couple guys even in these

few minutes of loitering around, which made him smile, at least. Maybe this whole socializing thing was a good idea.

"Nic! Hey, there you are!" Evie was waving at him from the other side of the bar. She beckoned him over and he smiled and nodded. Halfway there, Nic spotted the distinctive flash of bright green hair, though Kyle's back was to him.

Oh, boy. I should have known. He probably won't want to hang out when I'm here. It'll be awkward, right?

But when he approached, brushing by Kyle's elbow to join Evie, Kyle looked over at him and brightened up. "Oh! Hey! Evie said you were coming."

Evie nodded at his drink. "All set?" There was a woman standing close to her, her arm wrapped around Evie's waist— almost definitely her partner, then.

"Yeah, thanks," Nic smiled. He'd make this double last a while. Better to take it slow while he met them and their friends. "I'm Nic. Hi," he introduced himself to the other woman.

"This is Dana, my partner. Nic's new at the company," Evie told Dana. "He's the guy Greg sent to work for Kyle's project."

"I hope you got a referral fee out of that," Dana grinned. "Nice to meet you." They nodded at each other casually, Nic slightly disconcerted that not everyone out here seemed to believe in handshakes as a strictly necessary form of greeting.

It was a little overwhelming here, but he stuck close to Kyle and Evie and now Dana as a couple other people joined them: River first, then Ash, whom he recognized from the charity, and finally Joe, who almost instantly bounced to the other side of the bar to hit on the group of leather daddies there.

"He's hard to keep around," Kyle grinned conspiratorially

at Nic. Even though Nic didn't know him, he felt welcomed into the little group of friends and grinned back at him.

"Can't blame him. There's... a lot to see here."

"I guess compared to Minneapolis, huh?" Kyle nodded. "Welcome to the land of mega-clubs and partying 'til dawn!"

"And close to the land of accidental weddings," Evie smirked, giving Dana a sideways glance.

Dana scoffed. "If I didn't know better, I'd say she's hoping to get me hammered tonight and hitched tomorrow before I knew what happened."

"We can start by talking about moving in," Evie teased while Kyle laughed.

Nic leaned against the bar, staying quiet as he listened to them talk—River and Kyle the most. It was good to see Kyle beaming and laughing at everything River said, but he felt bad that he was *glad* he didn't detect a romantic vibe between them.

River was the campest guy in the place. He was all-in with eyeliner, eyeshadow, and a bunch of things Nic couldn't even name. No wonder he held Kyle's attention.

God, why was Nic focusing on Kyle? Yeah, he was gorgeous and his type, and also gorgeous and his type, and...

No, he reminded himself. He was *not* here for Kyle tonight. It didn't matter how much he wanted to squirm with pleasure every time Kyle grinned at him like that smile was for him alone.

Besides, it wouldn't be appropriate to hold Kyle's interest for too long. They had a work relationship right now, and would for another three or four weeks, if the timeline held.

The topics at hand sparked and died off in the natural ebb and flow of bar conversations, and Nic participated now and then, but mostly stayed off to the side, watching everyone else get along. Maybe next time he'd let them draw him into the center of attention.

Or maybe next time he'd be bold enough to try to be the center of *Kyle's* attention. They caught each other's eyes more than once, and when he brushed past Kyle to lean against the bar and reorder, he felt the thrill between their skin every bit as well as Kyle did, judging by the way he shifted on his feet.

If he wants me... I need a signal. Nic wasn't going to dive in head-first after a man he was sure wouldn't be interested in him for more than a good conversation.

Well, no, that was a lie. He *wanted* to dive head-first into his bed, but he was trying his hardest not to follow that impulse.

As Kyle bumped his side playfully to get his agreement on something to do with the music, Nic beamed at him and nodded while he blushed, willing to agree to anything Kyle said.

Oh, boy. One drink was not enough, which was why he had a two-drink rule. He was going to need that second drink to handle it if Kyle touched him one more time.

Don't come on to him. Play it cool.

Nic was hot already—burning with the desire to dance close to a man, and feel hands all over him. And not just any man—Kyle.

Kyle's hand touched his hip on accident as he gestured while talking. Nic barely stifled his gasp, turning away to the bar to watch for his drink.

Okay, fine. Next time, I'll hit on him.

He curled his toes in his shoes, trying to focus on the bartender pouring his drink.

Next time.

10

KYLE

The moment Evie introduced Nic to River, Kyle could feel his best friend's eyes cut straight over to him.

Yes, he's that guy. No, don't make it obvious, Kyle mentally begged River.

For the first few minutes, he thought he'd won that psychic exchange. Turned out he was wrong.

The moment Nic turned away to reorder, River sidled up and put his arm around his shoulder, stopping Kyle from talking music with Nic. "Hey. Come here. Dance."

"What?" Kyle laughed as River pulled him toward the dance floor to shimmy with him. He mirrored River's moves, swishing his hips back and forth. "You and Evie look like you've been plotting."

"What if we have? He's the same Nic you were talking about before, isn't he?" River exclaimed. "No wonder Evie wanted to get him here with you."

Kyle wagged his finger. "No. Nuh uh. You know my thoughts on that."

River completely ignored him, so he tried to wag his finger in River's face. He just grabbed Kyle's hand and raised it overhead, shimmying to the music and shouting along for a few verses.

Kyle relaxed into the movement and laughed at his best friend. "You are ridiculous."

"Your shyness all of a sudden, that's what's ridiculous," River called back, then leaned in to talk to him closer again. "Go chat with him. Hit on him."

Kyle stared at River. "Really?"

"Really! He's here to dance. He's as gay as three repressed Mormons. Small town kid? He wants to explode onto the scene. And by explode, I do mean..."

Kyle grabbed River's other hand before he could make any obscene gestures. "Okay, okay. Jesus. I get the idea."

River spun him around and grinned at him. "Come on. You start blushing when you're standing next to each other."

"No, we don't! Do we?" Kyle felt like he was in middle school again, which was about right since Evie was giggling in the background with Dana as she watched him awkwardly dance. He was a *good* club dancer, when he wasn't being distracted by very bad ideas.

And the *very* bad ideas that those ideas gave him. Like Nic, pinned to the bed, gasping and squirming and crying his pleasure, Kyle's mouth on his cock.

River smacked his hip. "Go do it before I twist your arm."

Kyle hesitated, glancing away and moving to the beat. The darkened lights, the touch of alcohol getting to his head, the pulsing music that vibrated his chest... it loosened his inhibitions just enough. Work relationship between them or not, life was meant to be lived, right?

He drew a breath, downed the rest of his beer, and handed River the bottle. "You're such an asshole."

Nic was too fucking adorable to resist.

"Love you too, baby," River blew him a kiss as Kyle made his way back to the group and straight to Nic's side.

Nic had been subtly pulling away from the group, shyly watching for the last half hour. No more of that.

"Dance with me?" Kyle beamed, holding out a hand.

Nic went a funny shade of pink, his lips parting—and such delectable lips they were, too. Even in the dim lighting, they looked pink and full and soft. Kyle would kill to feel them on his own.

Don't shoot me down. Or do, and get this whole silly thing over with.

His heart leapt when Nic nodded. Kyle tried not to get invested in every guy he asked, but hell, it was impossible not to hope that Nic had eyes for him.

They found a relatively clear spot on the dance floor where they didn't instantly have to grind together, and then Kyle rested his hands lightly on Nic's shoulders. "Having a good night?"

"I am now," Nic beamed back at him. Oh, that was a good sign.

Kyle winked. "We'll get you having a *great* night."

"Is that a promise?"

"Absolutely." Kyle grabbed Nic's hand and traced his finger over his heart in an "x" shape. "Cross my heart."

And hope to die... The catchy pop lyrics overhead made Nic laugh, and Kyle thanked the universe and the queen of pop for the perfect timing.

It worked. Nic's hands came to rest on his sides and they

shimmied up closer, still keeping a little space between their bodies.

Kyle's heart raced. He kept his hands where they were for now but put a little more effort into rippling his body from head to toe with each move until Nic's eyes were drawn to his chest, stomach, and further south to watch the undulations.

Nic's eyebrow arched, and then he grinned, mimicking the same slow roll of his hips toward Kyle. His hand slid up Kyle's back toward the back of his head.

That was as clear an invitation as any. Kyle let his hands run down Nic's back toward his waistband, resting them on his sides for a few moments. He stepped close enough that their thighs started to brush.

With Nic's full attention on him, the sexual and playful side of him coaxed out, Kyle barely remembered anyone else's existence. He ignored it whenever he stumbled from an arm or elbow. He couldn't tear his eyes off Nic's face, except to admire his body.

And then the moment came: they stumbled close together, high off the beat of the music pulsing through them, dirty suggestions vibrating through their chests... their bodies nestled together, arms slipping around each other's backs and running over each other's asses and thighs, clutching at the back of each other's heads as they play-fought who was going to lead this kiss.

Nic's eyes sparkled as he pulled his head back from Kyle's and cocked it, licking his lips slowly.

Kyle half-closed his eyes and tilted his head, and then they both leaned in together to close the gap.

Soft and surprisingly intimate for a first kiss in the middle of the dance floor. And *chemistry* flared between them, so hot that Kyle felt like his whole body was scorched.

Suddenly, Nic's lips weren't enough, but they were all he wanted to taste.

They leaned in for the second kiss and teeth caught lips, tongues teasing, Nic's stubble scraping his cheek. Kyle pulled Nic into his body until they stumbled together, losing the beat of the music.

I need him.

11

NIC

Being approached by Kyle was enough of a surprise. Being led to dance with him? Nic was stunned.

He had just been planning his graceful escape and slow approach—maybe he'd flirt with Kyle a little next week, take a few weeks to suggest getting a drink for him...

But Kyle was here, shimmying against him on the dance floor, his arms looped around his shoulders, his gaze dripping with innuendo every time he looked Nic over.

Right here, sweeping him away to a whole new world again.

Nic was beginning to suspect that Kyle was exactly the force of nature he craved tonight. Nobody else had caught his eye all night, even when he'd tried to look for someone.

So being singled out, having Kyle look him over like he was deciding his best approach, was making Nic's cheeks burn. His brain was paralyzed with shock, amazed pleasure, and... desire.

Oh, yeah. He wasn't immune to Kyle's charms, even if he knew Kyle was deliberately turning them on him. With Kyle's hands gripping him, channeling the thrum of desire that ran through him, it was an easy decision to put his hands on Kyle.

The second he did, he knew he was lost.

Only a matter of time, a few songs, more brushing of their bodies, more moments of getting lost in that intense eye contact that never seemed to end...

And then they were kissing.

Kyle's lips were warm and soft, but his kisses were intense. The air left Nic's lungs and gravity itself seemed to shift to center Kyle. Nic was floating, pulled out of his world, hands fisted in Kyle's shirt as he desperately pressed into him.

Their cocks ground, and Nic's cheeks flushed as he pulled back.

Kyle pressed forward, stumbling into him and running his hand through Nic's hair. He gripped lightly before letting go, a spark of mischief in his eyes. "We should go somewhere private."

Nic nearly leapt with joy. *He wants me!* "Yes. God, yes."

It felt like he was caught up in Kyle's wake as Kyle gripped his hand. Their fingers laced, and Nic held on tight so he wouldn't get swept away as they pushed their way through the growing crowd toward the exit.

Kyle didn't even stop to say goodbye to his friends.

With us both going missing at the same time, everyone's going to know. Oh, hell. I don't care. I want them to know he... chose me.

Probably not for more than a night. This was probably just a fling. But a guy could hope, and it felt like the whole world stopped when Kyle looked at him like this.

As it turned out, Kyle lived closer than Nic and the taxi ride to Kyle's place passed in a flash. The apartment building exterior didn't look welcoming, especially at night, but Kyle took Nic's hand to pull him along.

They were in a bubble, safe from the rest of their thoughts and worries as they focused only on tonight.

The courtyard looked neater than the exterior, and Nic breathed in the cool, fresh air from the tropical plants. A few palm trees stretched up to the second floor, where Kyle's apartment was.

Kyle dropped his hand to unlock the door, then pushed it open and held it for Nic, his hand resting in the small of his back in the sexiest fucking possessive move.

Before Nic could even express his appreciation, Kyle stepped in afterward and flicked the hall light on. "God, you're sexy."

Nic knew he was blushing, but he offered a bright smile, too. "Yeah? Glad you, um, like the nerdy boy look."

"Don't undersell yourself," Kyle advised him, his words as certain and confident as ever. Nic would kill for a fraction of that confidence. Their shoes were off now, and they were stumbling for the bedroom. "You look at me with those pretty eyes and it makes me want to do the *filthiest* things to you."

Nic was thrumming with pent-up desire again, and he let a moan slip from his throat. This must be Kyle's bedroom— gorgeous, big double bed, but not much else in the room.

He pulled Kyle in by the waist, brushing their noses together affectionately before capturing his lips for a brief kiss. "I gotta tell you something."

"You're a virgin." Kyle mock-gasped. "I'll warn you, I rarely believe that... and almost never the second time."

"Ha ha." At least a bit of the tension in Nic's chest uncoiled at the second of levity Kyle brought to the moment. "No, I'm trans."

The usual second of surprise worked its way through Kyle's expression while the tension nearly killed Nic, and then Kyle nodded. "Do you top? Bottom? What does this mean in terms of... what you want from me?"

Nic wasn't sure anyone had ever taken it so casually and turned it into *these* questions: what he wanted, not who he was.

He might have loved Kyle a little for it.

"I still want you to fuck me. But my cock's pretty small. So, just a heads-up."

Kyle's grin was back, and he pecked Nic's lips. "Every guy worries about that. All I want is to make you come so hard you scream my name. Think I can do that?" Kyle's thumb traced Nic's jaw slowly, teasing the hairs along his jaw but not touching skin.

"I... please," Nic whimpered as heat flushed through him. His cock was throbbing, his heart pounding... he was falling into Kyle all over again.

"Let me see you, then. Anything else you want me to know?" Kyle whispered, gripping Nic by the hips to maneuver him to the bed.

Nic licked his lips and shook his head, unbuttoning his shirt. The distinctive double scars across his chest under his nipples had faded to white by now, but there was still no missing them. "I guess... testing-wise... I haven't been laid in too fucking long, but I got tested since then and. Um. Nothing. So." *Totally just admitted I haven't fucked anyone in too long. Smooth.*

Kyle nodded, his eyes gleaming with amusement. "Do you give every guy that speech?"

Nic hesitated, then shook his head. "I try to. Sometimes I don't ask. If someone's into me, I..." *Shit. This could get way personal, way fast.* He decided not to get into it. "I just see how it goes."

"I appreciate it," Kyle murmured, kissing him lightly and swaying with him. "If it matters, I'm negative for everything, too, as of a month ago. And I haven't done anything risky since."

"Oh. Cool." Kyle made it sound so casual. So easy to talk to him.

And then Kyle was pushing him to the bed, straddling him and running his hands down his chest and stomach. "You feel anything in your nipples? Are they too sensitive?"

"You've fucked a trans guy before," Nic surmised in a whisper, raising his brow. He shed his shirt and tossed it aside. That was too specific for just anyone to think of. "I... yeah, I feel things. I like it when—nnh! Fuck."

Kyle was running his thumb around Nic's nipple slowly, teasing the nerves to life. "Good. And I have, if it matters. Ooh, they're big. That's hot. Christ, your chest muscles are *ripped*."

"Cool." Nic had been pretty sure Kyle wouldn't just give him a boner-killer moment, but this upgraded his status from *please fuck me now* to *please please please you're perfect.* "They are. I work out a lot. Gives me something to do."

Kyle didn't just sweep him off his feet—he made him feel safe in his current.

Nic grabbed Kyle's shirt and pulled at it while Kyle laughed, stripping it off as fast as he could. The lean torso and dark fuzz along his chest caught his eye, and he licked his lips.

"I want you now," Kyle breathed out, unzipping his own jeans and pulling them off. He was hard in his underwear, the distinctive thick line of a hard cock pressing against the thin fabric. "Can I suck your dick?"

Kyle didn't even know what to expect, since he hadn't

asked about bottom surgery. That meant... he cared about making Nic feel good. Nic closed his eyes for a second to let the excitement wash through him, then moaned, "God, yes."

He was hard, too, and Kyle's firm palm running down over his crotch made his hips reflexively jolt and push up into him.

"Easy, boy," Kyle teased, unbuckling Nic's belt and unzipping his jeans. He pulled the fabric down to his thighs so Nic could take over and kick them off, but left on his underwear so far.

Instead of going straight down, Kyle braced himself on one arm over Nic to kiss at his neck and throat, then worked his way down.

"Oh, fuck," Nic breathed as Kyle's hot tongue trailed along his skin, igniting a burning line under his skin from throat to chest. It turned into a throaty groan of desire when lips flicked over his nipple. He squirmed, pressing his cock into Kyle's hip and grinding in quick, needy movements.

It was like a direct line to his dick, a promise of things to come, when the wet warmth closed around his nipple and sucked hard.

Nic jolted and gasped, his hands flying to Kyle's shoulders to dig his nails in and squeeze. "Yes!"

"Mmm," Kyle moaned, the faint vibrations echoed in the trembling of Nic's body. He swirled his tongue around, then rapidly flicked the tip over the sensitive nub.

Nic squeezed his eyes shut with how fucking *good* that felt. "Kyle, please..." he moaned, grinding harder in a quick rhythm. "Please. Fuck. Oh, fuck..."

"You're *so* sensitive," Kyle whispered, sounding delighted. "God, I'd love to tie you down and tease you... all... fucking... night." He punctuated each word by pressing an openmouthed kiss against his chest.

Kyle breathed the last word out over Nic's other nipple, then closed his lips and sucked it firmly into his mouth, flicking his other fingertip over Nic's still-damp nipple.

Nic whimpered open-mouthed, choking his sound of desire when he ran out of breath. "Yes...!"

"Mm," Kyle gasped. "Oh, you're a fun one."

Nic nearly covered his face from embarrassment at the way Kyle told him that. Just knowing Kyle found him irresistible made him feel appreciated. It would put a spring in his step for weeks.

Kyle was kissing his hipbone and stomach, licking his way down the treasure trail. He pressed his lips against the fabric over Nic's throbbing shaft, and Nic grabbed Kyle's hair.

"Oh, man," Kyle whispered, hooking his thumb into Nic's underwear to drag it down to his thighs. He kissed along Nic's inner thigh. "You make me wanna lick your cock until you're whimpering for me."

Up close, Nic's cock looked like any other small cock, his balls heavy in Kyle's hand as Kyle cupped them. It wasn't quite long or thick enough to easily fuck. And still, Kyle was looking at him with those hot, lidded eyes.

Nic breathed out heavily as his dick twitched under Kyle's lustful gaze. "Fuck, please. Yes, fuck... fuck, please..." He'd do or say just about anything to get that hot mouth on him.

"Are you comfortable without a condom?"

"None fit me anyway," Nic breathed a quick laugh. Finger cots were too small, most condoms off the shelf too big, dental dams meant for flatter body parts. "So, yeah."

Kyle frowned, rubbing his thumb along Nic's shaft to the head and circling it slowly. "Christ. I hadn't even thought..." He looked sheepish. "And Plus... wow."

"Don't worry about it," Nic brushed it off. They could talk

about Kyle's work later, when he wasn't five seconds from having Kyle's pretty lips wrapped around his dick.

Kyle smirked at the urgency in his voice. "You need me that much, don't you? You're so hard." He slowly rubbed his fingers up Nic's shaft, playing with his foreskin, then back down again. "Fuck, you're hot."

"*Kyle,*" Nic begged, out of breath and out of patience. "*Please.*"

The moan that slipped from Kyle's throat sent shudders through Nic, but they paled in comparison to the surge of desire that made his thighs tremble and his stomach muscles tense. His whole body drew tight. For half a second, he thought he'd come on the spot.

Nic's nerves were on fire as Kyle's tongue circled the head of his cock and flicked over it. "Yes! Oh my *fuck*—" he gasped.

Kyle slowly drew his head up and down, pulling the shaft between his lips as he bobbed his head.

Nic couldn't help his little moans of need as Kyle sucked hard, the wet sounds making his cheeks flush. "Oh, fuck, yes. Oh my God. Kyle..."

Kyle flicked his tongue around and along the underside of his cock, then the head again. He palmed Nic's balls in the other, teasing the insides of his thighs. Every little prickle of pleasant sensation made Nic's taut muscles vibrate, making him arch off the bed and squirm again.

Kyle slowly pulled his mouth off Nic, ignoring Nic's moan. "God, you're sensitive. And so," Kyle licked the underside of Nic's cock from base to tip, "damn," he suckled on the head for a moment, "hot." He blew lightly across it.

"Fuck. Fuuuck," Nic groaned, grabbing Kyle's hair and tangling his hands in it. It was all he could do not to shove himself back into Kyle's mouth. "I *need* it, baby. Please. Fuck. I'm so close... I wanna come before you fuck me."

His self-consciousness was gone. There was nothing left to be shy about when his dick was red and throbbing, Kyle's lips swollen and pink, both of them panting with desire as they writhed together on the bed.

"God, yes," Kyle breathed out hoarsely. When he sucked Nic into his mouth again, this time, he meant business. Fast and hard, he bobbed his head, keeping the wet, tight pressure while running his tongue across the head nonstop.

"I can't..." Nic started to gasp, but it was too late. His climax blinded him, making him push back into the mattress with his shoulders as he thrust into Kyle's mouth with each shuddering clench.

Waves of pleasure hit him like the hurricane that was Kyle, blotting out every thought except how fucking incredible Kyle's hands were, how filthy good his mouth was. And naturally, Kyle swallowed, because he couldn't get any more perfect.

When Nic's moans subsided, his thighs still trembling, Nic collapsed onto the mattress again, letting go of his grip on Kyle's hair. "S-Sorry. If that was... rough."

"Fucking *Jesus*, you're hot," Kyle breathed out, his eyes wide but dark with desire. "That was... *fuck*. I didn't know you could, uh..."

"Come? Yeah." Nic's head spun as he grinned at Kyle. "Sorry. Tried to warn you. You were too good. Thank you. Shit. I can't..." His brain was in that disjointed, fuzzy place where his pleasure was making him giddy, his thoughts hard to corral.

Kyle licked his lips and grinned back. "The pleasure's all

mine." He hooked his thumbs into his underwear and pulled them down, his cock springing free.

Oh, *that* was big... and thick. And looking in dire need of attention.

"It is now," Nic breathed out, drawing his knees up and spreading his legs.

"You take your time."

"No. Now," Nic ordered. He wanted to be filled by that manhood as soon as possible.

As Kyle scooted up his body and over to the bedside table to grab lube, Nic grabbed his wrist. "No condom."

Kyle stared at him. "What? Are you sure?"

"Yeah." Unsaid was the, *I trust you, of all people, to be honest.*

Kyle read it in his face anyway, and his expression softened. "You don't have to..."

"I know," Nic snorted. "This isn't... gratitude or desperation. You choose, but I want it. I never get to do this."

"Me neither," Kyle admitted, half-smiling. "And I did just suck you off without one, for the first time in *forever*... what's gotten into me?"

"Hopefully me, sometime," Nic winked as Kyle's lean, wet fingers slid into him.

Kyle's cheeks turned red, and then he laughed. "Okay then. Yeah. We'll see."

"Yeah?" Nic's cheeks heated up. He wanted to be marked as Kyle's, fucked hard and left wet. If this was one night, he was going to make it count.

"*Hell*, yeah," Kyle winked, and Nic shivered with delight. It was Kyle. Kyle sent all the filthiest thoughts straight to his head, and he couldn't stop himself.

The head of Kyle's cock pressed at Nic's opening, and Kyle

ground against Nic's cock, blanketing his body with his weight. He was going to be hard again within minutes if Kyle fucked him like he looked like he meant to.

Filled by every inch, Nic choked back his gasps so he could hear Kyle's quiet moans. He was hot and thick and *perfect*. He squirmed and curled his toes into the bed, grabbing Kyle around the shoulders to haul him down until their chests crushed together.

"Hi," Kyle breathlessly laughed with surprise as Nic hitched up one knee to slide his leg around Kyle's upper thighs. "Jesus, you make me wanna fuck you through the bed," he whispered, pressing his lips against Nic's jaw and behind his ear.

"Hnnh!" Nic's thighs twitched, heat flushing his face as Kyle flicked his tongue along the sensitive earlobe. "Fuck!"

"You like that, huh?" Kyle whispered, pushing his hips into motion at long fucking last. "Maybe I can make you come again..."

Nic nodded slightly, his nails digging into Kyle's back as he ran his hands down to the small of his back.

Kyle thrust, slow and steady at first, the heat pressing deep into Nic and then out again, leaving him with a twinge of disappointment and need each time. That pace didn't last, though. He was too desperate. His breathing was heavy against Nic's neck, his body trembling with tension.

"Fuck me, baby," Nic breathed out, slapping Kyle's firm ass. God, what a great *smack* sound it made, ringing out through the room. Then he pulled Kyle close again so his cock ground against Kyle's stomach, grunting with pleasure. With a few minutes having passed, the oversensitive stage was over. He was stirring to life again. It was always trickier to get off the second time—way harder than it had been years ago—but with enough effort, he could sometimes manage it.

And with the smoking hot visuals he had right now.

Kyle obediently braced himself on an elbow above Nic's head, shifting his weight, then drove into him hard and fast.

"Yes!" Nic whimpered, his arms locking around Kyle's back while Kyle moaned and gasped for breath close to his ear. He wanted Kyle's thick, throbbing manhood in him all fucking day.

"I'm so close, baby. Watching you... and feeling you get hard again..." Kyle panted for breath. "You want me to come in you or on you?"

"In me," Nic whispered instantly, squeezing Kyle's ass again. He slid one palm between them so he could grab his own dick and start jerking hard and fast.

Kyle's gaze flickered down between their bodies for a moment, and then his cheeks turned even redder. "Oh my God, yes!"

Nic turned his head to catch his lips for a hot, wet kiss. He only had to tease the tip of Kyle's tongue with his own and suck on his lower lip for a few moments before Kyle was pulling back, his eyes widening.

"I'm—baby...!" Kyle's nails dug into his shoulder and his hip as he thrust hard, and suddenly erratically. "Yes... yes, Nic, oh, fuck..."

And Nic was wetter than ever. Each quick thrust of Kyle's hips only added to the mess, and he thought he might die happy when Kyle finally slid out of him and collapsed on him.

He jerked himself off hard, knocking away Kyle's hand when Kyle tried to reach between them. "My turn."

Kyle laughed softly and instead rolled onto his side to

watch, running his toes up Nic's leg. "Fucking fuck, that's hot."

It took Nic a few more minutes before his body could manage it, but then he growled with pleasure. He replayed every moment he'd just experienced, squeezing his eyes shut.

Then it hit. Pleasure blinded Nic for a few long moments and he came, arching off the bed.

Kyle's hands ran along his thigh and side, the back of his knuckles along his jaw. Nic's muscles were already tight and twitching, but now his nerves were on fire from every little touch, and he didn't want it to stop.

All he could manage was a loud, senseless moan as he thrust into his own fingers. When his body started to relax, he rubbed the wetness down his shaft for a few final, slower strokes, and let go. "Jesus."

"So good," Kyle whispered, his lips close to Nic's ear. The soft kiss behind it made Nic's chest warm up. Then his brain kicked in again, and he let out a long breath, pressing into Kyle's side. Kyle's arm slid around him, pulling him in.

Exhaustion hit at last.

Best night ever.

12

NIC

The sheets were warm, cozy, and blue.

That was wrong. Nic's sheets were supposed to be white, and these were distinctly dark blue. The same moment he saw the answer, he also smelled its faint musk, felt its body heat, and tasted the faint aftertaste of its lips.

I'm at Kyle's.

He hadn't meant to fall asleep, but Kyle's arm around him had been strong and warm, and surprisingly tender after their fun night. He'd closed his eyes to doze against Kyle's side, and then sleep had claimed him.

It was definitely early Saturday morning now.

Been a while since I've done the walk of shame. Nic's lip quirked at the corner, and then he shifted in bed slightly to watch Kyle. *Totally worth it.*

Kyle was already stirring, as if his body and brain were in disagreement over the next step. His fingers twitched against Nic's ribs. The absence of his hand, when he pulled it back toward his own face to rub his eyes as his wakeful mind won the battle, left Nic aching.

"Hey," Nic greeted, then cleared his throat of roughness.

Kyle cracked an eye, then closed it again and sighed, wriggling against the bed as if wishing for another few hours of rest. "Morning," he murmured.

Kyle was painfully pretty. His hair was rumpled, some green bits stuck up, while others were almost long enough to get into his eyes. It had felt stiff but not tacky when he grabbed it last night—he must use clay or wax. Nic found himself wondering what Kyle's grooming regimen looked like.

He stole a look around the room while Kyle convinced himself to wake up.

An elegant, simple, understated room, but not overdressed. Every detail was carefully chosen, and there was a definite dark, rich color scheme at play. From sheets to curtains, Kyle had chosen jewel tones, much like the green of his hair blended into the darkness of the rest. The walls were cream. He had an art piece above the bed that Nic couldn't really see from this angle, and a painting of a seascape on another wall.

It felt sophisticated but youthful, like Kyle himself.

The blinds were cracked, and sunlight streamed across the floor. When Kyle finally swung his feet out of bed, he padded over to the bedroom window to pull them apart.

Christ, it was already daylight. Nic had no real plans this weekend, but Kyle probably did. He seemed busy.

"Up to much today? Hope I didn't keep you sleeping in," Nic half-smiled, pushing the covers off himself. He felt Kyle's gaze trail down his back and looked over his shoulder to make eye contact.

Kyle winked when he made eye contact. "Nah," he shrugged, yawning and stretching. He rose onto tiptoe, and God, it was hard not to admire him naked as his stomach muscles pulled tight and back rippled. "It's only eight."

"Oh, that's early for a Saturday," Nic grinned, tearing his eyes off Kyle and glancing toward the bathroom.

"You can shower if you want."

"Nah," Nic shook his head. He'd rather wait until he got home and could properly relax. He didn't have anything to do except shop for groceries and whatever anyway. And this time of morning, getting a taxi would be almost instant. "Thanks."

But Kyle was so fucking gorgeous, and when he smiled sweetly back at Nic, Nic's heart throbbed.

"Okay. You gonna get home all right?"

"I'm fine," Nic assured Kyle. He slowly approached, not even thinking to be self-conscious. They both moved to slide their arms loosely around each other's waist, swaying to and fro in the sunlight.

The hand running up his back to the back of his neck made Nic smile. He felt *safe* in Kyle's hands, but he had with other men, too. With Kyle, there was something else, too. He didn't want to think about it, but boy, did he *feel* it warming his chest.

Nic knew he should know better. He *really* should. Before he opened his mouth, he knew it was a bad idea, but he couldn't stop himself.

"Can I take you out again? Dinner sometime?" There it was. No point mooning around and hoping for more. He had to make a move if he wanted more.

Kyle's expression gentled, and he leaned in to press a kiss to Nic's forehead. *Uh oh. Bad sign.* "Thank you, but no. You're..." Kyle cleared his throat.

Too what? Nic's brain filled in the question, and a host of possible answers that he tried to ignore. Too trans? Some guys could fuck one but not date one, even post-transition like he was. Too young? Some guys wanted a silver fox to take care of

E. DAVIES

them and look the part as well as paying the bills. Too quiet? Some guys needed a boisterous, outgoing guy who could be the life of the party.

Sometimes, it felt like everyone was just searching for someone who ticked the right boxes, without paying attention to *this*—the chemistry that still sizzled between them, the way neither of them had dropped their hands from each other's backs.

The pause was only maybe half a second, but Nic's thoughts raced as his heart sank way harder than he'd anticipated.

"You're really sweet," Kyle went on, rubbing his thumb along Nic's jaw before pulling his hand away, stepping back half a pace. "You don't deserve to be led on."

God, Nic would let Kyle lead him on if he'd hold him like that again. Which was the lamest thought he'd ever had. Nic cleared his throat and shifted from one foot to the other. "Yeah, yeah, cool," he mumbled, hoping to disappear into the ground any moment now.

"It's *really* not you," Kyle said, and something in his tone caught Nic's eye. He sounded... disappointed? Was that self-reproach? This wasn't a rehearsed speech, not like Nic had heard and given. "I'm not looking for a relationship, that's all. So if you want more..."

Nic wanted to give the answer his dick told him to—that he didn't care about relationships, that he'd just fuck Kyle without getting his heart involved—but he already knew it was a lie. If he landed in bed with this man again, he was going to fall for him.

Shit. Maybe he already had.

Whatever the case, it would be the worst possible idea to

push his luck. He'd gotten Kyle for a night. If that was all, it had still been a great night.

"Yeah, I think I am," Nic admitted with a quick smile. "But that's fine. No hard feelings. Well... lots of *hard* feelings..."

Kyle's face split in a grin of relief and amusement, and then he slapped Nic's ass. "Get out with you, before I break my no-guy-twice rule."

"Could I tempt you to?" Nic winked, wiggling his ass and glancing over his shoulder as he turned to grab his clothes from the floor and sort them out.

"If I didn't have something this afternoon, perhaps. You're a bad man." Kyle licked his lips and headed for the bedroom door, clearly looking to break this sexual tension. "Coffee for the road?"

"Sure."

Nic let his own breath of relief escape when Kyle was out of the room.

It was, after all, relief and not disappointment making his heart sink and slow to its normal rate, holding his movements back to slow and lazy ones.

It was relief that made his eyes sting with the morning light when he stepped outside for the taxi a couple minutes later, caffeinated and fully dressed and aching for a goodbye kiss. He hadn't gone for one, and Kyle hadn't offered.

It was relief, wasn't it?

It's a good thing. Somehow. At least I won't waste time wondering.

Nic's throat was tight as he leaned into the taxi door. After he gave his address, he was silent for the drive home.

13

KYLE

Wallet, keys, phone—it all went into Kyle's pockets, which made him grin deliriously. This skirt had *pockets*.

It was hard finding clothes that worked for him. Women's jeans fit his narrow hips better than some men's jeans and gave him room for his ass, and as a bonus, they rode his hips lower. That showed off more V if he had a crop top on. On the flip side, there was no extra room downstairs. Crowding there got uncomfortable fast.

Kyle had the confidence to wear a lot of skirts and dresses, but many cuts relied on chest padding he didn't have. Others pulled too tight around the waist at the wrong point, or around the thighs, which would result in *really* showing off his bulge— sometimes welcome but not always the look he wanted.

And shirts—fuck, he'd been self-conscious about his wide shoulders and defined biceps some days. Some sleeves pulled tight or looked wrong. Shirts also had the *no-boobs* problem.

This was his weekend to have Kevin, and when he'd told River he was looking for something purple to wear out with his son, River had conjured up this piece of pure *magic* a day later.

He could kiss his best friend sometimes. If they'd ever felt a spark of chemistry, they'd have made goddamn perfect boyfriends. As it was, they settled for fiercely vetting each other's boyfriend choices, but River didn't have someone like he deserved right now.

And Nic was a sweetheart, like River, in his own way. Kyle half-wondered if Nic's liking for femme guys extended to drag queens, but that sent a weird prickle through him. Probably just because they weren't the kind of friends who shared guys —at least, on purpose. Accidents happened in this one-degree-of-separation world.

As Kyle climbed into the car, he grinned again as he had to reach into his skirt pocket for the car keys. A purse wasn't his style. He hated carrying things for longer than he had to; he'd just put one down and forget it.

By the time he got to Evie's house, Evie shooed him inside and straight for the kitchen counter, handing him a cup of coffee.

"I, uh—Kevin?" Kyle questioned as he found the mug of coffee scorching his palms. He set it down and blew into his hands, then picked it up gingerly again.

"He's getting ready. He can't choose tights. He got a run in his favorite black pair last week," Evie told him with a sigh. "I have to pick up more. Cute skirt, by the way. You two will match."

"That's the plan. We'll get tights for him if we're near a store this weekend," Kyle promised.

"Mmm." Evie leaned onto her elbows and folded her hands, propping her chin on them.

"Why are you looking at me like that?" Kyle knew damn well why, and he couldn't keep up the innocent pretense longer than a few moments before he cracked and grinned.

Evie clicked her tongue. "Of *course* I saw you two leaving together. So?"

"I..." Kyle glanced down at his coffee, watching the ripples settle in the mug, then looked up at Evie.

Her dark eyes were wide and curious, hopeful but not pushy. She clearly wanted good news, but the truth, too. She'd sniff out anything else too fast anyway. She knew Kyle better than he knew himself some days, and that was saying something.

"I almost... I've got some..." Kyle shifted the mug to hold it by its handle so he could wave with the other hand. "Almost feelings for him."

"Oh, shit," Evie whispered, then smiled gently. "This happens now and then, though, right?"

Kyle cast his mind back. He'd gotten little crushes here and there on guys he'd fucked, but usually *before* he fucked them. They didn't usually keep his interest afterward. But it had taken every ounce of strength not to let Nic flirt with him longer.

Not to lead him on.

"I wanted him to stick around this morning."

Evie whistled under her breath. "I *knew* there'd be something there."

Kyle's cheeks were hot. He sipped his coffee and set it down, then pushed her shoulder, trying to get her to stop grinning like the cat that got the canary. "Don't get worked up. I turned down a date."

"What? Oh, God. Kyle. Why?" Evie groaned. "Is it the coworker thing?"

"I... Yeah. I don't know how to handle working with him if I'm seeing him, too. You know. There's no rules against it, but..." Kyle waved a hand. It was paper-thin, as excuses went.

But there were other, more solid reasons, when he took the time to think of them. Focusing on his work and his son, for example. Kyle didn't know what it said about him that those were the last concerns to mind. Normally, they were the first.

"I think I want him," Kyle murmured, then smacked his head gently against his coffee mug. "Fuck."

Evie squeezed his arm and rubbed lightly. "It's *good*, honey. Even if things don't go somewhere... it's nice to like someone. He's totally into you, too. He was looking at you like his hero last night."

The memory of Nic's wide eyes following Kyle's every move at the club led to memories of Nic's wide eyes and eagerness to please in bed. But he wasn't desperate; his self-confidence was fucking *hot* as hell. Even being turned down had clearly disappointed him, but he hadn't tried to coax him, nor had he changed his mind on what he wanted just to suit what Kyle wanted to hear.

Nic might be shy and awkward sometimes, but he was a man, not a boy. Kyle needed someone with a strong will and straight priorities, like Nic. And Nic was smart as hell, and funny, and his heart was definitely in the right place. And open and generous in bed... God, their sex was hot.

The fact that Kyle was even thinking all this was damning. He didn't get attached so fast—he just didn't.

"Fuck," Kyle whispered again. He let himself start thinking about *what-if*s. "Denver would be okay, I think... I don't know about his boss."

"Nic comes off as professional," Evie told him gently. "I only know him a little, but I've heard other people talking about his work on the project. Greg will be okay with it."

"Yeah, but..." Kyle trailed off, casting his mind around for excuses. Again, Evie was silent to let him think through it.

He couldn't get the image out of his head: Nic's mournful expression for a few seconds before he covered it up with graceful acceptance.

Maybe Nic had clued into something Kyle hadn't. Nic *was* exactly his type, and from how Nic had acted around him, he was into him, too. He'd asked him out, for God's sake.

But he wasn't in the market for a relationship.

His son's footsteps shattered his thoughts, and Kyle grinned as he turned to Kevin. "Hey, gorgeous! Love the dress!"

"Thank you, Daddy. Wanna go to park? Ready to go? I'm ready!" Kevin bolted for the door.

The dress was a cute purple A-line dress, simple but elegant. From the closet, Kevin grabbed bright yellow shoes. When Kyle saw them, he raised his eyebrows and opened his mouth, but Evie kicked him, silently forbidding him to say anything.

Oh, great. He likes Crocs.

"That's all you," Kyle told her under his breath.

"Probably," Evie giggled. "Sorry."

Kyle dramatically groaned, then came around the coffee table to sweep Evie into a tight hug. He kissed her cheek. "Thanks, Eve."

"Always, Kyle," Evie promised gently and squeezed him back. "Go have fun."

Kyle smiled at her and turned to his son. "Okay, buddy. Time to head for the car."

"Are we going to the park?" Kevin was still bouncing up and down on his toes, even in those horrible Crocs. "I wanna go to the park. Mommy said if it's a nice day we can go to the park and it's a nice day. It's sun."

"It is sunny," Kyle agreed, his eyes sparkling already as he smiled fondly at his son. "Yeah, our first stop is the park."

Kevin's cheer lasted all the way to the car as he hopped over to it. Kyle had to sprint after him to stay between him and the road.

It was going to be a great weekend.

14

NIC

Being outside in fresh air and sunlight wasn't supposed to feel this odd. Nic squinted up at the afternoon sun and shook his head ruefully.

Time management, man.

He'd been largely on-track for developing the new database until this weekend. The days off had thrown him out of his rhythm. Now it was Wednesday, and the last time he'd been out of the house was on Saturday for groceries.

But the prototype was *ready*, and most of the bugs were probably squashed. There was a lot of finishing work to be done—they were a couple weeks from the end of the project, even if it would look to the inexperienced observer like they were almost there.

This time, Nic remembered where he was going and didn't get lost on his way to the Plus office. He parked and grabbed his laptop bag, then headed for the front door.

The building was way more secure than Nic had first envisioned. He wasn't working from it, so they hadn't given him a key card to get in. He buzzed and waited.

There were about four secure doors in between here and there. He didn't want to think too closely about why.

"Hey! Nic? I'll be down in two... in a sec!" the speaker grill chirped in Kyle's unmistakably bubbly tone.

"Okay, thanks." Nic's cheeks burned as he shifted his laptop bag from one hand to the other, his mind not at all on work for a few moments. It was going to be their first time seeing each other face-to-face since sleeping together several days ago. He didn't know how Kyle was going to act.

Keep it professional. He didn't usually sleep with coworkers, so that bridge was already in ashes, but he could salvage his pride, if not his reputation.

"Hey!" Kyle pushed open the glass door abruptly, making Nic jump with surprise. He'd been caught up in thought. "Oh, sorry!" Kyle instantly gasped, reaching out as if to touch his arm but not quite doing so.

"It's fine," Nic brushed it off with a quick smile. "Hi. I've got the specs ready."

"The specs. Great. Okay, come on up. Did it all go well? Do you have a prototype? Can I click on things and see what happens?"

Kyle was exactly the same as he had been the first time— bubbly and vivacious, beaming at him like he was the only person in the world.

Phew. Not awkward at all. By the time they were at the office door, Nic found himself chatting about the function he couldn't get figured out, encouraged by Kyle even though Kyle had no idea what he was talking about.

Flustered, he cleared his throat and followed after Kyle. "But I'll—I'll debug it."

A few of the guys in the office waved to him on the way past, so he smiled and nodded back.

They settled in a little office next to the meeting room they'd used last time, both of them sitting on the same side of the desk. Kyle folded his hands in his lap attentively. "So, hit me with your *best shot*." His voice rose into a melody, and he danced with the tune for a few seconds.

Nic was beaming again. Yeah, he was crushing. Christ, it was hard not to stare at Kyle and let on his feelings, but he tried. He just couldn't help himself. "Okay, here's the basic interface."

He opened up the program and clicked around a little, explaining what would connect to what, and how the resource database would integrate with email in particular.

The reporting function—email categorization and tagging, allowing them to generate reports of the services they provided —made Kyle gasp with delight.

He was so fucking adorable... so vibrant. It was hard not to take Kyle's rejection personally when they got along so easily right now, but Nic reminded himself that that was because it *wasn't* personal. They just wanted different things, and that was okay. It made this whole situation less awkward.

And the sex *had* been great. Hot. Phenomenal, even.

"This is so cool!" Kyle kept exclaiming before leaning in to ask what another button did. This time, he was poking the inventory button.

"Well..." Nic wasn't sure anyone had ever felt happier about his work, and it made it hard to think straight. When he leaned in to put his finger on the trackpad, Kyle hadn't quite drawn back yet.

Their hands brushed, and a jolt shivered through Nic's whole frame.

Holy fuck. That chemistry isn't spent.

They'd both felt it—they shifted, glancing sideways at each other as if to measure up what had just happened.

There was a light knock on the door, and Kyle's hands were suddenly in his lap again.

"Sounds like there's fun happening in here." It was Denver, poking his head in and then stepping inside before closing the door after him. His eyes were twinkling with amusement.

"You should see this thing. It's so cool," Kyle instantly told Denver. "Nic's doing great with interpreting our instructions. I didn't even think to ask about reporting..."

Nic's cheeks were hot at the praise. "Automatically generated reports, which I can also integrate with your inventory database so you know how many condoms you gave away in a year or whatnot," he explained. He tried not to blush at the word. This was not his usual professional environment.

Denver sank into a chair on the other side of the desk. "Oh, that *is* helpful. Kyle and I waste a lot of time figuring that out manually."

"I know. Hopefully this can free you up," Nic told them both, then started going over the system basics again with Denver.

Denver picked up technology as intuitively as Kyle did, which was a great relief. He was only a few years older, but that could make a big difference to how fast people caught on when he taught them anything.

"You guys have fun at the club last weekend?"

The question startled Nic. *Did he know about us? Did someone say? Shit, is this a test?*

Before he could even answer, Denver added, "Sorry I couldn't make it. I do every now and then," he said to Nic.

"Ahh. Yeah."

"It was great. Great fun," Kyle said with a smile and a nod. He was casual as all get-out.

"Fun, yeah," Nic agreed, trying to adopt the same easy-going tone. *Totally not suspicious at all.*

Denver's eyes flickered between them, and then a smile flickered over his lips. "I'm glad Evie recommended her company to us, and they could send you. It's nice to keep it in the community where we can."

"Yeah," Nic murmured under his breath, clearing his throat. *Kyle and I sure did.* "Um. I haven't done a project for an organization like this before. It's all been medium to large businesses, really... impersonal."

"That's why you're putting all those extra touches in," Kyle murmured.

Nic blushed. *Busted.* He didn't want to take credit for going above and beyond the job description, but it was true. These guys worked fucking hard at their jobs, they all clearly felt passionate about it, and they were doing good work. Way better work than he could do from behind a keyboard. It was the least he could do.

"Careful," Denver warned, rising to his feet with a wink. "We might kidnap you and keep you as our IT minion. The catch is that we pay in pizza. I hope that's fine..."

Nic clicked his tongue as if considering it. "Pizza *is* really good." He opened up a notepad file to write down the reactions he'd noticed—starting with the fact that both of them had tried to click a button that he'd intended as a nonfunctional menu label.

"I know, huh? He offered me the same gig," Kyle grinned while Nic typed.

"And did I lie?"

"He *does* feed us a lot of pizza. That's about all we eat

working after hours. Oh my God, that sound so bad," Kyle laughed, covering his face. "I eat things other than carbs occasionally. Don't judge me."

Nic snorted. "You're in fine shape." He only realized what he said after it had left his mouth. *Oh, shit.* He managed *not* to look guilty or look at Denver, but he was pretty sure he was blushing again. *Oh my God, don't tell his boss you saw him naked a few days ago.*

"Yeah. Stop complaining about your five-percent body fat," Denver rolled his eyes at Kyle. Thank God he didn't catch on. "You know better than to chase shallowness."

Kyle laughed quietly. "Oh, *I* know." It didn't quite sound bitter, but it was pretty damn close. If they'd been alone, Nic might have considered pressing it.

As it was, there was a moment of silence.

"*Awk*warrrrd," Kyle chirped, wiggling his fingers in the air like jazz-hands. "Joke. Laugh, damn it."

They both did, and then Denver leaned across the desk for another look at the laptop. "So, you're just progressing with what you have? Next progress report will be next week?"

"Correct. If you need any updates earlier, I can probably provide them, but there won't be a lot of excitement. I need to make these functions actually work," Nic warned them, half-smiling. A lot of buttons had been nonfunctional, and he'd alt-tabbed to show a mockup of what he was designing.

"That's perfect." Denver looked at Kyle. "Ready for your board meeting?"

Kyle made a face. "I was trying not to think about that."

"Oh. I should get going," Nic nodded, rising to his feet and closing his laptop. There was no sense lingering to try to get a few more minutes with this guy.

We don't want the same thing.

Despite that, Kyle lingered in the doorway, watching him climb into his car. He even raised his hand for a goodbye wave. Nic hastily waved back as he turned out of the parking lot to the main road.

The green of Kyle's hair was the last thing Nic saw before he disappeared around the corner. Nic's fingers itched to comb through the soft, thick hair and pull Kyle in for just one more lazy, naked hug in the morning sunlight.

Even if I can't have him, I can appreciate him. It made Nic's chest ache, but a lot of things about being adult did.

Maybe he'd treat himself to ice cream tonight. Or pizza.

Pizza it was.

15

KYLE

"Does anyone have questions?"

God, please say no.

"Yes, I have a few. Can we go over those slides again?" Of course it was Cal.

Kyle just smiled broadly at him. "Of course!"

The second time around, his nerves were much calmer. The board was not his ideal audience—not the guys in the trenches, like them. Largely, these people were stuffy old guys in suits. Some of them were interested in the charity from a medical or public health standpoint and had no investment in the gay community; others were the kind of gays who wore merino sweaters with quarter-zips and looked away from starving kids.

Several board members did care about the cause, and were genuinely great people, but bringing money into it always complicated things. This wasn't a regular board meeting. They were specifically meeting about bringing new donors on board, in the hopes of acquiring more funds to allocate to different programs.

Kyle had made his programming pitch, but it was up to the board to vote on it. And he had to convince them that they'd made the best use of funding, they just needed more.

"Of the students we surveyed at the entry fairs, few had heard of PrEP. The numbers are a little higher for LGBT-identified students. But if you look at even healthcare providers... it's still only two-thirds of them who have heard of it. Knowledge is critical at this stage."

"But, getting back to your LGBT students, that includes lesbians and trans. And... straight-curious men. The ones who just sleep with men but don't date them. They're not in our mandate to focus on the health of *gay men.*"

I could strangle him.

Kyle drew a breath, then smiled. "Our mission statement discusses gay men, that's true. But in our articles, we use the term MSM, which *includes* bi men. And those surveys cover lesbians and trans *people*, yes. Gender identity and sexual orientation are not mutually exclusive. Many trans women are at very high risk, and are frequently involved with MSM, or identify that way prior to transition. Other charities are focused on them, but they may come to us first. And finally, we don't know much at all about the risks to trans men. Trans MSM in this area have no other charities out there specifically looking at HIV education, prevention, treatment, and advocacy. Our remit is not solely cis people."

One of the better board members, Andy, was nodding along with him, his hand loosely raised.

Kyle nodded at him to acknowledge him and turned back to Cal. "And there's almost no research on nonbinary people, but our survey numbers have skyrocketed. Our definitions— MSM, FSF—that fails us when we talk about nonbinary or agender people who *we'd* see as gay men, but won't identify themselves that way, or even look like what we picture MSM to look like. So if we're only focusing on gay men, people who fall within our mandate according to slippery biological definitions are being excluded, and we're less effective and prepared. We can't do our work on assumptions. That makes us no better than the groups we're holding accountable."

There were grumbles and shifting. He could tell they were judging him for his loud hair and apparel, wondering if he was one of *those* people himself. Kyle carried on, though.

"Denver and I believe that educating all LGBT students at once does us a lot more good than trying to single out MSM. God, not to mention all the closeted kids who call themselves allies…! Not only do we want to reach high-risk individuals who form their own communities but wouldn't come to us, but we can help start those conversations among other risk groups. We can be there to help study, and listen to what they need."

It was a wordier answer than Kyle could have given, but it served its purpose. He sounded prepared, and some other board members were nodding. They at least respected him for his knowledge of the generations close to his own.

"This seems like a large budget increase you're asking for," Andy pointed out. It wasn't accusatory, just curious. "Your primary goal is awareness? What about access?"

Kyle clapped his hands together and nodded briskly. "Right. Good question. We have guides, and there are two online guides that go into more detail than we're allowed to on generics and nonprescription use."

"Isn't condom usage still our top prevention strategy?" Cal held out his hands and looked around the room. "Hasn't it always been? What happens when all these kids stop using them? Do we even know that PrEP will work like it's supposed to?"

Kyle had expected this one. He drew a deep breath and laced his hands behind his back, resisting the urge to tug down his skirt or neaten his hair. Cal needed a direct approach.

"First of all, yes, we know it works. Over 99%, near 100%, success rate when properly used, just like birth control. We still continue to advocate condom use, of course, as the easiest and cheapest and most reliable method, but all the data is incredibly promising. We've always been on the front line: studying medical research, giving people access to lifesaving measures before policy catches up with us. We can't fall down on that now, and we are right now. Other countries are looking at introducing PrEP access nationwide."

"So, PrEP is just Truvada taken before infection?" That was Joseph, one of the older men who tended to ignore the existence of everyone except attractive white gay men. He and Kyle never got along. "It doesn't build up a resistance, even when all those kids forget to take it every day?"

"Correct. It's a one-a-day pill, antiretroviral medication—Truvada, yes. There's no resistance if you miss a dose, but the protection rate is lower. The biggest priority is getting diagnosed ASAP if you *are* infected," Kyle explained, trying to stay patient. How Joseph could be on the board of this charity and not know these things boggled his mind. "That way doctors can test your viral load and adjust. The only way you build up a resistance is if the virus is *already* in your body."

"Got it." That was Andy, and he drummed the table. "Explaining that to people is definitely a priority."

"Well," Cal said, "can't we include PrEP education in other campaigns? Like the school presentations?"

God, he was worn out from battling Cal's questions all throughout the presentation. And they just didn't seem to stop. He'd objected to every aspect of the budget increase request, from start to finish. It was like he didn't want to ask any new potential donors for funding. But he didn't have to—Kyle would fucking do it himself if he had to.

"We do, but it's a *huge* topic in itself." Kyle shook his head. "We have to explain who's best suited, answer questions, talk about the anti-anxiety effect it has on people, set them up with a good doctor, help people figure out insurance companies... The materials all need to be updated, and we need to increase testing availability so we don't create other dangers like resistance."

"Right, right, but... I guess it seems like an inefficient use of funds," Cal spoke slowly. "What else... you said you're working with all the LGBT... non-gender... people... don't transsexual, or transgendered, or whatever, men have women's health concerns that we can't really cover? Would it be cheaper to focus just on men?"

Kyle narrowed his eyes. "Here's the sum total of the research we've got: trans men probably *are* more vulnerable because medically, they're more likely to experience bleeding in receptive sexual positions after taking testosterone, before bottom surgery. And we recently had it brought to our attention..." *you have no idea how, hah,* "that there are no standard safer sex options for post-surgery trans men who don't opt for a, uh, total phalloplasty. We're passing out thousands of condoms to MSM, but some of them can't use them. We just don't know what the HIV rates for trans men and nonbinary MSM are locally, if this is causing an undue mental health burden, if there's access issues... we know nothing. And knowledge is power."

"So we might not be able to help," Cal surmised. "Even with an increased budget."

"No. I said we don't know what we don't know," Kyle

patiently told him. "So maybe there are things we can't help with, but maybe there are. They're a small proportion of the population we're mandated to work with, but we have to start getting that right, too. The number one problem is making sure they aren't experiencing the kind of infection rates the charities for trans women have told me that *they* see. That's always been our first mission: prevention."

"Right," even Cal had to admit.

"Then we work backward," Kyle said, "and figure out how to integrate our findings with our mission, and include education about and for trans men as well as cis men like we've always done. Just like when we did studies on racial factors, this is important. But the survey groups are a really small proportion of the funding increase we're asking for. I think you're blowing it out of proportion." He flipped back a few slides, showing the group the total funding allocation request, where the money was going. The token payments for qualitative survey participants accounted for a relatively small proportion of the total. Hell, they'd pay triple that amount just in increased printing costs for PrEP booklets.

"So, time to vote? Anyone else have questions?" Andy asked, looking around. Cal was silent. "I'd like to get a move on this."

The next few minutes were the most nerve-racking, but Kyle glowed with absolute pleasure when the votes were totaled. Eleven to two, the PrEP program increase was approved. Eight to four with one abstaining on the expanded gender and sexuality resources, but he'd take it—it was still a win. They were turned down for the budget increase to hire another part-time staff member, but they'd expected it. It wasn't a top priority, now that the new email system should reduce that workload drastically. And they flat-out denied they had enough funding to pay him for his after-hours work—right now, meetings with a group of local doctors who had questions about PrEP after having seen their educational materials.

Kyle wasn't worried, though. He did a lot of unpaid after-hours time already. It would have been nice, but money was finite. If they wound up with more donations after the next donor recruitment dinner, maybe that would change.

He was proud of himself as he headed out of the board meeting to let them wrap things up, but exhausted.

Defending everything I work for gets exhausting sometimes.

For a moment, he had a flash of empathy for Nic. He'd seemed so relieved and grateful to learn that Kyle knew a little about what he was doing, and Kyle could see why. It was his life, just like this was Kyle's. Even if Kyle was negative now, this bled into every area of the LGBT community, so in many ways, it was still an enormous part of his life and had been for years now.

Kyle fought back the crazy impulse to call Nic and ask his opinion on the trans men's survey groups. They had a volunteer to handle that, and he'd specifically chosen Ash because he thought he could do it without damaging relations with that segment of the community.

For now, he had to celebrate the victories. He composed a quick text to River—*Got most of what we asked for! PREP A GO. Gender & sex yes. No to new staff and overtime funding. Thats OK.*

River's response was swift. *FUCK YES. Except that the cheap bastards always turn you down for overtime and you do it anyway.*

It needs to be done, Kyle told him, smiling as he climbed into his car.

Before he drove, the phone went off again.

You can put yourself first once or twice, darling. Then several kissing emoticons.

He sent back a few more and shoved his phone into the cup holder, then started up his car with a sigh.

The closest he'd come to putting himself first was when River had made him go flirt with Nic.

That had been nice. That had been *fun*. Nic made him feel sexy in public and in bed. And smart, talking to him like an equal at the progress update meeting, like Kyle knew what PHP or whatever was. And he made Kyle laugh, and he...

Fuck. Nic wanted more than he could give. River was right, Kyle did work a lot, but River also never said he should stop. His best friend knew too well that he wouldn't.

When was the next status update? Next week? God, an entire week without seeing Nic's cute face in his office was going to be hell. He could see him earlier, but then he'd have to call him up and invent some excuse...

It took him a mile to realize that he was daydreaming about a date with Nic.

Ohhhh, no. Fuck me if I'm doing that.

"Dinnertime," he said out loud to keep his thoughts on track, drumming the wheel in time with the radio. "Chicken? Maybe chicken. I can do chicken. Yes."

Though his lips were busy mouthing the lyrics to top 20 pop, his traitorous hands trembled on the wheel, and his heart kept racing all the way home.

16

NIC

"I'm going to be a superstar today."

Nic eyed himself in the mirror, turning his face this way and that as he dragged the razor across his jawbone. It had taken a few years to figure out how to get most of the hairs in one pass so he didn't piss off his skin.

He lowered his voice and mumbled, "I'm going to be a superstar today." He winced at how cheesy it sounded, then carefully smoothed his face for the last bit around the corner of his jawbone.

Before shaving his upper lip, he almost whispered his affirmation a third and final time. Self-consciousness prickled hotly at his ears. Even though he was alone in the apartment, and even though he'd done it for years whenever he needed a little extra confidence boost, affirmations had never grown more comfortable for him.

Once Nic finished splashing water over his face and rinsing the sink, he patted a towel against his cheeks and inspected his face again. There were always a few stray hairs, but he liked that. He'd had to wait damn well long enough to grow facial hair, after all. He may as well show it off.

He was going to get over this infatuation with Kyle by using the many positives of that one-night fling with him—the great sex that had left him feeling good about himself, the confidence he'd seen in action and could now mirror.

Kyle was so authentically *him*. What you saw was what you got, through and through, and Nic loved it. He wanted to be a lot more like that—not like Kyle, but like the Nic who was just a bit too shy to come out sometimes.

His finger trailed along his cheekbones. The fat on his face had shifted subtly over the first few years of testosterone. He couldn't see the girl's face underneath anymore, and hadn't for a long time. It left him striving to find a reference point for what he'd look like... well, dolled up like Kyle.

Nic's heart pounded as he absently rubbed silicone into the thin scars on his chest. They were nearly invisible now, so he technically didn't have to, but it was a self-soothing habit.

Nic loved how unapologetically femme Kyle was, and he had to admit that part of his attraction was exactly that. And hell, it was inspiring. Nic frowned at the mirror, then stared. He'd spent so many years learning and asserting his masculinity that he felt... well, out of balance.

Damn it, he *was* allowed to like feminine things just as much as a cis guy like Kyle. There was no reason he couldn't wear a skirt himself, or some colors now and then.

He had a weekday off, so the store wouldn't be busy, and he felt great. Perfect time to go shopping.

———

It turned out the stark walls of Nic's bathroom made it a lot easier to be bold than the aisles of Target.

Nic had chosen the store because, even though he could afford nicer brands these days, shopping there was still a habit. He'd bought his first new men's clothing there—a thrilling graduation from the thrift store racks.

It was easy to wander back and forth between the sections in this store. No huge gap between the sections, filled with judgmental salespeople patrolling their turf.

Still, there *was* an aisle between them. Nic lingered at a table, touching men's t-shirts to admire the soft cotton as he looked over toward the women's section.

It was only a few steps. People would think he was there shopping for a girlfriend, or girl friend. It had been at least months, maybe years now, since anyone had misgendered him.

The only one holding him back was himself.

It had been *years* since he'd worn anything remotely like what Kyle pulled off. Skirts, dresses, leggings, blouses, shawls... it was all alien territory to him by now, and his body looked and felt so different now that he had no idea where to start.

Nic drew a breath, then stepped across the aisle, wandering casually along the outside of the section as he gazed in.

There was some ugly stuff in there, too: neon graphic print t-shirts, ripped-up flare jeans, and colors even Kyle probably wouldn't be caught dead in. Not ugly, he reminded himself, but definitely not his style.

Wait. He had a style.

It made him feel slightly better that he still had *some* taste, so he kept walking the outside of the aisle.

No way would he be brave enough to grab something and

take it to the dressing rooms, so what could he buy that didn't need to be tried on first?

As Nic spotted the accessories stands near the checkouts, he perked up. A scarf? That was more androgynous than he usually wore, and pretty gay, too. Oh, yeah. A scarf could work *well*.

There were bright pink and blue scarves, flowery ones, but also darker, more subtle tones. He'd have to go for something subtle first, to build up his nerve. After a few weeks of conservative dark suits, walking into the office wearing a neon blue floral print would just make everyone think it was a joke, or a bet.

Dark grey flowers on black? It was thin, all-season. Nic ran the scarf through his hands, picturing himself with it on.

It would be almost too subtle, but it was the perfect place to start.

As Nic played with the tassels, he glanced up and around for anyone watching him, his cheeks burning. Even if he'd lost his nerve to try anything like Kyle's style, it was a huge step for him to be hovering near the women's section. He'd chalk the whole day up as a win.

A flash of green hair near the registers caught Nic's eye.

Think of the devil...

Nic broke into a smile and straightened up. He could have hung back and waited for Kyle to check out before heading for the tills, but that didn't even occur to him.

Instead, he was preoccupied with what Kyle would think of him buying this.

Nic found himself striding for the cash desks, his smile rueful but heart fluttering with excitement at Kyle's presence.

Once again, Kyle's orbit pulled him in before he even had a chance to resist. Who could expect him to defy gravity?

17

KYLE

Cheetos, pretzels, chips, a couple liters of Coke, and a Netflix gift card: one at a time, Kyle plopped the items in his arms onto the register belt.

He was almost bouncing on his toes with excitement. Kyle hadn't had a good movie night with River in months, and this was his reward for nailing the meeting. It was always cheap, since River bought the rum, and good for a memorable night.

Not that he and River had ever tried to Netflix and chill—they actually watched the damn movies. They usually made fun of them the whole time. Sometimes they turned on closed captions so they could try to read the dialog along with the actors in funny voices and make each other crack up.

Kyle shuffled along in the line, keeping his eyes on the items on the belt while he daydreamed.

Neither he nor River paid for a Netflix subscription every month. They took turns buying prepaid gift cards when money was good, then let the subscription run for a month at a time, binge-watching it when they had it.

This month was gonna be great.

Kyle stepped ahead when it was his turn, pulling out his debit card while the cashier did a great job not commenting on the particular combination of items he'd chosen.

He didn't expect the *declined* message that came up on the screen once he entered his PIN, or the carefully measured neutral look of the cashier when she told him his card had been declined.

Shit. I got my PIN right, I know I did. That doesn't make sense. I still have money in this account, don't I?

He wasn't sure. His back-of-hand math failed him in the moment as he patted his pockets for cash, already knowing he didn't have enough. His cheeks burned.

A warm voice near his ear said, "Add this to the transaction, please. I'll pay for it." Someone passed the cashier a scarf to scan.

"Oh, no. It's fine," Kyle started to tell the cashier. He turned to look behind him at the generous stranger, and the cashier paused, looking between them.

It was Nic.

Nic nodded at the cashier to signal her to carry on, and the cash till beeped behind him.

Kyle's chest tightened and he bristled. He didn't need Nic to do anything for him, and if this was Nic's way of trying to get in favor with him... well, he wasn't dating the guy because he'd bought him things.

This was *his* reward for acing the meeting, anyway. It didn't mean as much if someone else bought it for him.

He didn't have any other plan to pay for these things, but he couldn't let Nic have him over a barrel. No, it was an over-reaction. He knew it was.

"It's..." he trailed off, then clenched his jaw. They were starting to cause a scene, and he didn't need to make it any bigger. The line behind them was watching, and shame was already burning his cheeks.

He barely held his tongue until the transaction was over, then grabbed his bags and stalked out of the Target. He still had trouble getting a deep breath.

He didn't have to do that. I shouldn't have let him. I didn't deserve it.

Kyle didn't look, but he could feel Nic by his side and then behind him, tailing him out to the corner of the building.

"I'll pay you back," was the first thing Kyle said as he turned to face Nic, leaning on the side of the building.

Nic had a hand in his pocket, the bag dangling loosely in his other hand as he shrugged. Fifty bucks clearly didn't mean much to him. "It's nothing."

"It's not *nothing*," Kyle disagreed.

Nic eyed him, his expression wary, then nodded slightly. "Yeah. Sorry. I meant, it's not a big deal for me. I'd have done it to any stranger in line."

That made him feel slightly better, if not much. "And I thought I was easy," Kyle deadpanned.

Startled, Nic broke into a grin as his cheeks turned pink. "Oh. Um. I mean. Not... done *it* to."

Kyle snorted with amusement, then unlocked the back seat of his car to toss the bags inside. He slammed the car door and strolled back over to Nic, whose blush was fading now. "I'm not gonna Netflix and chill with you, if that's what you're hoping."

"That wasn't my intention." Nic licked his lips, and Kyle noticed him trying to keep his gaze on his face.

It was a compliment, as far as Kyle was concerned. He'd only worn tight jeans and a clingy pink t-shirt, but Nic still couldn't hide his interest. It didn't help him believe Nic was doing it for kindness and not sex, though.

"Oh, really?" Kyle smirked. "You're not looking for the sugar daddy lifestyle?"

Nic scowled, his annoyance clear. "No."

Kyle was weirdly pleased to get that reaction out of him—he wasn't sure why. Maybe he liked seeing Nic lose control. *Oops. Shit. Pull back.* "Then why not let me pay you back?"

"I don't... I didn't..." Nic breathed out a quick, annoyed snort and folded his arms as he looked at Kyle. God, he looked even hotter with a scowl on his face, his expression simmering in... what? Need? Desire? Annoyance? "You're stubborn as fuck, you know that?"

"Guilty. A very stubborn fuck," Kyle retorted, dropping his voice. *I can't stop myself. I want him too much.*

"If you're worried about my intentions, take the damn gift and walk away."

Instead, Kyle took a step closer, resting his hand on one of Nic's tightly-folded arms. The heat between them crackled nearly audibly as both of them caught their breaths. "I appreciate it, but I don't need anyone's help."

Nic tilted his head, pushing away from the wall. Their lips were just inches apart. "Never said you did."

"Good."

"Good."

Their hands tangled in each other's hair at the same moment, and Kyle pushed Nic into the wall hard. Their bodies crushed together, hard planes of heat angling against each other.

The soft growl that escaped from Nic's throat made Kyle get hard instantly, pressing into his hip while pushing his own thigh against Nic's hardening dick.

Hot, wet, and all teeth, their lips crashed together. They bit, sucked, and pressed against each other's lips until Kyle could barely think straight.

Kyle swore he could hear Nic's heart hammering, but that could have been his own. His skin tingled with his need to feel Nic's skin against him, under him, burning with him once more.

They stumbled apart seconds later—it must have been seconds, but the heat between them had made it feel like minutes.

Shit. Kyle had *not* meant to kiss the guy. His signals were getting too mixed even for him.

"I'm still fucking paying you back," Kyle told him and yanked open the car door.

"Isn't that what *that* was?" Nic half-grinned, and the sight of him freshly-kissed, hair messy, hand sliding into his pocket to adjust himself...

Fuck. Kyle had to back off now if he wasn't going to end up in bed with the guy again.

"It's nothing," Kyle told him with a smirk he *knew* would be maddening, then slid into the driver's seat, closed the car door, and prayed the car would start.

It did. He couldn't resist a peek as he pulled away. Nic was still slumped against the wall in the rearview mirror, smoothing the wrinkles out of his shirt and finger-combing his hair back into place while licking his reddened, full lips.

Thank God for tight jeans, or Kyle's boner would have hit the steering wheel.

18

NIC

Kyle was the most frustrating man Nic had ever met.

Nic was fuming. He glared as hard as he could after Kyle's car, but his body was tingling way too pleasantly for him to be truly annoyed with his friend... potential lover... *friend.*

He had to get home before he exploded. Nic strode to his car, grinding his teeth as he tossed the bag into the other seat and swung down into the driver's seat, started the car, buckled up, and flicked his turn signal on.

Nic made himself take a deep breath in and out, checking all his mirrors before he pulled out.

The moment of calm didn't last long.

"*You're* the one who didn't want anything to do with me," he said, as if Kyle were right there and willing to hear it. He thumped the wheel with his palm as his car glided to a stop at the sign.

So why the hell is he kissing me now?

"Mixed messages. And fucking rude." Nic clicked his tongue, tapping his foot as he waited his turn for the car to his right in the four-way intersection to go. It didn't and he scoffed, pulling into the intersection. "Fucking bad drivers around here, too. Yield to the right. Take your turn, or you'll rear-end me."

Oh, boy. Nope. That was unintended enough innuendo that it made Nic blush, but he tried to push it out of his mind. "I do not need anyone rear-ending me in any way."

Speaking of which, what had all that flirting been about? Before he shot Nic down with that last comment? Nic muttered, "It was nothing," and scoffed again, clenching his teeth at Kyle's behavior. "It wasn't *nothing*. I didn't mean that."

Wait. Maybe Kyle hadn't, either.

But that smirk—he'd meant the comment to get under his skin. He *knew* the effect it would have. He'd wanted to ruffle Nic's feathers.

It was a pride thing. Nic knew that damn well. He understood that on a personal level, but shit, he'd just tried to be nice. He hadn't said anything about Kyle not being able to afford it or needing help.

"He is the most insufferable, pissily stupidly stubborn, *frustrating...*" Nic trailed off, sharply turning around a corner onto his own street, "goddamn hot, mixed-signal-sending..." he flicked the signal on for his condo building's driveway, "flirtatious... *way overly flirtatious...* inappropriate... sexy..."

He trailed off when he had to roll down his window to scan the key card and get into his garage. Last thing he needed was the security camera catching some stupid rant, like he was having boyfriend problems.

Boyfriends. God, if he were so lucky, he could deal with Kyle's behavior. But no, as just friends, it was weird.

He stalked through the parking garage, tension threading

through his muscles and stiffening his body. Nic knew he felt—
and looked—like a cat in heat, but he couldn't fucking help
himself.

Just like he hadn't been able to resist unleashing that frustration in that damn kiss they'd shared—grabbing Kyle's lower
lip and sucking until Kyle moaned so softly even he probably
hadn't known he'd made that noise. In return, Kyle's tongue
smashing up against his own, teasing it, before Kyle caught his
tongue between his lips and sucked, filthy and slow...

Every rub against each other's sensitive lips, every panted
breath into each other's mouth, the heat multiplying between
them as Kyle jammed Nic up against the brick wall, the chemistry that made Nic want to rip his clothes off and *fuck* Kyle...

It was all coming back to him. The elevator ride was tortu-
ously slow, and mercifully solo.

Kyle just had that effect on him. And he was damn well
aware, judging by the way he'd noticed Nic trying not to check
him out, and immediately flirted.

"Damn him," Nic muttered as he unlocked his door and
shouldered his way through it, dropping his bag by the door
and locking it again.

On the way to the bedroom, he fought his shirt off and
threw it aside; by the time he reached the bed, he was kicking
his jeans and underwear off.

The apartment wasn't at all uncomfortable in his bare skin,
which meant he was burning too hot to stop now.

"Fuck, yes," he breathed out as he hit the bed. The sheets
were cool and soothing against his back, and he squirmed up
until his head indented the pillow.

He ran both hands down his chest, imagining Kyle's broad
palms and firm touch. He didn't have to imagine the hot, solid

body pressing into him—he remembered that well enough from not even twenty minutes ago.

His hands reached his hipbones and he fingered them lightly, then moved down to his thighs, spreading them and letting his fingertips brush along the dark triangle of hair until he nearly touched his cock—but not quite.

Nic was hard already, his eyes sliding closed as he brought Kyle's face back into his mind.

Especially Kyle's lips around his cock, his gaze flickering up to Nic's to drink in every reaction and expression.

He wanted to tangle his hands in the dark green hair and push up into his mouth, fuck his lips until he was trembling on the edge of ecstasy.

Nic closed his fingers around his shaft at last, pulling from base to tip in quick, rough movements. It wasn't hard to get lost in the vision of Kyle's lips around his shaft, the tight suction of his mouth all the way to the base, his tongue flickering around the shaft...

Oh, God, he remembered that wet heat like it was yesterday. And the gentle touch of Kyle's hand under his balls, cupping and squeezing them to add that extra *zing* of sensation...

Pricks of need shot through to the tip of his cock, and he rubbed his thumb across it before groaning. He was *not* going to hold out just for the sake of it. If he came immediately, so much the better. He'd been fighting this boner all the way home.

Kyle's cock in him was fucking perfect, too, though. The heat and weight of him filled Nic's hole perfectly. Fingers were a poor substitute, but with the power of his imagination...

Kyle could press him into the mattress and fuck him hard

and fast until they were gasping into each other's mouths. Kyle's arm braced on the bed above Nic, his mouth on Nic's, his cock buried to the root in him, his other hand jerking Nic off...

Wrapped around Kyle, legs locked around his waist, all Nic could do was groan his name, whimpering into the air and thrusting into his hand with every quick jerk.

No, there *was* one thing... his fingers could slip down to that perfect, round ass and inside, rubbing that spot deep inside Kyle until Kyle lost his fucking mind, trembled on the edge of pleasure, his cock leaking precum and pounding rhythm broken into a quivering, jerky one...

Nic clenched hard and came, a cry ripped from his throat as he rolled his head back against the pillows, his cock pulsing in his hand with each thrust into his fingers and coating his hand with hot passion while he rubbed at the spot deep within himself.

Kyle's face, twisted and tight with pleasure, that cocky arrogance of earlier utterly undone...

It was then Nic realized he'd been gasping Kyle's name.

Nic groaned again, this time hoarsely. Sleeping with Kyle hadn't settled their fizzling chemistry. Instead, that unforgettably hot sex had honed it to an explosive reaction.

Fuck. Who the hell was Kyle, that he could take Nic apart so thoroughly with a couple words, the right look, the right kiss? Why did he have to say he didn't want more, even when his body language, his behavior, and some of his words said otherwise?

The next time they saw each other—probably at the next progress update meeting—he had to find some way to take Kyle aside and talk about this.

As Nic idly rubbed his thumb along his softening shaft, he whispered into the stillness of the bedroom, "I want him."

The meaning of his words settled in for real, and Nic closed his eyes to acknowledge the ache in his chest.

"I'm so fucked."

19

KYLE

Goddamn it. Kyle hadn't meant to overreact. He hadn't been arguing with Nic at all, despite what it looked like. It was himself. Or worse yet...

"You are the definition of daddy issues," Kyle muttered, clutching the steering wheel. "Jesus, Kyle. Get it together."

He fiddled with the car radio, but none of the channels made him happy, so he turned it off again. God, he needed to burn another mix CD soon. He was getting bored with everything, and even shuffle didn't help. Or get a CD-to-iPod converter, if those existed.

Kyle was thinking about everything and everything, and he knew the signs of avoidance. He had a good ten minutes until he got to River's house, even if he floored it, and he couldn't avoid it forever.

He drew a deep breath.

If Kyle were really honest, Nic had reminded him of his father for a minute, and he was the last person Kyle wanted to think about. He barely spared his biological family any thought these days—he hadn't for years.

Not after the first few years of recovery and getting his shit together. It was such a fucking stereotype: flamboyant faggot gets thrown out by father for being gay, underwhelming support from his mother, and a second gay sibling left afraid to come out.

Four years after he'd left, his brother had come out as bi, and had dear old Dad thrown him out? No, and apparently he'd come around to thinking gay people *might* be okay—but only because his brother had been just about to graduate medical school. *He'd* made something of himself.

Only at Danny's insistence had their dad contacted him again to say he might be willing to compromise on his stance. Yeah, right. His dad knew what side his bread was buttered on. The side that expected a good retirement home after all he'd done for—*to*—him.

And his mom... seeing glimpses of the real her, the happy and enthusiastic mom she'd once been, had kept him going. It had made him certain that being authentic was the *only* way to be. Fuck being a puppet for someone else's desires. She'd never gotten to live on her own and *be* herself before she died, early last year. And from the brief interactions he'd had with his dad at the funeral, he hadn't changed a bit.

Kyle would take Danny's calls, but that was it.

Not that he'd had the luxury of that stance for the first year after moving out. His dad had tried to bribe him into coming home or stopping his disgusting behavior by holding money over his head. The moment he got his first Walmart job, Kyle had stopped trying to jump when his dad said to jump.

Money was a touchy subject—probably the touchiest of any for him. It wasn't Nic's fault he'd stumbled into it. Nic definitely hadn't meant offense. In his shoes, Kyle would have helped out a friend, too. He paid for River's coffees without keeping track.

Come to think of it, River had paid for something as dumb as today's impulse purchase, and that cost just as much. That enormous overstuffed beanbag had met an untimely end via a hookup involving handcuffs.

"Why does it bother me that much, then?" he muttered, fidgeting with the steering wheel.

Oh. Yeah. Because it was *Nic*, not River or someone else paying for him.

And Nic had been getting closer and closer to him—not romancing him, or overtly coming on to him, but still closer. Work, sex, now shopping... he was under Kyle's skin.

Kyle wasn't sure what to make of it, or his own reactions.

He parked in front of River's building and leaned into the door, rubbing his hand down his face. Thinking about his family always did this to him. God, he was in no state to have fun.

But he didn't want to sap River's energy, either. He hated being negative, and he hated himself for letting others make him feel that way.

This was a vicious cycle, and he was *not* going to let it get started.

"Kyle Everson, you are going to kill yourself."

"Is that at the top of your Christmas list?" Kyle spat back, his arms folded.

He was thin, it was true, and he was getting sick of ramen, but it was his ramen, eaten in his kitchen at one AM after fucking as many guys as he wanted and wearing whatever he wanted without a lecture that would leave him crying into his pillow half the night.

"Don't be such a little asshole. You don't deserve half of what we've given you, you filthy little—"

"Roger."

His mom's interruptions were carefully timed to spare him from the worst of his dad's words, but they did nothing to change Kyle's knowledge of what his dad wanted to say. What he had said, the day he kicked Kyle out.

"You can't keep surviving on your own," his father's voice boomed. Kyle wasn't looking at him. Nor was he looking at his mother, who had just slipped an envelope into his backpack near the front door. His father was still blustering. "I bet you're behind on rent already. Kid your age? Unemployable. Take a few hundred bucks. It doesn't matter to me. All that matters is seeing you on a decent path."

He wasn't going to turn it down, either. God, no. Kyle was too proud to take money from Dad, but too poor not to take money from Mom. It was the only reason he came back when his dad called, and his dad knew it.

Money. Fucking money. Dad had him over a barrel because of it. Otherwise, the day Kyle had moved out would have been the last time he'd seen him.

"I can survive, and in case you haven't noticed, I am," Kyle told his father, jutting his jaw out. "Did you come to yell at me for being a disgusting little perverted faggot again, or did you have something fatherly to say, for a change? 'Cause I've got some dick to suck somewhere, I'm sure."

"Get out."

Kyle rose to his feet, catching a glimpse of his brother's blond hair as he darted back into his room. He didn't blame Danny. Nobody wanted to get between him and his dad

113

when they were going toe-to-toe, and he wouldn't have let them. He wasn't going to cause casualties.

"You overuse that phrase," Kyle spat back at his father. He'd lost his fear of him last year, after hearing exactly those words for the first time, and then a lot worse. That day had hurt, yes, but it had led to... freedom. The worst possible outcome had turned out to be one of the best.

"I said—"

"Roger," his mom said again, louder this time. She swept Kyle up in a hug as he approached the front door. His father turned away and strode into the living room.

Kyle squeezed her hard, then whispered into her ear, "I'm okay. I got a job. Walmart. I can't keep visiting now."

Her hold faltered for a moment, and then she squeezed him so hard he lost his breath. "Baby. I'm so proud. I always have been. Always will be. Flaunt that big heart of yours. Don't settle—"

Kyle knew what she was going to say, and he shook his head slightly. "Don't settle for anything. Don't stop being me. I won't. I won't ever," Kyle whispered back, kissing her cheek. "I promise."

"I love you."

Kyle had never doubted that. He just wished he could help her be everything she could be, if she were free of this overgrown bully. His dad wasn't abusive to her, nor to his brother. Just to Kyle.

But she wasn't happy, either. She wasn't the beautiful, laughter-filled soul he'd caught glimpses of now and then when he visited while Dad wasn't in town.

"Love you, Mom. I'll be okay."

"I know you will be."

Kyle hugged her one more time, trying to memorize the

feeling of his mom's arms around him, the smell of her, the softness of her hair against the side of his cheek... the safety in her arms. "Call me if you need anything."

She knew what that meant. But, as always, she smiled slightly and sadly. "I've settled."

He could argue, say she didn't have to, but they'd been over that before. It was up to him to break free and be everything she wanted to be.

It was fucking terrifying to be nineteen and facing all the possibilities of a future he'd never thought he'd have, all alone.

But he was ready to spread his wings.

Kyle wiped his eyes roughly and cleared his throat, then checked his hair in the rearview mirror.

Yeah, he was kind of a mess. What he needed was River, Netflix, and a chill night.

When his best friend opened the door, he knew it, too.

"Movie time, baby." River took one look at his face and ignored Kyle holding out the bags. Instead, he swept him into a hug so tight Kyle wanted to bury himself in it forever.

Kyle breathed out a quick sigh. "God, I love you."

"Of course. Who doesn't? Tell me about it later." Despite his teasing tone, Kyle knew River was helping him change the subject. River knew something had happened, but he wasn't going to push it yet.

Kyle would tell him, too—he always did. He'd even include the angry kiss. River was going to make *so much* fun of him, and the thought already made him crack a small smile.

"That's it," River grinned, finally pulling back and taking the Coke bottle. "I've got the rum. You set up Netflix. Let's get this party started!"

20

NIC

Nic *had* to get himself a therapist.

It wasn't like he was having a mental health breakdown—he'd been through those before and survived relatively unscathed, all things considered. But he'd meant to do it as soon as he moved, and he'd been putting it off for the last few weeks.

And since it seemed like he was in the middle of tangling himself with an unavailable man, and nothing was stopping his seemingly solved abandonment issues from being jolted back to life, it was the smart thing to do.

He hated staring at the list of therapists he'd been given by his old therapist, who'd written him a referral note and a list of therapists to try. Nic had grown accustomed to phone conversations after his voice broke, but his anxiety about them lingered. He didn't *like* talking on the phone when email was faster and more efficient.

Still, it was the only way to find a good therapist. Few worked by email. He resigned himself to the task and kicked back on the couch, his cellphone in one hand and the list of numbers in the other.

Nic had to find someone who was trans-friendly—not just tolerant, but knowledgeable enough to want to write a surgery referral note, since phalloplasty was still on the table for him.

Metoidioplasty, the kind of surgery he'd already had, formed a small phallus of a couple inches, but it was all from existing bio dick tissue—which meant full natural erections, but not much thickness for penetration.

On the other hand, phalloplasty would give him a dick more the size of a cis guy's, and he'd be able to penetrate and probably retain sexual sensation once it came back. It would sure make it easier to pee at urinals, but the sensation of erection wouldn't be quite as natural since he'd need a pump or a rod if he wanted erections. That was why he'd avoided it.

It was a lot to talk about with a therapist, but he'd built enough of a bond with his last therapist that he trusted her and worked with her to get his referrals.

Plus, whoever it was had to be okay with gay issues and know enough that they could talk about his abandonment problems, and his feeling of not quite fitting into the community. He didn't like talking about those feelings, but sometimes he found them at the root of seemingly unrelated problems.

It wasn't like he hated therapy. He'd worked out so many of his issues with it, and he thought being proactive about it was good.

But setting up appointments to go under the knife had him anxious, even if booking the surgery itself was several steps in the future, *past* his appointments with this new therapist and other people, and... one step at a time.

One little step, that was all it would take.

He drew a breath, half-closed his eyes, and dialed the number before he could chicken out.

"Hello." It was a statement, not a question.

"O-Oh. Hi. My name's Nic Montero—"

"Are you a patient of the practice?" The secretary's voice was so abrupt that it made him flinch.

"Um. N-Not yet. I..."

"Dr. Lacks is only taking referrals at this time." He sounded so casually dismissive, like he was expecting Nic to stutter and hang up.

Whoa. That's an attitude and a half. He'd learned the hard way, too, that a good therapist was not worth putting up with a bad admin assistant.

"Okay. I guess this isn't the practice for me. Have a good one." Nic hung up without waiting for a response and let out a shuddery breath. "What a dick."

The second clinic didn't answer, but by the third name on the list, he struck gold.

"Hello, Dr. Barnard's practice, how can I help?"

"H-Hi. My name is Nic Montero. I was a patient of another therapist out in Minneapolis, Dr. Calvin. She recommended that I talk to you guys about becoming a new patient now that I've moved here."

"Well, welcome to L.A., honey! We'd be glad to have you as a patient!"

Even the pet name wasn't demeaning or dismissive like it would have been back home. She sounded warm and genuine, and it made him relax and breathe a quick sigh. "Great. That's awesome. Um, I guess I'll make an initial appointment, then."

The secretary—Mary-Ann—was efficient but kind, letting him know the therapist's fees, insurance coverage, and schedule. Before he knew it, he had a first appointment booked and a friendly rapport with Mary-Ann over the spelling of her name —he spelled Nicolas without an H or K, and she spelled Mary-Ann with a hyphen and no E. Most people tried to insert unwanted characters into their names, and Nic found himself laughing over it.

"So, we'll see you next week, Nic. Looking forward to meeting you!" Mary-Ann told him.

"Thanks so much. Have a great one."

"Why, thank you. You too, hon!"

Nic found himself smiling with the weight of one more burden lifted from his shoulders. He was doing pretty okay at this whole moving thing.

Time to rummage through the cupboards for chocolate and reward himself for making those calls.

21

KYLE

"Go check out the other side of the baaar."

"There's never anyone good on that side of the bar. You should know that by now." Kyle eyed River and snorted, waving off their attempts to convince him to do it.

River pushed a hand back through their long, blond hair, patting the curls back into place. They were in full drag tonight—a long shimmery blue dress, green eye makeup, gorgeous highlighter and lip gloss and all.

Kyle occasionally wished he wanted to be that pretty. People understood drag queens better than guys like him, though as River always told him, they didn't *really* understand. Some queens used it to feel better about themselves, or to make fun of women. That left a bad taste in Kyle's mouth. Others used it to experiment or validate themselves while transitioning to female. Others just liked playing dress-up, and didn't care about the gendered aspect of it as much as everyone around them.

For River, they'd always described themselves as not fully male, but much less a woman than a man. Something in between, kind of a bit of both but not either. Kyle never pressed them to put words on it, but when others occasionally did, they'd say they were nonbinary or genderfluid. Drag had helped them figure that out, and as gorgeous as they looked in full femme mode, they sometimes presented as androgynous, too.

In drag, Kyle called River "they" or sometimes "she," since River didn't care what pronoun people used in general. They said they didn't really like any of them anyway. They only used "he" in everyday life because most people defaulted to it. It amused Kyle to watch people's confused reactions, but he also felt protective of his best friend. He would fuck up anyone who took offense to them, no matter what they were wearing.

River was dancing at the bar with a now-empty shot glass in their hand, grinning at him. "Isn't there? Nic was over there a couple weeks ago."

Below the belt. Kyle glared and rolled his eyes, finishing his beer and pushing the glass across the counter.

River leaned in and told him, "You can find someone else to dance with, baby. Or hook up with. I know you. I can find you someone cute you won't turn down."

"I'm easy, am I?" Kyle laughed. "Thanks."

River winked. "Anytime. You can't say I don't know you."

They really did. Normally, Kyle would be cruising everyone in the place for something to wash away the taste of the last hookup. Tonight, though... Kyle wasn't sure he was interested, and he didn't know what that was about.

Instead, he hung out closer to Evie and the usual crowd, occasionally glancing for the door. Evie had said Nic told her he was busy this weekend, decorating his new apartment.

Fair enough, but it did seem a bit like avoidance. But then again, he wasn't required to come out to this every week. None of them were. It wasn't a scheduled thing, just a spontaneous thing.

God, he had to stop thinking about Nic.

"—someone's going to end up doing body shots." Evie was laughing. "And it'll be *after* I go home."

"Awww. But you're such a good mom. You barely let the babysitter babysit." Joe beamed at her. "I don't know how you do it."

Kyle shook his head. "Because she likes adulting better than the rest of us. Makes us all look bad. Getting back to the body shots..."

River was flirting with the bartender, but even they looked back over their shoulder. "Are we doing that now? Can we do that?"

"Not in public, baby," Ash teased, giving them an exaggerated wink.

"Good. I need to get my good tits on for that," River winked back.

Kyle almost doubled over with laughter at the look on Ash's face. Ash was mostly used to River by now, but he was the easiest to embarrass.

None of the rest of them—Ash and Joe, who'd been here last week, or Ben or the others who hadn't been—knew about Nic. Nobody but Evie and River had noticed them slipping out together, thank God, or he would have had the whole group pestering him to get with him or get over him. And he was *not* thinking about Nic again. Jesus.

"Is that a promise?" Ash managed after a minute of everyone laughing.

River sidled up and slipped a shot glass in their cleavage. "If you want it to be."

"Careful." Kyle grinned at Ash. "You can't unsee anything."

River flipped him off and he winked, then took another look around the place.

Still nobody interesting out there. A few cute little twinks on the floor, but he wanted a nerdier guy. No, that wasn't right. He always avoided getting stuck on one type, and his last... hookup... had been nerdy. Sweet, well-dressed, but nerdy. Some big muscled military guy was more what he should be looking for.

But none of them were really out there. A few showy gym dudes who clearly spent more time there than at home, but they weren't catching his eye, either.

Ash was staggering to his feet, grabbing River's shoulder and the bar to stand upright. A quarter of the shot had gone down his shirt, and now River was leaning in to lick it from his neck, to uproarious laughter from the rest of the group.

"Your turn," River teased Kyle. "Unless you have anyone... any*thing*... better to do."

The others giggled, but Kyle waved them off. "No, no, I don't want to make your new boyfriend jealous."

Ash gasped. "Oh, God. Don't tell Ben."

"Don't tell me what?" Ben swooped in from across the room and grabbed Ash's ass.

Ash jumped. "That was a quick leak."

"I hurried. The stalls are busy tonight. Didn't want to risk slipping it in anywhere. And what did I miss?"

"He was slipping something of mine down his throat." River beamed, less than innocently, at Ben.

Kyle had to sit down on a bar stool, he was laughing so hard.

Ben eyed them solemnly and yanked Ash close to him, his

arm around his waist. "I don't want to have to hit a lady, so tell me: that sounds hot. Why the hell didn't you wait for me?"

"Good thing I'm *far* from one," River told him. "You can take the next shot if you like."

"Oh, shots? I can do shots," Ben started. His jaw dropped as River slipped the other one into their cleavage. "Oh, shit."

Ash was giggling half-hysterically, and even the patrons around them were grinning.

"No take-backsies." River pressed a finger to their pink lips. "I won't tell."

"Everyone else will, though," Evie helpfully piped up. "For weeks. On the other hand, if you chicken out..."

"You need a guided tutorial on how these work?" River winked, jiggling the breast forms at him.

Ben bent over in one swift move, slurping the top of the shot, gripping the rim of the glass between his lips, and throwing his head back to down the rest of it.

When he straightened up, everyone stared at him.

"Uhhh," Ash drawled, sliding an arm slowly around his boyfriend's waist as he stared at him. "How are you... an expert?"

"Two things you could look up in the dictionary: bi and spring break."

"Holy shit." Kyle laughed even harder. "We *need* to hear about this."

It didn't take much more alcohol to convince Ben to tell all —a week in a party hotel, two nights following a random invitation to a yacht with his very open boyfriend at the time.

Kyle wished he'd had the money for spring break at that age. That threw him out of the mood to look for guys, if he'd even been convincing himself to get in that mood in the first place.

Fine. He clearly wasn't getting any tonight, and his head wasn't in the right place. That happened sometimes. Wrong time of the night, wrong crowd out that night, Jupiter out of alignment, whatever. It had absolutely nothing to do with Nic. Really, it didn't.

He'd just go home, then. And if Kyle imagined undressing Nic on the walk between the front door and the bed, he didn't have to tell a soul.

Kyle wasn't thinking a goddamn thing about Nic.

NIC

Bzzzzt.

Nic nearly fell over himself to scramble over to the buzzer. He crashed against the wall where the panel was held, spreading his hands instinctively to spread the weight against the wall so he didn't dent it. The condo was solidly built, though, and the wall didn't buckle.

"Hello?" he answered, pressing the button.

"Package for a Nic Montero."

"That's me. I'll let you in. I'm on the fifth floor." Nic let go of the button and pressed the door open button, then waited by his apartment door.

The moment he heard the knock, he pulled open the door and smiled at the delivery guy, signed the screen of the electronic device he handed over, and took his package.

Just in time. He had to work from the office today, which meant leaving in ten minutes. The Amazon purchase he'd made over the weekend had next-day delivery and he'd hoped that meant this morning. Apparently, it had.

Nic tore open the package and discarded the wrapper, then held the shirt up to the light. In the stark, cold light of day, held up against his own body, it looked different from the photo online.

The shirt was nothing that special. It was menswear, a standard linen button-down business shirt, not the soft silk or pretty floral embroidery he wanted to experiment with. But it was light pink, a shade he hadn't worn since middle school. And it would go well with the charcoal gray of his scarf under his winter coat.

He shrugged off his dark blue conservative shirt and swapped it out for the pink one, buttoning it up. A little wrinkled, but under his suit jacket, those would smooth out throughout the day.

This was the most feminine outfit he had now—the scarf plus pink shirt—and he was feeling brave. Time to see how the office took it.

The drive to work was quick, luckily. He'd chosen a condo reasonably close to the office so he didn't have to worry about traffic on the days where he didn't get to work from home. That distance meant he didn't really have time to worry about the what-ifs.

Other people wore more casual clothing, but he'd already gotten a reputation for bland, masculine suits and occasionally business casual clothing. Nothing risky, nothing with color to it.

As soon as Nic walked through the first section of the office, Evie stood up and waved him over. He was confident that at least she'd like it. The way she was beaming confirmed it.

"Hey, good-looking! That's a great color on you. You should wear it more often."

"I will," Nic told her, relaxing into a quick smile. "Thanks. Good morning."

Now that he knew Evie was good friends with Kyle, he couldn't risk getting attached to her. Hanging out with Kyle's best friend would just be weird, after... angrily making out with him just late last week.

Not an appropriate thought for work, he reminded himself.

"Morning. Here for the day?"

"Yep, except the progress report with the charity. Boss wants to make sure I'm actually coding and not hiring it out to, like, eight little monkeys with matching hats and diplomas."

Evie snorted with laughter. "I'm not sure I shouldn't do that," she admitted. "This project's getting on top of me."

"What's going on?"

"It's Perl. I hate Perl."

"Oh, I'm good with Perl," Nic told her. "Five or six?"

"Five."

"Great. If you want to send anything over, I can have a look at it."

Evie looked relieved. "Would you? Oh, God, thanks. It's hideous. I'm only using it to grab some old data before I give them something that actually works."

"Hey, Perl's ugly but it works. Usually." Nic grinned.

Evie laughed. "Thanks. I'll send you something later. Only after you're finished with your work, though. How's that going?"

"Really well. I'm ahead of track and I have to slow down so I don't go off-track with what the client wants," Nic admitted, though he kept his voice down. He didn't want to be the office show-off.

"Great." Evie high-fived him. "Okay. I gotta get back to this script. It's calling my name, and not in the nice way."

Nic dropped his voice and growled like a video game boss, "*Evie.*"

"Something like that." Evie laughed, louder this time. "Oh, someone brought in donuts. Go grab one before the good ones are gone."

"Happy Monday to us!" Nic waved and trotted off.

On his way to the donuts, Nic heard a snort and turned for a look. Hank's office door was open and he was eyeing Nic.

"Morning to you, too," Nic answered coolly. He hadn't forgotten the comments at the status update meeting, but he wasn't going to harp on them. He just didn't trust Hank now.

He was right not to. Hank's next remark was, "Did you get caught in a Pride parade on the way over? I think you got a little—on your shirt there—"

Nic glanced down, but there were no smudges or stains on his new shirt. Then, he clued in and rolled his eyes. "A little pink?"

Hank paused for long enough to make it clear that wasn't what he meant. He was totally implying there was cum all over his shirt just because it was pink. Bastard. Then, Hank answered in a mocking tone, "Yeah. Sure."

"It's a common color. In RGB terms, lots of red and a little green and blue. Keep up with the times. They just discovered it," Nic dryly answered. He snorted with laughter as he headed past Hank's office to the lunchroom.

He kept chuckling all the way there. How damn insecure was Hank that the color of Nic's shirt offended him and made him assume he sucked cock? Wow. Speaking of fragile masculinity.

The donut was totally worth walking past Hank's office

twice. His favorite kind of glazed treat, and in suspiciously perfect timing, he was just licking his fingers—thoroughly—as he passed Hank's office on the way back to his own. He didn't look over, but he heard the strangled noise of offense.

Victory, and it's not even 10 a.m.!

As he flopped in his chair, he scrubbed his fingers clean with hand sanitizer, then leaned over to press the message light on his phone and tucked the receiver between his ear and shoulder while starting up his laptop.

"Hi, Nic. This is Kyle. Sorry I couldn't reach you in person."

His good mood ballooned. Then, it sank.

"Uh, I have to reschedule our progress meeting that was supposed to be today. Sorry, things are crazy here."

Shit. Now he's avoiding me at work. Every red flag was going off in Nic's head. This was why mixing business with personal feelings was such a bad idea.

"I'll give you a call tomorrow and hopefully I'll reach you, we'll figure out a better time. Hope this doesn't slow things down—sorry for the short notice. Okay, talk to you soon."

Well, Nic had half-expected him to say that Denver or someone else had to interface with the company on the charity's behalf now. That could still be the next step of—

Whoa, Mr. Abandonment Issues. Nic caught himself short and shook his head. This didn't mean anything yet. He couldn't jump to conclusions.

But Nic's Monday was gloomier without Kyle's bright hair and brighter smile to look forward to seeing later.

23

KYLE

Kyle's oral fixation was a real problem. He stuck out his tongue at the rubbery taste of the pencil eraser he was chewing on. He'd be chewing on it again within minutes if they didn't hurry up and take him off hold.

He hated calling insurance companies, especially when he was chasing up on an information request from months ago. They were trying to find out which common group insurance plans covered PrEP and which didn't, and one insurer was still holding out on the details.

He was nearly at the stage of requesting a meeting with a company representative to discuss it. The insurance company office closed in an hour, so they were probably trying to make him go away. All he needed was one damn simple answer.

There were so many damn balls to keep in the air today that he didn't even have the heart to make a joke about not neglecting the shafts.

Kyle grabbed the stress balls—his favorite giveaway from a prostate cancer awareness campaign—from his drawer and kneaded them a few times, then put them down. He grabbed his cellphone, opening the app to order pizza again. No, maybe he'd check the office fridge and see if there were any frozen pizzas there first.

It had been a really long fucking day, and to top it off, he'd had to reschedule his meeting with Nic. He knew how it would look to Nic, but it really wasn't about his personal feelings. Ash and Ben had both gotten the flu on Sunday, and he believed them—they'd been looking rougher than their drinking would justify on Friday night. That left him juggling both their workloads plus his own.

Once the insurance agent came back to him, *finally* with the authorized answer, he took careful notes on it, added it to his file, and switched to preparing the donor presentation Powerpoint slides for Cal's next event.

Kyle lost track of time again, but when he finally checked back in and realized he'd just done a day's work in a couple hours, it was dark outside. He worked late without pay a lot of the time, and didn't really mind. He knew it was that attitude that led to burnout in many charity workers, but he'd also worked longer hours in shittier jobs just to make ends meet. This? An office job with a salary? He could handle this.

He smelled smoke. Crap. He leaned his head out of his office to look around the main area. Nobody else around, just as he'd thought, which meant it was just him and Denver as usual.

"Denver! You're burning the fucking pizza!"

No answer. And there it was—the smoke alarm.

Kyle banged his head on the desk. Last thing he needed was having to clean the oven tomorrow. Last time, the pizza had been partly thawed. When Denver threw it in the oven without a pizza sheet for a crispier crust, it had melted clear through the bars and covered the whole thing in burned cheese.

No sense putting it off, then. He'd deal with the pizza situation himself.

When he got to the kitchen, though, there was no smoke billowing from the oven, and no sheepish Denver flapping a towel at it and screeching.

But there it was, in his nose. He definitely smelled it. It took his brain a few seconds to put two and two together: the smoke wasn't coming from the kitchen. Which meant something else was on fire, and Denver was MIA.

"Shit! Denver!"

Denver wasn't in his office, and the smoke was visible now. It was just like they drilled into his head at school as a kid: don't worry about possessions. Everything suddenly became irrelevant except finding Denver and getting out of the building.

A quick scan of the offices and meeting rooms showed he wasn't there, and he wasn't in the bathroom, so where the fuck was he? Kyle was breathing fast now, fear making it hard to think.

Wait, maybe Denver had been out on the front step. He didn't smoke, but sometimes he went to get fresh air there or wait for food delivery.

Please, God, let him have been outside and not wherever that fire was.

It was hot in here now—several degrees hotter, and he was sweating. Shit. Kyle was out of time.

Kyle pressed his hand to the office door and swore with relief under his breath when it was cool. He yanked it open, keeping low as smoke rushed into the office, and scrambled down the staircase.

There was Denver—on the floor, in the hallway between the front lobby and the staircase to their office. The security locks automatically released when the fire alarm went off, thank God, so Kyle shouldered his way through the final door and dropped to the ground by Denver's side.

Denver was definitely unconscious, but he didn't look burned. He had... a swelling black eye? How the hell had he knocked himself out?

The flames were licking against the floor upstairs—he could hear them, and it was goddamn terrifying. Nobody had ever said you could hear the fire *eating* things all around you. And he could see them.

Shit. He could see them eating through the wall from one of the ground floor offices, licking rapidly along the walls.

Fuck, Denver was heavy. He wasn't sure he could lift him, standing up into the smoke that was filling the air from the top down, and get them both out safely. Dragging him would have to do.

He looped Denver's arms around his shoulders and pulled hard, his muscles straining and lungs burning. Smoke was filling the hallway from top to bottom. He was choking, even though he wasn't in the thickest blanket of smoke, and his eyes wouldn't stop stinging.

At the same moment Kyle realized he was only ten feet from the front door, he also realized he might not make it. The closest he'd ever felt to this was when he'd worked laying sod for a groundskeeping company in the dead of summer, even further south than here. 110° days with full humidity, where he thought he was going to pass out and all he could do was lift one thing at a time, take a deep breath, and assess if he'd still be on his feet a few seconds later.

He'd made it through then—because fainting might have

meant getting fired, which would have meant being broke and very quickly homeless and hungry. That, and a dose of luck.

Now, Kyle was going to lean on that survival instinct and his sheer luck again. Fainting might mean death again, and *fuck him* if he'd gone this long only to die now.

He covered his mouth with his arm and breathed as deeply as he could, then grabbed Denver's arm once more and pulled him across the carpet. He made it most of the way to the glass front door. There were shouts from outside—the janitor had been around. Kyle recognized his face dimly as he collapsed through the door when the man pushed it open for him.

He heard sirens, and hands were on him, helping him sit down. He had to lie down, though, coughing too hard to breathe.

He swore he saw a few other faces, unfamiliar ones, in the alley by the building, but everything was spinning. Maybe he did know them. Oh, no. They were firefighters. Maybe they'd come to save him.

His heart was going too fast. He wiped his forehead with his arm as his ears rang, but he couldn't feel his hand.

Fat lot of good they were, just standing there. He'd had to save himself, for God's sake.

"Too late, bitches," Kyle gasped.

And then he passed out.

24

NIC

The last few reps were almost impossible. That was the way a good workout should be—if Nic wasn't ready to puke by the time he was lifting the bar the last time, he wasn't pushing himself hard enough.

Just as he collapsed on the bench and tried to let sensation return to his arms, Nic's cellphone went off. "Oh, Jesus," he muttered, smacking his thigh with his hand a couple times before he managed to get it in his pocket. His arms were not going to thank him tomorrow.

The prickle of annoyance he felt faded when he saw Evie's name on the screen. He winced as he raised the phone to his ear and grunted, "Hey."

"Nic! Hi. Oh, thank God I got you."

Shit. Something was wrong. Surely it was a work thing, right? But Evie sounded frantic. *Please let it be a code problem.*

"Evie? Hey, what's up?" Pushing himself upright was a superhuman feat. Nic had to gulp some water before he could stand and leave the bench free for the guy waiting nearby. He leaned on the leg press while his world spun and reoriented itself.

"I'm not trying to impose, I know it's late, I'm so sorry—but I tried some other people and I haven't gotten an answer, and I had to try you, so I did—"

"Evie, whoa, whoa," Nic urged. "It's okay. I was just at the gym." God, his arms ached. "You're not bothering me. I need to know what's wrong."

"There was... shit, of course, you were at the gym. You didn't see the news on Twitter."

Nic's chest kept tightening, but he kept his voice calm. "Evie."

"There was a fire at Kyle's office building. He's in the hospital—he's alive! He's okay. I think. I don't know, they wouldn't tell me more."

"Oh, shit," Nic whispered. Luckily it wasn't leg day, so he jogged to the changing room. "Oh, my God. He's okay?"

"He's not in critical condition or anything. But I need to go to the hospital, and... and I know this is a big favor, but can you watch Kevin?"

"Kevin..." Nic trailed off, his brow furrowing. *A dog? A baby? Her baby? Why her kid? Me, of all people?* He couldn't remember either of them mentioning any of the above, so he took a stab in the dark. "Your kid?"

"Yeah. Kevin's our kid."

"Ohhh. Sorry, yeah, of course," Nic instantly apologized, even though he hadn't known.

"It's okay. I'm so sorry. I know it's totally out of the blue and probably not how you wanna spend your Monday night, but Kyle likes you, he'd trust you to watch him. Oh, shit, right. He probably didn't tell you, did he? And Dana's out of town. I don't want to be a bother—" Evie was losing her breath.

"Evie, it's okay," Nic interrupted, keeping his voice calm, even if his heart was racing. Shit, Kyle could be hurt or worse right now. With HIPAA, anything was possible. "I'll watch Kevin. Text me your address. I'll shower and be right over."

"Are you sure? Really? You don't have to say yes—"

"Of course I do," Nic told her. He pinched the bridge of his nose and looked around the locker room, thankful he'd gone late when it was empty. "I care about Kyle, too. Anything I can do for him, for you... I wanna do. A few hours watching Kevin is nothing, okay? I'd want someone to help me out, if I had a kid, and a... Kyle."

Evie's shallow breathing caught in her throat. Then she swallowed and answered, "Oh. You're serious about liking him."

"Yeah. And more, if he'd let me." Nic didn't want to waste time talking about his feelings, so honesty was the only route forward.

"Oh, Nic," Evie whispered, breathing out a quick sigh. "For what it's worth... it's not your fault he didn't tell you about this. It's too much for some guys to deal with, and—God, if I messed this up for him..."

Nic grabbed his clothes out of the locker and started pulling his shirt off, awkwardly jamming the phone against his neck. "You didn't. Evie, it's okay. I gotta go so I can get over there. Text me the address now, before you forget."

Evie breathed out quickly. "Sh—shut the front door, Nic, thank you. You're a lifesaver."

"Course. See you in a bit."

With the urgency hanging over him now, Nic had never showered or changed faster. His hair was still damp when he hit the road, his hands tight on the wheel, swearing at the local news channel for playing radio ads instead of breaking news.

He *did* care about Kyle. A lot.

And Kyle trusted him to watch Evie's kid. Not just that; the conversation had made it clear Kevin wasn't just Evie's kid, he was Kyle's. *Our kid*, she'd said.

No wonder Kyle didn't want to rush into anything. It wasn't about him not being enough. Hell, Kyle had said he trusted Nic to watch Kevin.

Christ, Nic could kick himself for moping all day over that rescheduled meeting, feeling sorry for himself.

Helping Kyle and Evie in a moment of need was its own reward. But on top of that, now that Nic realized the complexity of Kyle's life, he wasn't dissuaded. In fact, if Nic told Kyle as much, he might just have a shot with him. From the way Evie had spoken to him, he had at least one of Kyle's good friends' approval, and a big hint as to why Kyle was acting this way.

It felt like being handed another chance. Nic was grabbing on with both hands. The way Kyle made him feel, anything was worth a try.

KYLE

"Not a chance, but thank you for your concern. You have enough patients to worry about. Have a nice day." Kyle closed the reception door firmly and leaned on the outside wall of the hospital.

After such minimal injuries, he was not going to let them fuss over him any longer—especially since he'd barely been able to afford the copay from this minimal treatment alone. Hanging around long enough for the cops to interview him had been about all he wanted to do.

He'd come out of this relatively well. The smoke inhalation, oxygen deprivation, something something he hadn't paid attention to, had made him pass out. He just had a couple scrapes and a cough that might linger.

Denver had experienced blunt force trauma. Whoever had started the fire had... according to him... fucking knocked him out. Left him to die. He hadn't said more than that. He was too angry to speak about it.

Kyle didn't want to think about it. Denver was alive. He

was going to be in the hospital overnight to make sure his lungs hadn't been scorched. But Kyle was free to go.

At least Denver was awake, thank God, and he was as furious and talkative as a man wearing a ridiculous plastic mask of oxygen could be. Kyle hadn't been able to get many words in edgewise, or understand many of Denver's.

Thank God Evie pulled up right on time. Hiding out from the nurses in Denver's room had been his backup plan, but now that he thought about it, not a smart one.

"Oh, my hero," Kyle groaned and dropped into the passenger seat of her bright green Prius.

Evie just about attacked him, unbuckling to dive over the center of the seat at him and hug him tightly. "You... bloody idiot."

"Is that Kevin-friendly swearing these days?" Kyle teased, but he hugged tightly and rubbed her back.

"He can deal with a few new vocabulary words. Did you already pay up and walk out? You didn't rip your IV out or anything, did you?" Evie pulled back and eyed him suspiciously.

Kyle laughed and shook his head, showing the backs of his hands. "None needed. Just a little smoke inhalation, a few bumps and bruises from fainting."

"Jesus, you fainted? Inside? Did the sexy firemen have to come rescue you?"

"Sadly, but also luckily, they did not," Kyle confirmed, his lips twitching into a smile. "I love that your priorities are aligned with mine." He held up his hand for a high-five and Evie rolled her eyes at him but slapped their palms together.

Their back-and-forth was almost enough to make him forget about everything on his mind.

Kevin, mainly. Christ, that had been a scare. If he hadn't

been paying attention, or if he'd been in the wrong place at the wrong time, he might never have made it home from work.

Evie sensed his shift in mood and leaned in again for another hug.

Kyle looked away, over her shoulder, trying to will the swimming tears in his eyes away. He was fine. He was going to be completely fine.

And he was fine on his own.

Only now he wasn't so sure about that. In fact, as he thought about it more, he realized that was the opposite of fine.

Kyle cleared his throat when the hug had gone on a little too long and nudged her shoulder. "Get out of the fire lane, loser. Unless you wanna stay here."

"Hoping for a second chance with them?" Evie teased, patting his shoulder as she straightened up and buckled up again.

Kyle laughed. "You know it, baby."

"God, are you okay, though?" Evie asked more seriously as she pulled away from the curb. "That must have been terrifying."

"It... it was," Kyle admitted softly, leaning back into the familiar passenger seat and closing his eyes for a second. "Makes you think about things. Family." Kevin, of course, but... Nic had come to mind, too.

Facing the very fragility of life had shaken him more deeply than he wanted to admit. The wrong place at the wrong moment and boom, that was it. No second chances, no do-overs.

No take-backsies, River would say.

Kyle rubbed his hand down his face. It was more than the fire that had him scared. He wanted to sweep Kevin into his arms and hold him all night, but that wasn't the only ache in his chest. His own stance against relationships had left him here, without anyone to wrap his arms around *him* and tell him it would be okay.

Evie, River, Denver, or many of his other friends would hug him, sure, but... it wasn't the same. It scared him shitless, but he wanted more.

And Nic was the first guy that came to mind—the *only* guy that came to mind—when he thought about who it could be.

I'll call him tomorrow.

Kyle drew a breath and opened his eyes again to glance at Evie. "Don't drop me at home. Can we see Kevin?"

"Of course, hon," Evie murmured, squeezing his knee. Then she looked sheepish for a moment. "Um, I hope it's not the wrong time, but... Nic's staying with him. I couldn't find anyone else, and..."

A smile spread across Kyle's face, but he also couldn't breathe.

Oh, my God. This could be it.

That was serendipity, wasn't it? Or was it flat-out fear? They felt like the same thing: tottering on his toes on the edge of the same chasm of possibility that lay between him and his expectations.

"Okay," Kyle said simply, because he couldn't think what else to say.

Yeah, it was more than okay that Kevin was with Kyle. He *had* mentioned off-hand to Evie that he'd trust Nic around Kevin. Of course Evie would have remembered that.

"I thought you wouldn't mind." Evie's voice was a lilting, gentle tease. God, how much had he talked about Nic without even realizing it?

Kyle's cheeks were hot, and he didn't answer. He couldn't,

until he knew how Nic felt about being kissed and left in the parking lot.

They had a lot to talk about, and a lot to make up, and Kyle had no idea what to say to Nic or how he'd say it.

As it turned out, it didn't matter. They were at Evie's house within what felt like seconds, and the moment the front door was open, Kevin came barreling into him at top speed, shouting, "Daddy, Daddy, Daddy!"

Kyle laughed and bent over to scoop his son into his arms. He barely had time to say hello to Nic before he was swept away by Kevin's enthusiasm, his own spirits lifting.

"Fly!"

Kyle made Kevin fly, holding him under the arms and spinning him around the living room while Kevin lifted his hands.

"It's late for even big boys," Kyle told him after one flight. "We're going to fly to your room."

And then he was going to hug Kevin like he'd never hugged him before, and tuck him into bed. His little boy, whom, for a minute, he thought he'd never see again.

"To my room!" Kevin giggled.

"Yes, sir," Kyle beamed, wiping his eyes on his shoulder as he turned Kevin to face the hall and trotted off toward his son's room. "And I shan't spare the horses."

26

NIC

It was kind of awkward just hanging around, waiting for Kyle. Nic wasn't sure how long bedtime was supposed to take for a four year old.

Before she left, Evie had given him the easiest possible babysitting gig: plopping him with Kevin on the couch, one of his favorite Lego sets, and his favorite cartoons.

Kevin had only asked for one snack in that whole time, and otherwise, had been completely happy to eat Froot Loops, put together Legos, and watch Batman cartoons.

It had been really nice, actually. Nic could get used to doing that all day. A lot easier than his childhood babysitting jobs, and one step better: from the little he did get to talk with Kevin, it was breathtaking how much like his father he was.

It filled Nic's heart with all kinds of sappy emotional crap just to see a mini-Kyle being just as joyful and carefree.

Evie was in the kitchen, making tea—she'd asked if he wanted any and he said no. So while she tidied the kitchen, Nic fidgeted on the sofa, looking around at the half-assembled

Lego town on the coffee table and the paused cartoon on the screen.

It was a warm, cozy house, and even though it was unconventional, a cozy family. It was the exact opposite of his own growing up, in every way. Not for that reason alone, he ached to be part of it.

But he couldn't force his way in. If Evie was right and Kyle did like him, but he wasn't ready to deal with that, he had to wait for Kyle to be ready on his own terms.

Hanging around was even more awkward under those circumstances. He really wanted to tell Evie he was just going to go home, but he assumed Kyle wasn't staying the night, and then how would he get home? A taxi? If he couldn't afford fifty bucks for snacks and a Netflix card, he couldn't afford a taxi. But on the other hand, would he take this as a gesture of charity, too?

It seemed like hours, but it was probably just a few minutes before the hall door opened and Kyle came out.

"Hey," he breathed out, heading straight for the living room.

Nic swallowed and raised a hand in an awkward wave. "Hi. Sorry, I wanted to make sure you were okay..."

Kyle's expression flickered, and now that he was closer, Nic saw the tired lines around his eyes before he offered another quick, bright smile. "I'm okay. Can I ask another favor...? Could you drive me home?"

He pressed his palms together, his cheeks pink. It was clearly hard on him to ask anything—he was grinding his teeth slightly, shifting his weight from foot to foot.

If Nic hadn't already been set to do it, he sure as hell would now. Anything. "Of course! Yeah. That's why I waited."

"Thank you," Kyle told him, breathing out a quick sigh and holding Nic's gaze for a few moments too long.

Just as Nic's heart started to thud, Evie came out of the kitchen. "You're going home? Good. Rest up."

They hugged, and then Evie came to hug Nic.

"Like it or not—" Kyle started to warn Nic, "she'll do this now."

"Shut up. You hug more than me," Evie told him.

Nic laughed and held out his arms for a quick hug. "It was no trouble," he assured Evie every time she tried to thank him, then pulled back and almost sprinted for the door.

"I'll get you donuts. So many donuts. You'll be fat off donuts," Evie told him.

Nic burst out laughing, and so did Kyle. "Thanks? I think?" Nic tilted his head.

"Thank *you*, sweetie," Evie told him. Nic could already see it—she was warm and open-hearted, just like Kyle. No wonder they got along so well. He was dying to know the story between the two of them, but there was really no good time to ask yet.

Once they were in his car, Nic let silence fall as he pulled away from the house and started to get out to the main road. The first time he looked over, a couple minutes later, his mood sank again.

Kyle looked... broken.

Of course he did. What did he expect after a near-death experience? Sunshine and rainbows?

But he sure as hell didn't expect his own heart to break at the sight. Nic dabbed a thumb along one eye and blinked a couple times, waiting until they were dry again before he cleared his throat and pulled over.

That got Kyle's attention. He slowly looked over at Nic

and blinked once. "Mm?"

"Feel free to say no, but... can I take you to my apartment?" Nic asked slowly. Kyle didn't look like he could handle complicated questions. "You don't look like you should be alone."

If he'd found it hard not to tear up at the sadness on Kyle's face a minute ago, the look of relief on Kyle's face now was even harder.

Don't cry. Keep it cool for him, for fuck's sake. Nic blinked and pulled himself together with the art of practice.

"Please," Kyle murmured, his shoulders even sinking. "I'd really... I need... yes."

They didn't say anything more as Nic nodded, pulled back onto the road, and did a U-turn.

The nervous anticipation when he led Kyle inside his condo was less awkward than Nic had expected. It was still impossible to miss the way they both caught their breath when they moved at the same moment for the living room and just the backs of their hands brushed.

Nic blushed from the heat that crawled along his whole hand, to his arm and chest, but he refocused his mind. He had to say this, now, too.

"It's awkward to say out loud and all, but..." Nic trailed off, clearing his throat. "I'm not expecting anything."

"I know," Kyle murmured, and then he took Nic's hand.

Oh, God. His hand was warm and strong, and now he was cupping Nic's hand between both of his own, kneading gently.

"I'm sorry for... flipping out at Target. I, uh. I have issues, I shouldn't have put them on you."

Nic opened his mouth, but sound wouldn't come out for a second. He wasn't sure how to react to someone apologizing for treating him badly and owning up to it so succinctly.

"Uh. I." He cleared his throat, but those earnest eyes

searching his own made it even harder to focus. If Kyle weren't touching him, he'd have stood half a chance at saying something coherent. "It's okay. I've had issues too. I... got that."

"Still," Kyle murmured, "I know you're not that kind of guy. The sugar daddy kind, or whatever I said when I was... freaking out."

Nic's heart was thumping now. Kyle wasn't letting go of his hand. Instead, Kyle let their palms rest together, and he was touching the backs of Nic's fingers with his own thumb, staring down at his hand as he gently traced along it. Then, Kyle met his eyes again.

"I need someone to hold me. I want it to be you. If you're not... if I haven't been..."

Nic smiled slightly and waited for him to finish the sentence, even though he wanted to wrap his arms around Kyle and pull him in forever.

Kyle cleared his throat. "...If you're still interested. For tonight, at least."

Tonight? Christ, Nic had no words for how much he wanted to hold him. Trying not to be overeager, Nic nodded once. "I'd love that, too."

Their fingers laced as Kyle lowered his hand, then looked around. "Where's your room?"

"This way."

Nic had daydreamed enough about Kyle's green hair and radiant smile against his pillow, but when he saw it for himself, he lost his breath for several seconds.

"Something wrong?"

"No," Nic breathed out. He yanked off his t-shirt one-handed and tossed it aside, then slid onto the bed and straddled Kyle with a knee on either side of his hips while Kyle ran his hands up his sides. "Not at all. You're gorgeous."

When Kyle's cheeks went pink, their saturation was as rich as the green of his hair. It was hard *not* to sit back and admire him, and Nic took a moment to do just that as he ran his hand up Kyle's chest, then unbuttoned his shirt slowly.

By the time he trailed his fingertips along the bare skin he'd revealed, all the way from his chest down to the elastic of his underwear that peeked out from his waistband, Kyle was squirming under him.

"I'm going to need you to do more than that," Kyle grumbled when he noticed Nic watching him.

Nic grinned. "Like what?" he teased, letting his fingers very gently run over the fabric covering each thigh.

"Hah!" Kyle twitched hard and then shivered, rolling his head back. "Naked. Please."

God, and how could Nic turn him down?

I want to tell him. But I'll only scare him off. I have to tame him, let him get close to me before I try to harness the typhoon that's his spirit.

He slipped the button free from Kyle's trousers and slid them down, running his hands along bare skin the whole way to his knees. While Kyle kicked them off, Nic rubbed his palm along the package that was stiffening under the thin fabric.

Kyle's squirm and grunt of pleasure was totally worth it. Nic grinned, watching Kyle's eyes squeeze closed while his lips parted, the tip of his tongue darting out to moisten his lips.

God, they were kissable.

Nic leaned down over Kyle to kiss him hard and suddenly, and Kyle pressed up into the kiss with teeth and a low growl.

Yet, after a few seconds of fire running through their veins, the second kiss was exploratory, delicate, maybe even... tender. He needed to be held, and Nic wanted to do that. He didn't want this round to be uncontrollable passion like last time.

Nic pulled back enough to tug Kyle's underwear down, then unbuttoned his own jeans, yanking them down along with his underwear. Kyle helped him push them off his body, but before long, his hands were just in the way.

"Gettoff—you can't—stop that—" Nic laughed as Kyle's hands got in the way. He could swear Kyle was doing it deliberately. And there it was: a playful sparkle in his eye. He *was*. "You little..."

Kyle beamed innocently and held his hands in the air. "Wha'? Me?"

"Yes, you," Nic chided, rolling onto his side so he could kick the damn things off. "Jesus. They're tight."

"I like your ass in them, though. Much better than trousers."

"Thanks. I should wear them more often."

Kyle grinned playfully at him. "Welllll. I might have to see them again before I judge *that*. Just for science."

"We'll see what we can work out," Nic winked.

The fact that Kyle was joking around didn't fool him, though. He knew defensive mechanisms like the back of his hand, and Kyle? When he was too wounded to be his usual open book, hurting too much to be sweet and vulnerable, Kyle was the type to hide it behind a grin.

"I wanna suck your cock this time," Nic told Kyle.

Kyle's jaw dropped. He stared at Nic, his parted lips so tempting that Nic leaned in for a quick kiss or three. That was his aroused look, and it was so damn hot. "You sure?"

"Really fucking sure," Nic breathed.

Kyle's cock was hardening now, rising in front of Nic's eyes. When Nic cast a quick, appreciative look at it, it twitched.

"Hnh. Uh. Condoms in the... over there," Kyle gestured, losing his vocabulary for *bedside table* for a moment.

Nic smirked and leaned over to grab a couple, plus the lube. God knew what they'd need next, but it was better to be prepared now. When he tore open the package and looked back at Kyle, Kyle was watching him with a strange expression.

Not just lustful, not wistful... like he wanted him, but not just his mouth or his ass.

Oh, fuck. This is real.

It was nerve-racking, but Nic's heart soared once again. He grinned, unrolling the condom slowly down Kyle's cock one-handed while cupping Kyle's cheek with the other hand. He kissed him hard.

"Mmm," Kyle groaned in appreciation, thrusting his hips into Nic's tight fingers. Nic let him fuck his hand one or two more times, then pulled back from the kiss and pressed his lips into Kyle's neck, then his chest.

By the time he reached his nipples, Kyle was panting for breath.

"Speaking of sensitive," Nic breathed out.

"S'perfect," Kyle moaned, his thighs trembling—Nic could feel them against his own legs. "Just hard. So fucking hard. I need you, Nic."

Nic did, too. He needed to make Kyle feel good. He needed Kyle close to him, and he needed Kyle all around him.

As a one-night stand went, he'd never felt so... *intimate*, so fast. Two-night stand now. Nic was so glad of that fact.

He licked Kyle's nipples one at a time, regretting that they didn't have all night for him to find every spot that made Kyle whimper his name. Sometime, if he was very lucky, he'd get that chance.

For now, he lingered around his hipbones and kissed once

or twice along the inside of his thigh, then wrapped his mouth around Kyle's balls, gently pulling them between his lips.

Kyle's were more sensitive than his, and their core was softer. Nic was a fan, though. He loved their shape, their weight in his mouth, and how they drew tight when he was about to come...

Nic licked his way up the shaft to the tip, enjoying the way Kyle's thighs pressed against his shoulders, squeezing his arms by his side. He unhooked his arms to get them free, pushing Kyle's legs further up the bed, and licked around the head now that he could grip the shaft with one hand.

"I'm—Jesus fuck, Nic, if you take much longer I'm going to come on the spot."

Nic clicked his tongue. "The art of foreplay is a dying one. 'Tis a pity."

Kyle managed to swallow his moan of frustration, but the choked noise was audible—and so fucking hot. "Yes, Sir Nicolas," he hissed.

"Sir? If you insist," Nic smirked, wrapping his lips around the warm, firm pointed head. He sucked the swollen shaft into his mouth, running his closed fingers down to the base of the shaft ahead of his mouth, then stroking back up in time.

Kyle *was* big, but not impossibly so. How the fuck he managed to control it under his skirts and things, Nic wanted to know. Nic was sure even his boners would show if he wasn't careful.

"Oh, God, Nic." Kyle's hands slid into his hair, his thumb caressing Nic's jaw. "Oh, my God. Yes..."

Nic swallowed it as deep as he could and moaned, sucking hard enough to make Kyle's thighs tremble around his sides.

Kyle's breath caught as he grunted, then pushed his hips up into Nic's face. "Yes!"

Nic held still to let him thrust a few times, running his hand along Kyle's thigh and up to his hip, then under to feel the strong muscles in his ass pushing his weight up off the bed.

Fucking. Goddamn. Perfect.

He'd let this man ride his mouth all damn night.

"Oh, fuck, you make me want you," Kyle breathed out, his voice hoarser than it had been a minute ago. It was rough and low, and laced with desire.

Nic slowly pulled his mouth up off his shaft, then grinned as he shifted his weight further up the bed, his toes curling in anticipation. "You wanna show me how?"

Kyle rolled onto his side and pulled Nic into his front, their thighs sliding together and cocks pressing into each other's hips. The warmth from chest to thigh ignited the simmer under Nic's to a rolling boil again.

"Fuck," Nic whispered, wrapping his arms around Kyle's waist to maneuver him over top of him. "You feel good."

Kyle's hands were tight on his hip and ass, keeping him crushed between Kyle's body and the bed so the friction burned as much as possible.

Kyle's weight over him *was* good—his heat even better. But best of all were his lips pressing soft and gentle and thankful kisses against Nic's lips.

He drank them in greedily, gasping against Kyle's mouth. "Wha'?"

"Shh. Thank you," Kyle breathed out.

"You didn't even come yet."

His eyes were open enough to see the fondness in the smile Kyle gave him. And now he couldn't look away, couldn't break the dark gaze that was fixed on him from just inches away. "Don't have to," Kyle whispered. "Sex is more than orgasm after orgasm."

Kyle was crushed between Nic's thighs, his nails running up Nic's side to hold him down by his hip and shoulder.

Sex is more than orgasm... Nic nodded wordlessly, not because he disagreed, but because he'd forgotten the last time he'd hooked up with someone who thought that. "For what it's worth, your blowjobs are great, too," he mumbled.

Kyle grinned at him, pushing his hips forward slowly until their cocks pressed together. "Are they?"

His hard length was still damp from Nic's mouth, and the wetness made for the perfect friction as their dicks slid along each other's.

It was Nic's turn to roll his head back into the pillow and grab at Kyle's back. "Ah! Nnnh!" Nic couldn't think straight, couldn't bear the sensation, but couldn't bear to be without it.

Kyle leaned down and sucked Nic's lower lip slowly into his mouth, and Nic gave up on anything except panting into Kyle's mouth and arching his hips against Kyle's, rolling them so their manhoods slid together at just the right speed.

Already, Nic couldn't hold back. He needed it faster and harder. He wrapped his arm around Kyle's back, combing his other hand through Kyle's hair and running it down his back to grab his ass. "Please..."

"Yes, baby," Kyle breathed out, his lips pressing at the crook of Nic's neck. He thrust harder against Nic while he kissed up to behind Nic's ear until his nerves were on fire, his whole body tensing up as his muscles pulled tight. "You're so fucking hot."

"Y-You... too." Nic moaned, then whimpered as his shaft pressed tight against Kyle's, the whole length of Kyle's dick rubbing against his from base to tip. Every time the heads rubbed against each other, the edge of Kyle's head caught on the tip of his dick and sent an extra thrill through him.

"And your dick feels amazing," Kyle breathed out, his voice faint and harsh. "Fucking perfect. I'm so close..." He pressed his mouth hard against Nic's, open-mouthed, their tongues twisting and twirling as Nic moaned into Kyle's mouth again.

The kiss was short, but incredibly hot because it was the kind neither of them had the energy to follow up on. Their bodies were too wrapped up in this dance, their climaxes so close Nic could taste it...

"I need... I'm gonna... Kyle!" Nic clenched hard and then thrust up against Kyle's cock, grabbing his ass with one hand and digging his nails into his back with the other.

He thrust hard as his dick pulsed, the wetness between them making Kyle's cock run along his own easier. He squeezed his eyes shut, but that didn't stop Kyle kissing him hard as he came. Kyle drank in every second of his bliss with that intense fucking focus that Nic only associated with him.

And then he realized that Kyle was moaning his own name into his mouth. "Yes...! Nic, fuck, yes, Nic... Nic!"

He opened his eyes and pulled back from the kiss to watch the pleasure roll across Kyle's face. Kyle's gorgeous lips were swollen from kisses, reddened, and he leaned up to catch and suck one of those lips while Kyle's whole body trembled and shuddered against his. "You're fucking gorgeous, Kyle. Come on, baby."

"Nnnh. You're too hot," Kyle whispered, out of breath. Nic couldn't move, his whole body trapped against the bed by Kyle's weight as Kyle used his cock for friction and hard texture, his hips jerking in rhythmic, unconscious thrusts he couldn't control.

"Oh my God, yes," Nic moaned his approval when Kyle

collapsed onto his shoulder. He wrapped his arms around Kyle to hold him close.

Kyle moaned and slowly rolled off him to give him space, then plucked at the condom.

Nic breathed out a quick laugh. "We could've done without, you know."

"Nnh." Kyle slowly opened his eyes. "Habit. Plus, if you've been..."

"Sleeping with anyone else? Lame, I know, but no." Nic's cheeks burned. *Don't question me on why. I'm not even sure what I'll tell you.*

Kyle didn't question it, though. He just gave a slow, lazy smile as he tossed aside the condom, then rolled onto Nic again, this time shifting so their softening cocks weren't pressed too hard against one another's.

That felt good. That felt... *really* good. In return, Nic looped both his arms around Kyle's waist and held him tight, pressing his lips into Kyle's neck, then against his ear.

He found himself idly kissing the rim of Kyle's ear, noticing which spots made him flinch and quiver with pleasure.

God, it would be fun to sleep with this man every night.

Don't get ahead of yourself. This might be it.

In his blissful euphoria, Nic felt Kyle's fingers run along his ribs, gently along his nipple and down his side to his hip. The affection wasn't lost on him.

The last thing Nic remembered was planning how he'd kiss his way back to Kyle's lips just as Kyle pressed his forehead into the pillow by Nic's head.

He'd do it soon, then. After a moment's rest.

27

KYLE

Even the bathroom had shiny white switch plates. Kyle stared at them for a moment, then looked at the tiled shower—rainfall shower head! He'd always wanted to try one.

The washcloths and towels were easily in sight on a shelf, and... was that a heated towel rail?

Kyle shook his head. It was a cozy bathroom despite being spacious and modern-feeling. He could see why it suited Nic. And, surprisingly, the place felt comfortable.

He really shouldn't fit in here. Not only was it not his own place, but... well, it was clear Nic was wealthy.

That wasn't a surprise, given his job, clothing, even his attitude at Target. Was it an unpleasant confirmation? Not really. Nic was more than his money. He'd shown that over and over now, in tiny ways.

And Kevin had liked him. When Kyle put him to bed, he'd said several times that he wanted to see Uncle Nic more often. His son had a good instinct for who was a nice person.

Kyle's head was still spinning after his near-miss yesterday. It had taken him a few moments when he woke up to remember where he was, and then *why*, and then the next deep lungful of air had been like taking the world's biggest hit.

He was high off being alive.

Nic had been so sweet last night. He'd been dead right— Kyle's pride wouldn't have let him ask Nic to come home with him, but Kyle wasn't sure if he would have had the courage to invite Nic inside his place, either. And holing up was the wrong thing for him. Being around people was what he needed.

And the sex. Christ. Nic was the hottest guy he could remember sleeping with—not just for his body, but his attitude, his confidence, the way his shyness fell away when it came to asking for what he needed...

I could do him again and not get bored. Three times? That was a habit. That was more than a fling.

Once Kyle used the bathroom, washed up his face, and sort of finger-combed his hair, Kyle eyed the clean bathroom counter. That wasn't much help.

Yanking open a few drawers, he found them empty, but the bottom drawer... wasn't.

Kyle swallowed and stared at the drawer. There were only a handful of things in there, but they were unmistakable: a palette of eyeshadow, a tube of mascara, a few eyeliner pencils, and several shades of lip gloss and lipstick.

He heard stirring from the bedroom and glanced back that way, then closed the drawer and opened the cabinet.

There they were: toothbrush and toothpaste. In the cabinet, like a weirdo. Kyle squeezed some paste onto his finger and scrubbed his teeth, then followed that up with floss and mouthwash.

Nic pushed open the bathroom door as he was rinsing his mouth out, then smiled at him. He was wearing only boxers.

God, he was hot. Kyle was too busy just checking Nic out to realize he'd said good morning for a second.

"Oh. Morning."

Nic's cheeks were sweetly pink as he grinned. "Subtle."

"If there's one word that should never be applied to me..." Kyle laughed, putting the mouthwash back. "Hope you don't mind."

"No, go ahead."

"I, uh, fished around your drawers first," Kyle confessed. He wasn't going to keep secrets. "And found..." He nudged the bottom drawer open with his toe.

Nic's cheeks flushed, but he didn't look down. He knew exactly what Kyle meant. His expression was carefully guarded as he nodded. "Right."

Kyle knew that look. He wanted to hug Nic and enthuse with him about makeup, even if it wasn't his area of expertise, exactly. But Nic wasn't ready for that yet. "Sorry, I didn't mean to rummage."

"No, it's okay. I should have put things on the counter."

"Yeah, what's with the cabinet, dude?" Kyle smiled, leaning on the counter while Nic approached to grab his toothbrush and paste.

Nic shrugged. "I was cleaning the counter yesterday and put them in there." He started brushing his teeth.

"Oh. It's not a permanent home. I thought you needed your counter clean for... reasons." Kyle wiggled his eyebrows.

"No," Nic laughed, blushing again. This time, Kyle caught Nic giving him a quick up-and-down glance as he brushed.

He still wants me, too. Perfect. I mean, if I'm doing this for real with him sometime. We've done this twice and we don't hate each other yet...

Kyle nudged the drawer shut again and scooted to sit on

the counter while Nic rinsed out his mouth. "Do you ever wear that stuff?"

There it was again—Nic looked wary. He shook his head. "Not much. I, um..." He paused, clearly selecting his words, so Kyle gave him a chance. "I don't like being seen as... not manly enough."

Kyle breathed out slowly, letting the words sit there for a moment as Nic avoided his gaze by looking in the mirror and running his hands through his hair. Then, he spoke up. "You know I wouldn't think that."

"Yeah."

"But that doesn't make much difference, does it? It's more about you."

"Yeah."

Kyle watched the worry lines form on Nic's forehead, then reached out to run his thumb along one of them and cup his cheek.

Startled, Nic paused, then looked up at him.

"Don't be afraid. You know what Oscar Wilde said?"

"Be yourself, everyone else is taken? That's so overused," Nic grumbled, but he was smiling slightly.

Kyle winked. "Because people like a succinct truth. And it's good for us to hear, in particular. Big, buff gym bros don't need to hear it the same way we do." He let go of Nic's cheek but held his gaze. "Would you wear some for me sometime?"

A flicker of recognition went through Nic's face, and then he nodded slowly. "We'll see. Are you a cereal or cooked breakfast man?" He pulled away to dry his hands.

It wasn't a refusal, just a subject change. Kyle would take it. "I can be a cooked breakfast man. I just can't make it myself. Well, no, I can do scrambled eggs."

"Pancakes?"

"Oh my God, you do pancakes? I knew you were perfect," Kyle teased.

Nic opened his mouth and stood there for a second trying to form a response, blushed, and then hurried out of the bathroom at a brisk stride. "Better get them started."

Oh, he was adorably easy to fluster. Kyle beamed after him, then hopped down from the counter and slowly wandered after Nic, pausing to take in the details of the apartment as he walked.

What a gorgeous man, in a gorgeous place. Maybe money *could* buy happiness.

28

NIC

The quiet sizzle of pancake batter forming round, fluffy disks in the pan, the crackle and pop of bacon... it always made Nic smile.

"Can I set the table?"

"Go ahead." Nic didn't take his eyes off the surface of the current pair of cooking pancakes. They were almost ready to flip. "I'm sure you can find things if you rummage," he added, keeping his voice light and teasing.

Once he flipped the pancakes, he looked over at Kyle and grinned. Kyle was blushing, but had the good grace not to defend himself as he set out placemats, knives, and forks.

He didn't really mind that Kyle had found his makeup stash, but he was also far from ready to wear that stuff for himself, let alone for other people. It still looked strange and artificial to him, no matter how much work he did on his own thoughts to remind himself that it was no more artificial than the masculinity the gym bros Kyle had referenced worked for.

"What do you want to drink? And what do you *have* to drink?" Kyle asked.

Nic laughed. "Juice, and... juice, water, milk, or booze."

"A little early for the last one." Kyle poured them both orange juice, eyeing the carton. "Are these free-range oranges?"

Grinning again, Nic shook his head. "I know, I know. I buy the organic stuff when I can. Whole Paycheck, etc. You can make fun of me now."

"Okay, will do," Kyle winked and sat at the table as Nic portioned out the pancakes and bacon onto their plates.

Nic could see himself doing this every morning.

He swallowed hard and pushed the thought away. Thank God he was able to work from home today, in case Kyle needed a place to stay. But reality sank in: he was going to need to go home at some point, surely.

An unfamiliar phone chime rang: It's Raining Men.

"Seriously?" Nic stifled his laugh and looked at Kyle.

Kyle was bright red as he answered. "Hey, Kyle here." Then, his suppressed embarrassment faded, his face going serious. "Seriously? How many? Jesus. No shit. Everyone's okay?"

Nic set the plates on the table and eased himself into the chair by Kyle's—but not opposite—as quietly as he could. He didn't want to get lost in those beautiful blue eyes.

"Okay, let me just..." Kyle hit the speakerphone button on his phone. "Denver, I'm at Nic's place."

Denver's voice crackled over the phone. "Oh, that's perfect. Hey, Nic. A few other employees at the charity were targeted overnight. Everyone's unharmed, but... someone burned a cross on the front lawn of one of the board members."

A chill ran down Nic's spine as his head jerked up and he met Kyle's gaze. *No way.*

Kyle nodded slowly, his expression grim.

"Fuck. I'm... wow. I'm sorry," Nic breathed out.

Denver sighed. "It's all right. But, look, a couple of the others had their cars smashed. Someone was having a field day all night long."

"Are you okay? You were in the hospital, right?" Nic asked.

"Yeah, I'm fine, I'm free to go. But I've been giving the police a statement about the guys—I caught them in the act and they jumped me. Long story. Anyway," Denver brushed it off, "it's obviously orchestrated, if they got away from this *and* got to those other places all in one night. I would prefer it, Kyle, if you had a place to stay."

"My place, obviously," Nic spoke up, raising his hand.

Kyle looked at him quickly and nodded, then licked his lips. "Okay, we'll chat about that. Nic or River or Evie, someone's place. I'll be fine," Kyle promised Denver.

Come on. Accept my help. Nic gave Kyle a look, but Kyle was staring at the phone.

"Okay. Good. I'll call when we have more news—no work for now, obviously. Everything's a mess. Insurance and cops and fire investigators..." Denver trailed off.

"Call if you need anything," Kyle told Denver. "Anything at all."

"I will, darling. Rest up. We have work to do." Denver sounded tired, but there was a spark of fight in his voice. Even Nic recognized it. "Thanks for looking after him, Nic," Denver added.

"Of course. No problem." Once Kyle hung up, silence settled for a few moments before Nic nudged Kyle's leg with his foot. "Eat up."

They'd finished their breakfast before Kyle spoke up about it. "You really don't mind if I stay here? I have other people who can help."

"I don't mind at all," Nic assured Kyle firmly, straightening up in his chair as he arranged his cutlery in the twelve-o'clock position. "I don't want you going home by yourself."

Unspoken was the other thing hanging between them: he didn't want to push Kyle away at all, let alone sometime like now when he was vulnerable. Nic wanted to be there for him, more than financially.

Whatever Kyle said about it, he felt like he had something to prove now.

"And there's no strings attached," Nic added quietly and caught Kyle's gaze. Those long lashes fluttered as Kyle blinked a couple times, glancing between his eyes. God, he could look into Kyle's eyes all day... but now wasn't the moment to give him romantic eyes.

Kyle smiled, sighed slightly, and murmured, "We're a little past that now."

Nic hadn't expected those words from him. He drew in a sharp breath, then nodded silently. It hadn't just been a one-time thing, then, last night. Kyle was up for *something* more. But Nic didn't want to fuck anything up by pushing harder, and now wasn't the time.

He hoped Kyle would say yes to his offer, but for now, he just enjoyed the moment. It was a cozy domestic scene: the breakfast plates between them, both of them shirtless and leaning back to look at each other sideways.

"Do you have to go in to work today?" Kyle finally broke the silence and the gaze between them to murmur.

Nic shook his head. "Just work from home. Your program is nearly done. I can show you my progress, unless that counts as work for you... and you're off..."

"I don't mind," Kyle smiled. "I'd like to see you at work."

Nic blushed. "It's kinda boring. A lot of typing gibberish and cursing."

Kyle winked. "That sounds adorable. Go grab a shower and I'll clean up the dishes."

"Okay," Nic chuckled.

This was cool. This was... really, really cool. His brain was failing at coming up with other adjectives except *cool*, maybe because Kyle was being such a considerate houseguest already.

Well, no. It was mainly from Kyle saying they had strings attached already, and... maybe he'd stay for longer. Nic desperately wanted to know, but was too afraid to ask yet: *what strings?*

So, for now, he showered and daydreamed about Kyle's warm body wrapped around his own all night, every night.

29

KYLE

It felt a little repetitive to keep thinking about how nice the place was, but even after a morning of wandering around Nic's condo loft, Kyle couldn't get used to it.

He hadn't answered Nic's offer yet, but he also hadn't made a move to contact River or Evie or anyone else and ask for a floor to sleep on. Every time he thought about it, it made his heart ache.

It wasn't that he couldn't turn down a warm bed. It wasn't even sexual... although he wanted to fuck Nic against every wall in this place when he watched how limber Nic's fingers were on his keyboard and how his tongue darted across his lips distractedly while he typed.

Maybe it was his company. Nic was home more than the others—except Evie worked from home a lot, too, and his son was also there.

Okay, so it was Nic.

What was holding him back?

So as not to disturb Nic, though it seemed like only an elephant stampede could disturb him now that he was in his mental work zone, Kyle kept his steps quiet. He wandered down the hall from the front door to the living room again, gazing up at the vaulted ceiling.

It was really pretty here. Spacious and light, and his heart rose every time he looked around at the tastefully-decorated surroundings. It was a lot like his own style.

But there was no avoiding it: it was expensive. And Kyle certainly knew Nic didn't use his money as a weapon, like his father, but it was... kind of overwhelming.

And that's my own issue, Kyle reminded himself yet again.

It was crunch time. He had to get over that issue sooner or later, and if he could, maybe something way better than he'd dared to dream for himself lay in wait.

There was rustling from the kitchen. Nic was up and getting snacks. Now was the perfect time.

Kyle slid his hands into his pockets to stop them shaking as he wandered toward the kitchen and leaned against the island.

"Chips?"

"Yes, please. I've been thinking."

"Uh oh." Nic glanced at him and half-smiled, dumping chips into a bowl. "Pop? About?"

"Yes, please. About... uh, your offer."

"Right." Nic turned to face him, seemingly steeling himself. "And?"

Kyle's gaze flickered over his face. Why did he have to prepare himself? Was he that accustomed to rejection?

It was a familiar expression. God knew, as outgoing as he was, as attractive as some people found Kyle, a lot of people... well, didn't.

You're just too much.

He'd heard it over and over. From at least one of his exes, some hookups, an old boss...

Maybe Nic was worried about the opposite. Kyle was almost positive of it, after the brief flashes of insightful conversation they'd had. Nic thought that he wasn't enough.

Kyle got it out there as fast as he could. "I want to stay with you, here, in the loft. *If* you'll promise me one thing."

Nic looked wary, but he nodded for him to go on.

"If you'll try to embrace who you are—who *you* really are." Kyle leaned in and tapped Nic's chest gently with two fingers, then spread his fingers and his palm against Nic's chest. Nic's heart was racing. "And not let anyone else dictate what kind of man you are. I'll stay with you, if you're brave enough to *be* you."

For a moment, he was sure Nic wasn't going to agree to it. He'd just scoff and say he didn't need anyone telling him what to do, or that he wasn't as girly as *some* men, or... one of the other responses Kyle was used to getting from someone who wanted to be femme like him but was too afraid of what that meant.

But Nic was gazing at him gently, his brow furrowed as he worked through it. No instant rejection.

Kyle held his breath and waited, his hand still on Nic's chest.

Finally, Nic raised his hand to cover Kyle's hand with his own, then stepped closer and tilted his head.

Kyle leaned in to press their lips together gently, raising his other hand to cup the back of Nic's neck. *Oh, sweetheart. I want to help you be... you.*

Nic's lips were soft and gentle, his kiss tender. Almost too gentle for what Kyle felt he needed right now, but he quelled the itch in his chest by shifting from foot to foot. He just wasn't used to tenderness, that was all.

Nic's hands tentatively rested on his shoulders now, and

Kyle nudged one of them to his hip. Given the permission, Nic's grip tightened, but his lips still ghosted over Kyle's in a slow exploration.

"Okay," Nic finally breathed out against Kyle's mouth, then leaned into him.

Kyle wrapped his arms around him to support his weight, pressing his chin against Nic's shoulder. Nic was just a little taller than him—not even an inch, probably. "Okay?"

"Yeah. I'll try. We'll go get some of your stuff after work."

"Okay." Kyle's phone was going off with a text message notification. "Shit. Sorry." He groaned, but Nic chuckled softly and pulled back.

"It's okay. I gotta work, and if you keep doing *that*, I'll never focus," Nic winked.

Kyle smirked and grabbed the bowl of chips, tucking it against his hip like a laundry basket and sashaying into the living room to grab his phone and collapse on the couch next to Nic's work spot. "I won't distract you. I'll just watch."

A glance at Nic's screen and Kyle raised his brow. No way could he understand the words on the screen. Some of them were real words, but there were too many symbols. He could understand basic HTML and CSS—who couldn't, these days? —but that was it.

"You'll just watch me," Nic repeated, snorting. "Way to sound creepy." Nic brought over cans of pop and sat next to him, handing one to him.

"What about in a sexy way?"

"And we're back to distracting me."

"I'm *capable* of non-creepy, non-sexy watching," Kyle stated with a grin. "In theory."

"Is this an unproven theory?"

171

"Very much." Kyle glanced down at his phone as the reminder vibration buzzed in his hand.

It was River. Actually, six texts from River, and a missed call. Shit. He'd muted his phone so he didn't disturb Nic, and he'd forgotten.

I will smack you six ways from Sunday if you don't text me, asshole.

"Oops. I'm in trouble with River," Kyle laughed quietly.

"Have you called him?"

Kyle blushed. "Just from the hospital. Not since last night."

He quickly responded: *I'm okay. At Nic's place.*

River's response was just: *???!!!*

I needed to be around someone and he looked after Kevin so it worked out.

River's response text had five winking faces in a row, followed by the eggplant.

Kyle burst out laughing, then cleared his throat and quieted, glancing at Nic. "Sorry."

Nic's lips were quirked into a smile as he glanced over, the laptop comfortably settled on his lap. He grabbed a couple chips and shrugged. "It's fine. I'm nearly done for work today anyway. And I won't ask."

"Better that way," Kyle agreed.

He answered with a single wink emoticon of his own.

River's text demanded: *DETAILS.*

Later.

SOON.

Soon later. Don't you have work to do? Kyle teased.

River told him, *Yes, so I'll throttle you later. Glad you're alive, asshole.*

This time, Kyle managed to stifle his laughter, but barely. *Me too. Love you, Riv.*

River sent back the kissing emoticon and: *u2*.

Kyle set his phone down beside him and propped his chin on his fist, his elbow on the back of the couch. Slowly, he worked through the bowl of chips and his pop while he watched Nic.

By now, Nic was focused again—so much so that he forgot to eat any of the chips or drink his pop, but Kyle wasn't sure Nic wanted to be disturbed and reminded. The symbols and words were flying from his fingers across the screen.

The soothing lull of clicking, the warmth of the blanket around his shoulders, a full belly of junk food, and the contentment of having a safe place of his own again...

He napped for an hour, his head against the back of the couch and a few inches away from Nic's shoulder. Kyle breathed in his scent, even if he was just far enough that he had to imagine his body heat.

Everything was perfect, as long as he didn't think about bringing Nic back to his place again in daylight, now that Kyle had seen the kind of surroundings Nic was used to.

Surely he won't judge me. I trust him not to. I'm sure of it.

Now that the thought had crept into his head again, though, Kyle couldn't sit still. He contained his fidgeting as best he could. Waiting for Nic to finish work quickly became an exercise in torture rather than a pleasurable way to pass the rest of the hour.

I trust him. Don't I?

30

NIC

Kyle was even more restless than his usual energy level—somewhere around a charged lightning storm. It had started right when Nic offered his loft as a place to stay, and Kyle had taken the whole morning to decide before saying yes.

By now, Nic was getting a feeling for him. He suspected Kyle was out of his depth and maybe totally unfamiliar with relationships. Plus, it *was* an unfamiliar place, so when he wandered around, looking like a lost puppy, Nic tried not to look at him and give him enough space to process whatever he was going through.

After all, he couldn't imagine how hard he'd take it, had *his* workplace been targeted by a hate crime. And Kyle's passion was wrapped up with his job. It felt like a personal attack to Nic, and he was barely involved.

"I'll need your address again," Nic told him. "I wasn't really paying attention when I, uh, called the taxi."

Kyle cast him a quick sideways glance and smile, no doubt remembering that first night between them again, too. He rattled off the street number and name, and Nic punched it into his maps app on his phone.

"Is that the GPS that got you lost on your first day with us?" Kyle teased.

"God," Nic laughed. "It is."

"I'm not sure I trust it."

"Me neither." Nic buckled up. "But it's the quickest way to learn a new city."

"By getting lost? Huh. I like your travel philosophy," Kyle told him.

"Thanks." Nic chatted about nothing in particular—places they both wanted to visit—while they drove to Kyle's house, hoping to put him at ease.

Waiting for him to collect his personal belongings was exactly as awkward as he'd expected, but Nic was starting to get used to awkwardly waiting for Kyle. With their difference in personality, he had a feeling it would be a theme if he was around him much.

The apartment didn't really have a good place to wait except by the door, and Kyle hadn't ushered him through to the living room, so Nic didn't want to intrude. Instead, he just leaned on the wall by the front door and played with his phone, opening and closing apps.

So far, Kyle had rushed past him several times on the way to get clothes, shampoo, and his laptop from different rooms.

"Sorry," Kyle told him breathlessly as he hurried past to the bathroom once more. He *was* cute when he was in a rush. "Just remembered one more thing. Do you have a blowdryer?"

"Yeah, I think so." Nic didn't use it much, but he was sure he'd brought one in the move.

"With any accessories?"

Nic tilted his head.

"I'll take that as a no." Kyle waved what looked like a plastic funnel at him and threw it into his bag. "Honestly. A little volume never hurt anyone. Okay, *that* should be it."

Nic smiled. "You sure? I don't mind waiting."

"Yeah, I'm fine. I'm sure this is the last place you wanna be," Kyle chuckled. "I'm good to go."

Nic wasn't really sure why he wouldn't want to be here, but he nodded and led Kyle back out to his car.

"Sorry. Not really what you're used to, but, you know. We don't get a lot of overtime," Kyle smiled crookedly as he swung his gym bag into Nic's trunk.

Oh. Shit. There it was. It was about money again, and Nic had learned last time to tread very carefully.

"Right, no. We're lucky to," Nic chose to answer. He wasn't igniting any fuses while they were stuck in a car together. Once they were on the road and headed back to his place, he glanced over. "You *should* be paid for everything you do. I guess with charities there's funding issues?"

"Yep," Kyle sighed. "I apply every year, but they usually turn us down. And the volunteers are great, but they can't do everything."

"You do a lot of work for free," Nic surmised. "And then something like this happens..."

Kyle's expression tightened for a moment and he looked out the window.

Nic reached out to squeeze his knee. "Sorry, I'll change the subject."

"No, no. It's fine. I just..." Kyle trailed off. "Sorry. I'd better answer these emails."

Nic let him type on his phone for the rest of the drive, his mind still turning over those comments. By the time he got back to the apartment, he'd put two and two together: maybe Kyle was uncomfortable here because it was so nice.

Not that he was the kind of asshole who'd call Kyle's place shabby. It was beautifully decorated inside, even if the exterior wasn't in the best shape, and Kyle clearly looked after it.

But it also wasn't a condo loft overlooking the city.

Yeah, Nic could see the problem now.

As Kyle entered, he glanced around again. "I can see why you chose this place. The windows are great. And the view."

"Kyle..." Nic trailed off, closing the door behind them and kicking off his shoes.

He couldn't just let Kyle think he'd always been this privileged, or that he didn't understand what Kyle was feeling. Not when it was such a wedge between them.

"Sorry, it's not your fault, I just... issues. Like I said." Kyle held up his hands in apology, then dropped his gym bag by the bedroom door while Nic approached him slowly.

Okay, do this like it's a relationship. Nic still felt weird about being too familiar with Kyle. He reminded himself that Kyle touched him all the time in little ways—brushed him when they passed each other or to make a point, rested his chin on his shoulder when napping, sidled up to him when teasing him... *Be brave.*

Nic went for it. He slid his arms around Kyle's waist. "Can I talk to you about the money thing? It's, um, pretty personal. We should sit down."

Kyle looked worried, but curious now. He nodded at Nic, then the couch. "There?"

"Sounds good."

Once they were settled, Nic was even more nervous, even though he had no good reason to be. He kept his arm around

Kyle's waist, leaning into him. "Um, I didn't always have money."

Kyle looked sideways at him, then turned to face him a little more fully, their knees brushing. His expression had softened already. "Yeah?"

He wasn't used to telling people this. Nic's chest ached with tension, and he searched for the quickest way to get it out there. "I grew up with my grandma and my uncle. Parents left when I was really little—God knows where they are. Never tried to find them."

Nic had Kyle's full attention now, and it was almost painful. Once again, Kyle was looking at him like the most interesting person in the world, the only one he wanted to see.

Now, Nic couldn't meet Kyle's gaze. He gazed down at their laps instead, and when Kyle took his hand, he fidgeted with Kyle's fingers. "So, um, we didn't have a lot of money, on her pension and my uncle's unsteady work and all. And then I was kind of homeless. They were pissed off that I turned out... you know... trans, *and* gay, after everything. I always knew. They were okay with me being a tomboy at first, but they wanted me to be ladylike, you know... stereotypes, blah blah. We fought a lot."

Shit, he hadn't meant to get into *that*, but he didn't know how to tell only part of the story.

Kyle's other arm had slid around his shoulder now, pulling him against his chest.

Nic rested his head on his shoulder and drew a breath. "I was pretty quiet, aside from the fights. I hid it for a long time. I knew they wouldn't like it. When I was sixteen, I snapped and told them, and they..." He trailed off, his throat tight.

He hated telling people this. Sometimes it felt like once he did, it was all they'd see: the usual narrative. Like that was all he was.

But somehow, it felt like Kyle would get it.

"Well, they didn't take it well. Hung on another year, until I graduated. Then they pushed me out the door the day after." He laughed, but he couldn't quite keep the bitterness from his voice.

"Shit." Kyle pressed his cheek into Nic's hair.

Nic's eyes stung and he blinked a few times, glad to be hiding his face in Kyle's shoulder. "Sorry. I didn't mean to talk about that, just..."

"No, thank you for telling me." Kyle's voice was a soft, warm lull, and Nic's hand was on his chest. He breathed along with Kyle, slow and steady, until his eyes stopped stinging.

"I got kicked out, too," Kyle murmured. "I get it."

Nic's breath caught in his chest and he looked up sharply. "No."

"Yeah." Kyle gave him a crooked smile. "I have this... gaydar, but for kids like us. Homeless, early fledglings, whatever you wanna call it. I find myself befriending them without even knowing it. Like we have to stick together."

"Right," Nic murmured softly, studying Kyle's expression. It wasn't pity—it was understanding.

God, that was a relief. He could breathe again. It sounded horrible to say, like he was glad Kyle had gone through the same pain, but... he *got* it. He didn't feel sorry or give a lecture about how things were getting better for kids these days or praise him on how the shitty things made him stronger.

"So, uh," Nic cleared his throat and swallowed. "I learned to make shitty websites as a kid, and better ones in high school... so when I was alone, I'd be able to make it work. Lived in a Super 8 for a while, off the highway. Once I had enough

E. DAVIES

saved, picked up computer programming, got some freelance jobs, finally got my first apartment, learned about half a dozen languages in as many years while I bounced from contract to contract..." Nic trailed off. "Programming languages, that is. And that got me here. So. Yeah. I get it."

Oh, shit. Kyle's eyes were watery, but when Nic opened his mouth to apologize, Kyle pressed a finger to his lips. "I'm sorry I made you say that. I didn't want to... to make you feel bad," Kyle murmured.

Nic shook his head. "No. You didn't make me. I wanted to tell you. It... feels good," he admitted.

"Doesn't it? First time I told River about my parents throwing me out, I cried like a baby," Kyle admitted with a shaky laugh.

Nic managed a grin. "So I'm not doing too badly."

"Nope," Kyle agreed.

It was then Nic realized Kyle had been rocking him softly against him, and it felt... incredible.

"You're really..." Nic trailed off, then cleared his throat. "Thank you. For getting it."

Kyle chuckled. "Given the choice, I'd rather *not* understand from personal experience, but I get it."

"Yeah. Sorry. I... Can we just punch each other's family? I mean, assuming yours was shitty. They had to have been, right?"

"Deal," Kyle laughed, a little louder. "Yeah. Mine... Mom was okay, but she's gone now."

Nic rubbed his cheek against Kyle's shoulder. "Sorry."

"Don't be," Kyle shook his head, but his voice was raw. "And Dad... I don't talk to him. My brother, if he ever calls, I do."

Nic wasn't going to push that sore spot. "That what made you... all... the way you are?"

Kyle nodded. He seemed to want to say something, but he was hesitating, his gaze flickering between Nic's eyes. Finally, he managed a crooked smile. "Promised Mom before I left."

Oh. It clicked into place, and Nic nodded slowly, then leaned in to brush his lips against Kyle's. "I'm sure she'd be proud."

Oops. Now Kyle was crying. What had he said? That might have been too sappy. Shit. Watching Kyle cry made *him* tear up, too.

"Sorry. Fuck. God, I'm bad at comforting people." Nic pulled away and flailed for the tissue box. He shoved it at Kyle, nearly hit him in the nose, and swore again. "Sorry."

Kyle was laughing as he wiped his eyes and grabbed a tissue. "I gotta say, this is a lot of firsts."

"Yeah?"

"Crying on guy's shoulders is not my style." Kyle grinned. "And I'm guessing it's not yours."

"It really isn't," Nic laughed. "But it's been a weird couple days, hasn't it?"

Kyle pocketed the tissue and drew him in again, loosely this time. "It sure has. Is it bedtime yet?"

"It can be," Nic offered. "We were up late last night." And he *was* tired, maybe from all this talking, or maybe from the late night.

Kyle nodded. "Let's sleep."

"Deal."

Before they pulled away to head for the bedroom, Kyle cupped his cheek and turned his chin to face his, then leaned in for one slow kiss.

Then he pulled back and smiled. "Last in bed's a rotten egg."

Startled, Nic laughed as Kyle bolted to the bedroom, pushing himself off the couch to scramble after him. "Who said you could have my bed?" he dramatically sighed, so Kyle would know he was joking.

"I think you did when you wrapped yourself around me like a fucking octopus last night."

"Not an octopus!" Nic was blushing as he grabbed his pajama bottoms from the dresser.

"Something with a lot of limbs. More than four. Definitely five."

"You dirty bastard. You were counting?"

Kyle winked at him. "You know it."

Still, the mood between them wasn't sexually charged like before as they pulled back the covers to climb into bed.

Kyle scooted closer, so Nic let Kyle spoon him. His eyes hurt now, and closing them in the darkness of the room felt good.

As they found comfortable spots, Kyle's arm over his side and his palm against Nic's chest, Kyle pressed his lips into the back of his neck. "Thank you for letting me stay. And for talking to me."

"Thank you... for everything," Nic whispered back.

Even if this was all it was—a few days, a fling—something had happened back there, in the living room, or maybe in the bathroom this morning when Kyle told him to be himself, or maybe the very first time Kyle had beamed at him.

Nic was a better man for Kyle being in his life, however long he stayed.

31

KYLE

It wasn't hard for Kyle to get used to this domestic routine. It was simple but sweet: sleeping in with Nic, sharing breakfast, cleaning up, and then settling in to read or play games on his laptop while Nic typed like a speed demon.

There was a kind of easy familiarity between them now that they suddenly knew each other's deepest hurts, yet still liked each other.

It was almost ridiculous. Kyle kept kind of waiting for the other shoe to drop. Within the week, part of him was convinced it would happen. But Nic had given him no reason to hold back, so Kyle was trying his hardest to be relaxed around him and his place now while he waited to see what would happen.

Taking Monday off had been hard enough, but by lunchtime Tuesday, it got weird not to be working.

Kyle checked his charity email remotely, but there was nothing in there he could answer without even the old database at hand. God, what had happened to that? He couldn't remote-dial into it. Had everything been destroyed? He didn't know anything yet, and the uncertainty was the hardest part.

And then there was the *huge* sword of Damocles hanging over his head: was he still going to have a job after this?

What the hell was going to happen with the charity? Did they have insurance coverage? Did it cover employee salaries? Were they going to have to move office buildings? Downsize?

It was enough to send him into shock. If Kyle were a nail-biter, they would have been worn to the quick. As it was, he was starting that habit by Tuesday afternoon, when he finally yielded to the temptation to get in touch with Denver. He didn't want to disturb him, but he also needed answers.

And there was the minor terror that he'd lost his car, parked next to the building during the fire, or that it had been smashed out, too. Or that his apartment had been vandalized, or someone else at the charity had been hurt...

In particular, Kyle was trying not to think about his car yet, because he had no idea what he'd do if that turned out to be the case. He wasn't usually one to stick his head in the sand, but he thought he was allowed a *little* leeway given the situation.

He had to focus on one thing for his text to Denver, so he chose: *I can keep working on the brochure today.*

A few minutes later, his phone rang and he moved to the front hall so he didn't disturb Nic when he answered.

"Hey, Kyle. How's it going?"

"Good, you?"

"Yeah, I'm all right." Denver sounded distant—of course he wasn't okay. If this charity was Kyle's closest friend, it was Denver's baby. But now wasn't the right time to press him. "You're probably looking for answers, huh?"

"Um... yeah. About things."

"Your job's safe," Denver started with.

Kyle's breath of relief was huge. "Okay."

"I should have texted with that, sorry. I didn't want to bother you... and Nic...?"

Kyle avoided that question. "No, it's okay. I'm almost over the shock, I think."

"Good. I saw you haven't picked up your car."

"Don't tell me. I'm figuring that out later," Kyle told him firmly.

Denver hesitated, but went on. "All right. The board's going to be taking a couple days to think over how to progress. Nothing further happened last night in the way of hate crimes."

Kyle let a breath of relief escape. "Christ. Is everything okay with that?"

"Insurance shit is all underway, and police investigations, but God knows."

"It's politically smart for them to push for a proper investigation," Kyle reminded Denver in a murmur. "It looks bad these days if they don't."

"Right. We'll see," Denver sighed. "We know they don't like us."

They'd skirted trouble with the police, before Kyle's time, for providing information on managing blood work for illegal prescriptions, and once, for not handing over the details of IV users. Not to mention their interactions trying to shield the street kids, the rent boys who were among the highest risk groups, from the cops. Denver still had an acute memory of every one of *those* incidents.

"We might be surprised," Kyle urged gently. "Let them do their thing, but keep following up."

"Believe me, I have nothing better to do than chase them

down. The fact that I was assaulted in the process made them pay more attention. It could be attempted murder."

"Shit," Kyle whispered. He hadn't thought of it that way. What if it was a personal enemy? Or was it just some random homophobe?

The burning cross on Andy's lawn still made him sick to the stomach to think about. Here in 2017, not some backwater town in Georgia in 1997. No wonder Denver was shutting down. An extra decade or so made a huge difference in life experience, and God knew Kyle had run into enough homophobia these days, too.

"I'm sorry," Kyle added, clearing his throat. "God. It's fucked up."

Denver was quiet for a few moments before he sighed. "I know. We're going to take a couple days before we get back to anyone, though. Get everything settled with the arson investigators, and... all that. Don't expect to hear anything until next week. But call me if you need anything."

"I will. You? You sound like you need hugs. I'll come hug you," Kyle threatened.

That got Denver to laugh quietly. "Nah, I'm okay. You let Nic take care of you, too." His tone was knowing.

"I will," Kyle promised. No way was he going to deny anything while he wasn't sure what there *was* to confirm or deny. "I am."

"Good. Talk to you soon, Kyle."

Kyle hung up and pressed his phone to his lips, his chest pained.

Who the fuck had such a grudge against them, or their cause, to do something like this?

Maybe it *had* been attempted murder. Maybe it was just

poor timing—but they'd surely seen cars outside the building, too.

So they'd known people were inside the building.

That hadn't occurred to him before now, and now that he thought about it, he was starting to have trouble breathing.

No. He had to put it out of his head. The cops were taking care of it.

He needed Nic. When he headed back to the living room, Nic's laptop was closed and he was leaning back on the couch, his arm along the back of the couch.

Nic raised his brow and patted the couch next to him. "Or would you prefer bed?"

Oh, boy. Kyle's whole body warmed with just that one sentence, and he grinned back at Nic. He really did want that. It had been so long since he'd been in a new relationship that he'd forgotten how intensely exciting it was.

But there was one thing outstanding on his mind, and when his smile faded, Nic frowned in question at him.

Kyle dropped onto the couch next to him. "Sorry. I *do* want to, but... I haven't seen Kevin today, or yesterday."

Now Nic's smile was back, but gentle. "Yeah, I don't blame you."

"I need to see him. I can figure out a car situation, or—"

"I'll come with you," Nic volunteered without hesitation. "You've got a cool kid."

Kyle blinked a couple times, then looked over at Nic. "Really?" He was surprised, but not unhappy.

"Yeah! Of course." Nic was gazing steadily at him, waiting for his permission.

Shit, yes. Kyle's chest lightened of one more load that had been on it. He hadn't sure how Nic felt about kids, but apparently it wasn't a problem. "Sorry I didn't tell you about him."

"It's fine. It was just surprising."

"Yeah, I bet," Kyle murmured, leaning into him. "That was one reason I didn't want to lead you on. A lot of guys..." He trailed off.

"I'm cool with it." Nic clapped his shoulder. "But you gotta lead here, tell me what you're fine with, and what he's ready for."

Kyle's lips quirked into a smile. "Well, he liked you, so that's a good start."

The look of surprise and pleasure that Nic clearly tried to hide was so worth it. "Really?" Nic said, stretching out his legs. "Cool."

Kyle laughed quietly. "Oh, yeah. He wants to do more Lego Batman things with you."

"That was fun," Nic admitted with a grin, then stood up. "So, we gonna go?"

Given a sense of purpose, he was almost as eager as Kyle. Kyle beamed at him with appreciation. "Yeah. I'll text Evie and we'll head over and take him out."

"Ooh, where?"

"How do you feel about monkey bars?"

Nic laughed. "I haven't been on them in years."

"Get ready to monkey around, then." Kyle leaned in for a surprise tickle at Nic's sides.

Nic squirmed away and hurried for the door. "Jerk. I'll get you."

"Hopefully later," Kyle winked, enjoying Nic's blush as he followed at a more leisurely pace.

Then, Evie's response to him proposing a playground date with Kevin came, and they were on their way.

With how reluctant Kevin was to like Dana, Kyle didn't

want to get attached to Nic until Kevin approved of him for sure, but it was futile.

It's way too late. I've got my hopes up.

32

NIC

Nic had told himself to wait at least a few days before he thought about where the relationship was going. But, at this rate, it was damn near impossible *not* to dwell on it.

Even though he'd been slower to come around to the idea, it had been all Kyle hinting that they were in a relationship now. But Nic wasn't going to read too much into it until Kyle was ready to come out and ask about it. He didn't want to scare him off now.

When they picked up Kevin, he'd run to Nic and greeted him as *Uncle Nic*, which wasn't too weird when Evie murmured that all their friends were *Aunt* or *Uncle* or *Unty Their Name*.

But the look Kyle had shot him at Kevin's immediate approval? Nic was, for the first time, glad he'd been volunteered for so many babysitting gigs as a kid. It was supposed to have made him more ladylike and motherly or something, his family had said.

Instead, it had helped him connect with this kid by

listening to him and making him feel he was treating him like a smaller grownup. Making him feel like... well, a father.

Nic just hoped he didn't say or do anything to blow it now.

"You excited for the park, buddy?" Kyle asked, and Nic followed his glance into the backseat where the booster seat was strapped in.

"Yeeeeah!" Kevin crowed, pumping a fist. "Can you do the monkey bar thing?"

Kyle gasped dramatically. "Would it even be a trip to the park if I didn't?"

"No!"

"Then I guess I'll have to!"

Nic couldn't help grinning. God, as sweet as Kyle was around adults, he was even better around kids.

As soon as they got to the playground, Kyle headed around to the back to get Kevin out. He held Kevin's hand, and Nic's babysitting instincts made him head around to Kevin's other side as the three of them strolled for the playground in the park.

"Do you go here?" Kevin asked him. Not looking where he was going, he stumbled and grabbed for Nic's hand, so Nic caught him and helped him back up, then let him swing from his and Kyle's hands as they walked.

Nic had to resist smiling as he shook his head. "No."

"Why?"

"I'm too boring for cool things like this."

"Why?"

"Uh." He cast a quick look at Kyle.

Kyle saved him. "A lot of grownups forget about these places. Thank you for reminding him."

"You *have* to come here!" Kevin ordered him. "It's so cool!

They have a pirate ship! I love pirates. Daddy got me a pirate book. I like books. Do you like pirates?"

God, he was a talker. Had Kyle been this bright at his age? Nic had no doubt he had been. Nic grinned at Kyle, then looked down. "I like pirates *and* playgrounds. I see the error of my ways. I'll come here a lot now."

The playground *did* look pretty damn cool, actually. The moment they were on the wood chips, Kevin let go of their hands and bolted for the swings. "Push!"

"He's going to get so many report cards about being a... self-directed player." Nic grinned at Kyle.

"I know," Kyle chuckled fondly, watching his son scramble around to find his favorite swing. "Be warned, he will make you push him as high as you can."

"Can he hold on well?"

"Oh, yeah. Can't pry him off."

"Good."

Kyle cast him an appreciative glance. "Did you have a sibling, or...?"

"Nope. I was an only kid. But they used to volunteer me for everyone else's babysitting jobs. Free, of course," Nic rolled his eyes.

"Ugh," Kyle groaned. "It's so different when it's your own kid."

They started taking turns pushing Kevin, getting him up to speed and letting him swing on his own for a minute until he called for them to push again. It was an easy workout, compared to Nic was used to.

"So, um... what about you and Evie?" Nic finally asked as they stood aside and listened to Kevin squeal above them.

Kyle gave him a quick smile. "She wanted a kid, and so did

I, and she needed help. We never dated. We just agreed to coparent. I wanted to be involved in Kevin's life."

"That's so cool," Nic murmured, but as Kyle turned to push his son again, his mind was turning.

Kyle was answering his questions, and asking him along on playdates like this. He doubted Kyle would be open to him coming and bonding with Kevin if he *wasn't* serious about wanting a relationship, on some level. He was at least open to it.

It was bittersweet to watch Kyle with Kevin. As much as he liked being around Kevin, his own feelings on kids were far from settled.

Nic had never felt like carrying his own child was the right option, and back when he started testosterone, he hadn't had the money for egg storage. So, when he got his meta surgery, he'd had no choice but to get a hysterectomy, and he hadn't regretted it.

Getting his ovaries removed at the same time had been a *need* for him—the last barrier to feeling male, and the only way to eliminate the risk of cancer. Doctors still didn't know what the long-term effects of testosterone were, after all.

But the biological impulse to have kids was still there. Sure, some people didn't experience it and didn't want kids, but many others like him did; being trans didn't change that. The impulse to have a child of his own blood had little to do with his need to be in the right body. It was bittersweet to see people who didn't have to think about how to fulfill their biological imperatives and weigh up their life plans at age eighteen.

He helped Kyle chase Kevin through the play equipment, laughing and joking around with them. Despite the tender

E. DAVIES

feelings around parenting for him, things between the three of them were so *easy*, so right, without needing to be forced.

What would it be like to coparent? Even if the kid wasn't biologically his, nothing stopped him from being a great dad to someone else's child. It sounded like he and Kyle knew equally well that fatherhood—the real kind, not the legal obligation—had nothing to do with conception and everything to do with everything afterward.

Watching Kyle hoist himself up the monkey bars, trying not to laugh as he pulled what was *absolutely* a pole dancing move to get up there, and hold himself up by the ankles... it was a glimpse at a future that Nic suddenly desperately wanted.

Kevin crowed, "Your turn!" Nic didn't hesitate to approach the bars.

He wasn't sure he could hoist himself up, but after a few seconds of awkwardly hanging from his wrists, he felt Kyle yank his ankles up. He squeaked and nearly let go as Kyle laughed.

"Come on, hook your knees over."

"I haven't done this in—argh! Years!" Nic squirmed and slipped his legs over the bar, then clenched it hard.

"Let go," Kyle urged. He dropped to the ground smoothly and stood next to him, a hand on his hip.

Nic eyed the ground uncertainly.

But Kevin cheered him on, and Kyle had a hand on his leg.

Nic took a deep breath and let go of his grip on the cool steel.

He swung but held on, the ground rushing into view. Suddenly, Kevin was at eye-level with him but upside-down.

"Me next!" Kevin bounced up and down, grabbing his dad's arm.

Kyle laughed and hoisted him up, then flipped him upside-down.

Dangling from the bar, all the blood rushing to his head, Nic watched with the world's biggest grin.

He felt like a kid again, in ways he'd never gotten to experience the first time around.

God, he'd never realized he needed this until now.

He almost missed Kyle's murmur into his ear when he finally let go of the bar and dropped to the ground again.

"Good job, darling."

Nic gave Kyle a startled glance.

Kyle's smile in return was soft, and Kyle slipped his arm around his waist as he stood next to Kevin, keeping a hand on him as he scrambled around the bars.

Nic's smile was so hard it hurt. "Thanks... honey?"

"Sure, but that's a little sappy for your aesthetic," Kyle winked.

"Baby?"

Kyle hummed. "I'll take it."

Kevin was starting to tell them a story about his classmates at preschool, so Nic focused his attention on him, but he couldn't stop grinning.

One day at a time.

33

NIC

"Hey, I'm home!"

The week and subsequent weekend with Kyle had been one of the best times in Nic's life, but Monday always rolled around. He'd had to go to work to get a status update on the charity project and let his boss see him working.

After all, Greg didn't care that he had a new boyfriend—sort of boyfriend, since they still hadn't had the talk even after this week—living with him, and wanting to be in bed with him 24/7.

"Shouldn't that be *honey, I'm home?*" Kyle's cheerful face peeked out around the corner of the kitchen.

Nic smirked. "I don't know. I haven't seen what you're making for dinner yet."

"Oh, rude!" Kyle gasped. "My dinner is delicious, thank you."

Nic let his gaze flicker up and down Kyle's body. "I know it is."

"Ohhh. Very rude." Kyle jutted his hip out and leaned in

the doorway, then flicked a tea towel at him. "Sit at the table for service, sir. Of the decent-for-company kind... first."

Whatever he'd made, it *did* smell good. Something with tomato sauce and ground beef? Nic grinned his appreciation at both the food and the innuendo. "Mmmm. Casserole?"

Then, he stopped dead in the living room.

What?

It was... filled with boxes.

"Yep! I hope there's no vegetables you hate," Kyle cheerily went on, rattling at the cupboards to get out the plates. "I timed it perfectly! You're just home now and it should be perfectly cool. Who's a boss?"

Okay. Let's see. Nic loosened his tie and blinked at the stacks of boxes lining one of the walls of his living room.

If there was one thing he'd learned in his job, it was the art of remaining calm in the face of disaster. If he could handle a table melting down and threatening to leak sensitive financial information to foreign hackers, he could handle a U-Haul moment.

He hadn't thought Kyle was *that* serious about him.

"Oh! I hope you don't mind." Kyle paused between the kitchen and dining room with the plates, then started making quiet *ooh! aah!* noises and ran to the table to set them down. Apparently, they were hot.

Nic winced for him, unrooting his feet from the ground to casually head for the table. "Right, no. What...?"

"We'd been just ordering in supplies to the charity, these new brochures, and now that we don't have a place... I had to call the shipping company and reroute them, and Denver was out of his house today, and..."

The relief that washed through Nic made him laugh, but

not deeply. There was disappointment there, too. *Whoa. That's fast. Stop it.* He shouldn't be *hoping* for Kyle to move in right now!

"No, no. It's all right. Just surprised me," Nic told Kyle. "Dinner looks great." He didn't dare let on what the truth behind his surprise had been, but it took him a few minutes not to be on the edge of hysterical laughter.

After they were official, he was *so* going to tell Kyle the truth about this.

"How was your day at work? Stressful? Anything I can help you work out?" Kyle asked, batting his lashes and passing the salt.

Nic blushed as he took it, sprinkling it across his mashed potatoes. "Uh. As a matter of fact..." He'd almost forgotten, but since Kyle was asking, it popped back into mind. "Something weird happened today."

"You got sent out on a job to this *totally hot* new client..." Kyle prompted.

Nic laughed richly. "No. The cops came by."

"What?" Kyle blinked. "Why?"

"They were asking questions about money, who's got it, and... I don't know what else. They only asked me that." Nic lifted his shoulders in a quick shrug. "I hope nobody's been embezzling."

"Why do you think it's that?" Kyle dug into his casserole, casting him quick, concerned looks. "Are you going to be okay?"

"Oh, yeah. I'll be fine. I'm only on this project—yours—right now," Nic told him. "But other people are doing more sensitive financial work, and..."

"Ahhh," Kyle murmured. "Right."

"If the company gets busted doing anything... it affects us all. I don't want to be under that cloud of suspicion, right?" Nic sighed.

Kyle nudged Nic's foot with his own to draw his gaze. "I'm sure it'll work out fine," he assured him. "If someone's screwing around, they'll catch him—or her. Man. Evie didn't tell me. I think she's working at home today, though."

"Yeah. So they wouldn't be able to interview us all at once anyway." The last thing Nic wanted was to be dragged in to talk to cops about anything. He was going to try to stay at home this week, if Greg let him.

"I hope it's important, whatever it is," Kyle grumbled.

"Important enough for four of them."

"Four?" Kyle exclaimed. "They could be doing things like... solving arson cases..."

Nic gave him a quick, sympathetic look. "I think that's a different department."

In fact, he was sure of it. Still, he couldn't blame Kyle for bringing it up. He had been on edge for the last week, waiting to hear back. Nothing definitive yet. And they hadn't even caught the guys who assaulted Denver.

No wonder the poor guy looked on edge right now. No more cop talk.

Nic changed the subject and murmured, "So, about dessert...?"

"I didn't—ohhh. I have dessert prepared," Kyle swiftly changed course mid-sentence.

Nic laughed. "Smooth."

"Yes, it is. Usually. It can be rough if you like."

"Mmm." Nic just about lost his appetite, but his stomach growled. If they were going to have energy for tonight, he had to eat. He squirmed in his chair and stretched out his leg to let his feet play against Kyle's. "Long day alone?"

"So long," Kyle groaned. "I hope they call me back and let me start work again soon."

"You must have so much pent-up energy."

"So much."

"Mm." Nic winked, then went silent until he finished his casserole. It took all his focus to eat and play footsie with Kyle.

By the time they were both done, neither of them even made a move for the dishes. Kyle grabbed Nic's hand and towed him toward the bedroom.

Nic slipped his hand out of Kyle's so he could grab his ass instead and bumped shoulders playfully. "Great minds."

"Oh, you have a great mind. And body. And cock..." Kyle trailed off, his voice dropping a pitch.

Nic couldn't hit the bed and strip Kyle fast enough.

Minutes later, gasping and writhing atop Kyle, thrusting his hips down into his mouth while swallowing Kyle's cock to the base, it struck him for the hundredth time that week how fucking perfect this arrangement was.

There was one catch: Kyle hadn't followed up on the makeup thing, and Nic had been carefully not mentioning it. And if he expected Nic to be as loud and open as he was...

Well, Nic didn't have to worry about that yet.

He was too busy grinding into Kyle's lips, flinching at every flick of Kyle's tongue dragging across the underside of his dick, moaning around the fullness in his mouth.

Kyle finally panted across his wet cock, "Nic! Baby, I'm gonna come!" His lips were shaky as he pressed open-mouthed kisses against Nic's dick.

As Nic swallowed the thick, warm passion, his only wish

was that he could see every second of pleasure on Kyle's face. Sucking each other off at once had that disadvantage.

A few seconds later, when Kyle's cock started to soften and his lips closed around Nic's manhood again, his body reminded him of the more pressing need: another of the best orgasms he'd ever had.

"Yes...!" Nic whimpered. He pressed his cheek against Kyle's thigh as he fucked his mouth, fucked his lips a few more times, and then... glorious release. The room spun, his cock pulsed and jerked, his stomach tightened, every muscle trembled... and his brain whirled through crazy thoughts.

Chief of which was: *Whatever this is, I never want it to stop.* It was a thought scarily close to the one he wasn't ready for.

Nic let it slip out of his mind as he rolled off Kyle and caught his breath. "Oh, God."

Kyle slowly rolled and turned until he faced the right way, then cuddled up against him, pulling him in with a quick, rough jerk against him.

Nic squeaked, then laughed. "Hey."

Kyle playfully growled, "I hope you saved room for dessert."

"Wasn't that...?" Nic grinned.

"That was just the appetizer."

Nic pressed into Kyle's body and closed his eyes. "Oh, yeah. Bring on the entrée, baby."

Kyle kissed the side of his neck. "My thoughts exactly."

How fucking perfect can he be? There has to be a catch.

But, as Kyle's lips pressed against the sensitive spot just above one nipple, Nic's toes curled into the bed and he grunted a quick gasp.

Yeah, he was perfectly willing to cross that bridge when they got to it. Someday, but not today.

Today, judging by the flare of heat as Kyle's wet tongue pressed against his nipple and the oversensitive throb of his dick in response, Kyle was going to drive him out of his goddamn mind.

And for him, Nic was willing to let everything go.

34

KYLE

"I'm seeing you today. I don't care if I have to drag you away from your hot new lover myself."

Kyle laughed softly. River had been texting him every day since the fire—not that that was unusual, but he'd been making even more of a point of it. He texted jokes in the morning, asked for input into his lipstick shade choices, and sent sneaky creeper photos of hot guys at the gym.

"Jealous?" Kyle teased.

River clicked his tongue. "Well, I'm not getting *nearly* enough details. I need someone to live vicariously through."

"Fine, fine." Kyle rolled his eyes. He glanced around at the loft that had become his home over this last week, but shook his head to himself. He didn't feel comfortable inviting people over—especially when Nic wasn't around. It still felt like taking liberties.

"How about that little hole in the wall by your work, uh... the thing with the orange door?"

"Perfect," River exclaimed. "That's dingy enough for a

good night. They have good whiskey. Well, bad whiskey at good prices."

"I look forward to experiencing it with you," Kyle laughed. "Gimme half an hour."

"I'll be there in twenty. I'll grab a table. We have a lot to talk about."

Kyle groaned. "That sounds ominous. See you."

He only had to straighten his clothes and find shoes before he headed out, so the walk to the bar was quick. By the time he made it into the dark, grimy place, River had a table and a few tumblers of dark amber liquid on ice sitting in front of him.

"There you are, darling! I started to worry I'd have to down yours."

"I'm early!"

"Like I said." River gave a disappointed shake of his head and pushed Kyle a glass while he laughed.

Kyle sipped and settled back in his chair, stretching out his legs. "So, hit me with it."

"How *are* you?" River asked, leaning in over the table and folding his hands around his glass. "I can barely tell through your texts. Is this a brave front thing?"

"It was at first," Kyle admitted, his smile fading. "It... fuck. You know how much I care about this, and someone wanted to wreck it, and we still don't know *who*. They could still be roaming around, targeting us."

"That's terrifying," River whispered, his brows pulling together. "Are you safe, though? Do you think?"

"Since that first night, there's no more signs of anything," Kyle murmured. "But I still haven't even been back to see if my car's all right."

"Hon..."

"Not yet." Kyle interrupted with a firm shake of his head.

"No. I'm all right, I swear, but I don't need it yet, and I can't afford to do anything with it if they *did* break in, and..."

And he didn't want to see the building.

"But you're not just holding it together." River said it as a statement, one thin brow quirked in a slightly ironic question.

"No. I'm a little spooked, but it's nothing I can't handle," Kyle told him. "And Nic and I will go get the car soon."

"Ahhh. Nic and you." River let the fire go and focused on that subject instead. Now that he'd changed the subject, Kyle wasn't sure he wanted to talk about this, either. But he needed someone to confide in. River's initial smirk faded to a curious, then a gentle look. "What is it?"

"I... I need to talk about him."

"Yeaaah, you do." River nudged the glass back into his hand and let him take a few more sips.

The cheap stuff burned all the way down, making Kyle's eyes sting, but he gasped for breath and came to a second later. "Christ. What *is* that?"

"I don't know," River waved a hand like it was unimportant and waited for him to talk.

Kyle drew a breath. "I haven't taken a chance on a relationship in... *years* now. You know me. I just..."

River was waiting so patiently that he couldn't meet his eyes. He knew what River would say to him about it all, but it didn't stop his brain offering up these worries. He had to get them out.

"I'm afraid I'm too much for him to deal with." There it was. Kyle swallowed hard now that it hung in the air between them. "We're so opposite. I'm so loud, and he's so quiet, and I'm so... open about *me*, but he's so repressed."

River's eyes sharpened at the word choice, but he still didn't comment—just nodded slightly.

"And I want him, I do. I know he's waiting for me to ask, and I'm afraid. I just... do I want this? Should I be following it?"

"Well, your heart sure wants it. You've never even asked me about another guy," River pointed out. "Not the same way."

Kyle laughed sheepishly. He'd mentioned guys before plenty of times, but not like Nic. His interest always faded, or they moved on, or they just didn't click. Nobody had fascinated him and gotten under his skin as fast as Nic. "Yeah."

"You might be a little more repressed than you think, too, hon."

Kyle stared at River. He was the last person he'd apply that word to. "*Me?*" He looked around for anyone else.

"Yes, you," River laughed warmly. "You're afraid of being too much for someone to handle, because you have been for other people."

"Shit. Don't pull your punches." Kyle's heart twisted, but he knew River was right. His parents, his old boss in his first job, his last serious ex and plenty of dates and hookups... they all found him *too much*. But toning himself down wasn't an option, either.

"Don't let your fear hold you back from what you need."

Kyle was hanging onto River's every word. "Which is...?"

"Companionship," River said simply. "You're happy being around Nic. It comes through even in your texts. Doing errands with him, watching him work. You like that."

Kyle's blush was creeping down to his very toes, he was sure of it. He cleared his throat and nodded.

"And intimacy. Not just sexual. You told me you told him about... the past?"

"Parts of it. Most of it," Kyle murmured. "Was that a bad

call? It was so fucking fast. I didn't plan to. But he told me things about himself and then I just..."

"You listened to your heart, and you two bonded over it. It's wonderful," River told him, leaning in to cup his hands. "Trust. You need that, too. You don't trust people."

Kyle winced. His chest was tight, but he recognized the truth in the words because he wanted to push them away.

He liked humanity—people, in general. Loved people, even. Wearing his heart on his sleeve, dressing and acting and speaking the way he did, seemingly without a care about others' thoughts... it made people think that was all of him.

River was right. Kyle showed his heart off, but he didn't trust anyone enough to give it to them.

Except, maybe, Nic.

"He's great with Kevin."

"Mmhmm."

"And he's good around the house. I've been cooking for him when he goes to the office but he cooks for me, too."

"Uh huh."

"He's really smart."

"Kyle." River was smiling at him fondly.

Kyle blinked. He realized he was tightly holding the tumbler, so he finished it, then pushed it across the table. "What?"

"You don't need to justify being attracted to him. Or should I say being in love with him?"

Kyle's jaw dropped. *What the—?*

River leaned in and puffed air in his face.

That distracted him, at least. He smelled vanilla from River's lip gloss. "Dude! What?" Kyle exclaimed.

"Just seeing if I could blow you over."

Kyle snorted at River and shoved his shoulder until he

collapsed back in the seat opposite him, laughing away. Kyle folded his arms, trying to ignore River's amusement.

"Honey, you are *so* blind to yourself."

Kyle fidgeted, tapping his toe against the table leg. "I haven't told him. We're not even boyfriends. Jesus, we haven't even had that talk."

"He's waiting for you to be ready." River winked. "You already said that. Do I need to check if your balls are still there?"

"Oh, no. I'm confident they are." Kyle took his turn to smirk back. "They've been getting enough use, thanks."

River's cackle of laughter pealed across the bar, making heads turn. Kyle grinned broadly. It was impossible not to laugh when his best friend gave one of those true, full, distinctive laughs.

Kyle winked and slid out of the booth to grab them each another whiskey. When he returned, River smirked. "You, of all people, fucking a guy more than once. And *liking* it. You're adorable."

"You'll get there, too," Kyle threatened. "And I will mock you to the ends of the earth."

"Oh, sure." River rolled his eyes. They'd always seen it in each other—that tendency to assume nobody out there would understand them. And until now, they'd been right. But if Kyle could find someone who seemed willing to try, so could River. "Until then, I have a lot of dick to suck before I find the one that fits."

"Poetic. You should be a writer."

"I should," River agreed. "I'll write happily-ever-after tales of a nerdy prince coming to sweep a dashing peasant off his feet."

"Why am I the peasant?" Kyle exclaimed. He fidgeted with the glass, but they hadn't drunk yet.

"Honey, he's in IT. He's got money."

Kyle groaned. "Yeah. I know."

River eyed him and put down his glass. "And you're not being an asshole to him about it?" When Kyle cleared his throat, River kicked him—hard.

"Ow! I said sorry."

River held his nail against his thumb, ready to flick his hand. "If you use this to drive him away..."

God, River *did* know him. "No, no," Kyle hastened to assure him. "We talked about it. He understands. That's what led to the whole... past-sharing thing."

"Good." River shook his head. "Now," he picked up his glass and waved it at Kyle, "here's to you and loverboy."

"Don't call him that."

They clinked glasses. "To you and loverboy," River repeated with an obnoxious grin.

Kyle's chest tingled in hot, satisfying waves of pleasure before the whiskey even touched his lips.

35

NIC

I'm not ready for this.

Nic's mind whirled as he kept his distance from Kyle, eyeing the makeup strewn about the counter around him. Kyle was perched on the counter, holding up lip glosses and eyeing his skin tone, looking gleeful.

But Kyle had waited patiently all this time, and Nic had promised. There was absolutely no harm in trying it on, at least once, and seeing what happened. Nic had put on lipstick around the house a few times, but he felt dumb and wiped it off after an hour. He'd never worn it around other people.

He'd already gotten into the cute blouse and skinny legging-like jeans Kyle had suggested for him. What was one more step?

"Ready?"

"Not even a little," Nic laughed.

Kyle fondly smiled at him, then leaned in and tilted his chin up in an invitation for a kiss.

There's no harm. Nic met him with a kiss, relaxing as

Kyle's hand ran down his arm and his fingers played with his fingers.

"You're gorgeous," Kyle told him softly. "Come on. Sit here." He slid down from the counter and hoisted Nic up where he'd been.

Nic gasped and laughed at the sudden sensation of being hoisted.

"You like that?" Kyle winked, manhandling him around the counter a little just for show.

Nic laughed, but his cheeks were flushed. He could feel the heat burning around his skin. He really *did*. "Jerk."

"I know." Kyle winked, then held up a few tubes of gloss. "What do you like most?"

Nic swallowed hard and looked at the shades of pink. Objectively, he could recognize the differences—one had a cooler tone than the others, another had glitter that was hard to miss, and the third looked like a flat, more beige color.

But on *him*? How the hell was he supposed to know what would look best? "I don't..."

"I didn't ask what you think will look good," Kyle warned, anticipating his next words and waggling the tubes in his face. "Just what you like."

"Oh." That was easy: the cooler pink. He said as much, then wondered if it was the right choice.

Kyle beamed and unscrewed the tube, then took his hand and flipped it to run the wand along the inside of Nic's wrist.

Nic flinched but held still, blinking at him.

"That's the most accurate color. If you see how it looks here, and then on your lips, you'll get a sense for how to predict things you try out in the store."

"You don't... just try them on?" The moment he said it, Nic made a face. Trying on lipstick other people had used?

"Exactly," Kyle laughed. "Most people swipe it across their hand or wrist. But hands get tanned more easily."

"Right." Nic memorized the information like a stepping stone to a whole new language. He turned his wrist this way and that, admiring the cooler pink. "That's nicer on than in the tube."

"A lot of things are really different on your skin and lips than they look in the tube," Kyle nodded. "Now, you're sure about no foundation? Not that you need it. God, your skin is gorgeous."

Nic swatted at Kyle. "Stop flattering me."

"Stop being so handsome." Kyle sidled between his thighs, scooting up to the counter and sliding his arm around his waist.

Nic couldn't look at Kyle, but he was beaming, too, trying to bite back his grin.

"Look at me."

"*You* look at me," Nic mumbled back like he was eight years old.

"I am."

Nic chuckled. "Oh." He cleared his throat and managed to meet Kyle's eyes again, and the warmth he found there... God, it was beautiful.

It made this whole thing so much easier. Admitting what he liked, even in a lip gloss, felt like the vulnerability of being stripped naked, but even worse. Instead of his skin, it was his innermost desires—the ones he'd struggled to reconcile with his very core for his whole life—and Kyle had them in the palm of his hand.

But he trusted Kyle to be gentle.

He let his smile fade and tilted his face up to Kyle, letting him swipe the wand along his lips—top and bottom.

Then, Kyle picked up the eyeliner pencil. "At least let me talk you into this."

"I—"

"You don't have to do it yourself. I'll do it for you," Kyle promised. "And if you hate it, at least you tried it. But your eyes are gorgeous. Draw attention to your eyes and lips, that's all you need. You can wear anything with that and everyone will see you."

Nic winced. That was exactly what he didn't want.

Kyle cupped his cheek. "I'll be shopping with you today. I'll kick their asses if you like."

"Fine," Nic laughed breathily and closed his eyes.

Kyle's fingers were strong and confident as he cupped Nic's cheek to keep his face still. Nic's shoulders relaxed after a few swipes.

The pencil pressing against his eyelid felt damn weird, but it wasn't his grandma trying to make him pretty for school photos or his middle school ex-best friend sneaking her mom's eyeliner into school and practicing on all the girls.

It was Kyle, making him look handsome.

Kyle's gentle rubbing of the pad of his thumb against Nic's cheek helped him forget anything was up. Even with the sharp pressure against his lids, by the time Kyle pulled away, Nic was almost able to forget what it had all been about.

"Perfect," Kyle murmured, his hand running slowly down Nic's neck to his shoulder. "Take a look."

Nic swallowed hard and pushed himself to his feet, spinning to face the mirror. Then, he caught his breath.

Holy shit. He looked *good* with eyeliner.

Kyle was already grinning like he knew exactly what Nic was thinking.

"Shut up," Nic laughed, watching the pink flush through

his own cheeks. The cool lip gloss was good. Not too obvious, not neon pink like some of Kyle's preferred shades, but it stood out against his skin and made him glow.

And the worst of his fears—that it would make him look like less of a man, that people would go back to stumbling over themselves to insist he was a tomboy but still a real girl—didn't materialize. His jaw was still square, his stubble still shadowing his upper lip and cheeks.

There was no way someone would look at him and make the assumption he feared. They might have other assumptions, but he could deal with those, just like Kyle did.

I like it. I actually do.

Nic straightened up, then glanced at his lips again. He was grinning like the Cheshire cat.

"I told you," Kyle crowed, slipping his arms around Nic's waist from behind. He stretched up on his toes to press a kiss against the back of his neck, just under his hairline.

The fact that Kyle was an inch shorter never failed to amuse Nic. He pretended to bend while he twisted so Kyle could kiss his lips. "You might be a know-it-all, but you're still short."

"My love is more compact."

"What does that even...?" Nic burst out laughing, but he gripped Kyle's arm around his waist. He never wanted him to let go. Kyle ground against his ass in response, and Nic laughed again. "Not until we shop. You said we had to. Where?"

"Fine. I did," Kyle agreed, winking and looping his arm around Nic's neck to lead him out of the bathroom. "Target time. Where else?"

"You like it that much?"

"Because," Kyle answered wisely, "there's only one set of

changing rooms at our local one. Which makes them gender-neutral. Good place to start, until you have your sassy comebacks perfected when they stare at you in the men's section."

Nic's cheeks flushed. He remembered that much from his own transition, in the awkward early stages of motel living and trying to put together a wardrobe that wouldn't raise eyebrows. Luckily, most thrift stores only had one set. "Oh. Of course."

The first twenty minutes at the store were a blur. This time, instead of lurking around the periphery, Kyle dragged him straight in and started handing him things: two skirts, a dress, and a couple of blouses.

"First lot. Go."

The dressing room attendant didn't seem to care what he brought in. So, one at a time, Nic tried on items. It was easy to start figuring out what fit him and what didn't. Some cuts were more flattering to his flat chest and different body shape these days than others, and Kyle had a good eye.

As for buying things, he wasn't sure. Some of the blouses were easy—they were just on the feminine side of what a flamboyant guy would wear without hesitation.

Best of all, though, was Kyle's last find: a kilt.

"Perfect. Perfect!" Kyle enthused. "Dude. You know you want it."

Nic laughed sheepishly. "Yeah. I do."

"Try it on."

It fit well. It looked good. It was unmistakably a man's clothing item, but feminine, too. The perfect kind of androgynous thing to wear in public.

He really wanted it, but he put it back.

It was only when they got home that he realized Kyle hadn't just been shopping for items for himself when he'd been gathering up clothing. Somehow, among the new blouses Kyle had bought himself, Nic's kilt ended up on his bed.

Damn it, he's sneaky. Now I have to do this, for real.

But he was far from annoyed. Instead, he grinned as he headed back to the living room.

Kyle had earned more than a cuddle tonight.

———

"From how you told me about this, it sounds like you feel Kyle was pressing you to come out of your shell. Did I get that right?"

Nic was nodding before Dr. Barnard even finished the sentence. "Yeah. Exactly. It was like an intervention makeover."

"Those are interesting words. Can we talk about *intervention*?"

Nic hummed, his mind turning over why he'd used that word. He glanced around the therapist's office, taking in the greenery and plant life here. It was his first session, and she wasn't letting him get away with an inch. He liked that about her. That was what he needed—not to be able to retreat to his shell. And she'd already said she was willing to write a surgery referral letter—he'd double-checked.

"Yeah. He thinks I need to be less... repressed. Closeted. I don't know the word, exactly, for it. But to be more open about what I want to be, and do."

"And you feel...?"

"Good." The answer was instant. Nic knew that much—it wasn't unwanted. Maybe, like the therapist, he needed someone who pushed him a little harder than he'd push himself. "It's actually really good. I don't know what I'm doing, exactly, but... it's fun. It makes me think about what I actually don't like and what I'm told I'm not supposed to like."

"That sounds a bit like coming out, to me."

"It is." Nic seized on it, brightening up. "It... yeah. It's just like when I realized I was gay, only that was more complicated because I knew I was a guy long beforehand, but I was stuck in limbo until my family... yeah." He'd told his therapist about being thrown out, but they hadn't gotten into the specifics yet.

They only had an hour this week. It would take a few sessions before he got it all out.

Nic tugged on his kilt for probably the third or fourth time that hour, then played with the hem. "But I... I actually *am* glad he bought it for me. People don't stare as much as I thought."

"And the attention would bother you?" Dr. Barnard made a note.

Nic laughed. "Yeah. I don't flaunt it, like Kyle does." Immediately, he felt bad for the word choice, though he wasn't sure if she knew the depth behind it. "Not in a bad way. Just in a loud way. A... proud way." That was jealousy. "I wish I could. I wasn't supposed to. But I want to flaunt... *me*."

"That's a big statement."

"Yeah." Nic drew a breath, his chest tight. "But I'm... I'm getting closer. This feels like a step closer."

They were drawing near the end of the hour, and he recognized Dr. Barnard drawing him down from the conversation into discussing where they'd go next week, if he returned, and how he felt about the session and their working relationship.

Oh, he'd be coming back, all right. It felt good to be talking to someone about this, establishing a bond... figuring out what he wanted, but was still too afraid to go for.

One step at a time.

36

KYLE

The weirdest thing about dating someone who worked with his baby's mother was that, instead of the phone call from Evie that Kyle expected from the Synergy return number, it was Nic on the other end when he answered.

"Hey, Evie. Is it Kevin?" Kyle asked as he answered the phone.

"A hit and a miss. Want to try again?" The warm voice bubbled with perfectly-restrained laughter.

"Huh?" was his eloquent response.

"Nic," his live-in lover teased. "Or have you forgotten where I go when I'm off to the office?"

"I—I just—what's up?" Kyle rubbed his face, then frowned. "Wait. A hit *and* a miss?"

"Yeah, it's about Kevin. Evie got the call right before when she got pulled into an urgent meeting. He needs to be picked up from preschool."

"Shit," Kyle breathed out. Thank God he'd swallowed his pride and let Nic pick up his car for him a couple of days ago. It was intact and functioning, making him feel stupid for putting it off for all this time. He only had to stop at Evie's to pick up Kevin's booster seat. "Why?"

Nic hesitated for a second. "Um, for fighting."

"God." Kevin had been getting more irritable over the last couple months, but he hadn't gotten into this much trouble before. Kyle would attribute it to preschool stress, but Kevin had handled the first months of preschool very well. The only new factors in his life were Dana and Nic.

Or it could be something else—a kid at preschool bullying him. Over the last few months, he'd been wearing more dresses. Evie and Kyle weren't letting him wear makeup in public until he was a little older, and he didn't seem interested in it anyway, but it could be that.

"Kyle?" Nic prompted.

"Yeah. Sorry. Um, jeez. You didn't sign on for parental duties," Kyle sighed.

There was a weird moment of silence from Nic's end.

Oops. I think I stepped in something there. But Kyle didn't have time to worry about it, if Kevin was waiting to be picked up.

"Okay. I gotta go pick Kevin up," Kyle told Nic, "but we'll talk about that later."

Nic let out a quick breath. "Yeah, of course. See you after work, baby. Text me if you're out with Kevin, and I'll have dinner ready. Good luck."

"Thanks," was all Kyle could say. "Just... thanks. Bye."

He hung up and cleared his throat, then hurried for his shoes and car keys. No time to think about Nic's easy acceptance of parental duties. He had to face another unscheduled parent-teacher meeting and hope he could figure out what was troubling his kid.

"Daddy!" Kevin stayed sitting on the plastic chair near the principal's office of the small preschool, but he bounced up and down on his hands. He looked delighted.

Kyle hated to break his heart, but he also had to show disappointment, or Kevin would learn that causing trouble helped him see his parents sooner.

"Hi, Kevin. Why are you sitting there?"

"The teacher told me I had to."

"Okay." Kyle crouched by his chair, bracing his wrists on his knees. "Why?"

Kevin's face fell and he looked down. "I'm in trouble. That's... why you're here," he concluded, the sadness on his face actually kind of sweet. He was taking it hard, but he wasn't in tears yet.

Kyle straightened up at the sight of Mrs. Green from the corner of his eye. "Yes, it is, buddy. All right. I have to talk to your teacher, and I'll be right back."

Kevin didn't answer, just kicked his heels and nodded.

Once they were in Mrs. Green's office, Kyle sighed and closed the door, then took a seat opposite her desk. "I'm sorry for the trouble, ma'am."

"Oh, no ma'aming me," Mrs. Green laughed. They were around the same age, after all. "Thank you for coming in so promptly."

Kyle nodded. "I've got this week off work, so it's good timing."

"All right. I was about to ask." *Shit. He isn't getting the week off, is he?* Kyle's panic must have registered on his face, because she quickly added, "Only about today, don't worry.

We'd like him to take the afternoon off and think about his behavior."

"Right." Kyle steeled himself. "I heard it was for fighting?"

"He did start a fight," Mrs. Green frowned. "It's very out of character for him. Has he been going through any...?"

"Life upheavals? I've been racking my brain," Kyle confessed, leaning in. So often, this anxiety struck him: that he and Evie didn't know anything about being good parents, that they were somehow screwing up their kid and they wouldn't find out until it was too late. "I don't know."

"Well," Mrs. Green said, nodding, "I'd like you to talk about this with him and see what can be done. Something must be on his mind, and I've been watching the kids closely. Especially because of his progressive fashion sense."

Kyle chuckled at that way of putting it. "Of course. Thank you for keeping an eye on him. That was my first thought."

"Mine, too. But the other children involved have never shown signs of bullying. Nobody who's still enrolled here has," she added firmly.

Kyle's heart lifted, then sank. If it wasn't something happening at preschool, it was something at home, and that raised a million questions and fears. "Okay. I'll talk to him today." He rose to his feet. "I'm sorry, again. Has he apologized?"

"He did," Mrs. Green nodded. "Promptly, with that enviable vocabulary."

That went some way toward mitigating Kyle's disappointment in his son. He smiled his appreciation and nodded. "Great. Okay. We'd better get going, then. Thank you for your time."

"Thank you," Mrs. Green echoed, letting him head out and collect Kevin.

Kyle didn't say much to Kevin, who was much quieter than his usual chatty, bubbly self as they headed out to the car.

How the heck am I going to break through to him? There isn't a manual for this. And why would Nic want to sign up for this, anyway? No, that can wait until later.

"In you go, buddy," Kyle told him, hoisting his son into the back and making sure he was buckled in securely.

He leaned against the car for a moment before he got inside.

At least he had one failsafe question: *What would my dad do?* Whatever the answer, as long as he avoided that, things would work out okay.

37

NIC

"It's still going ahead?"

"To the best of our knowledge, yes," Greg assured Nic, leaning back in his chair.

Nic breathed out a quick sigh of relief and glanced around the room to hide the emotional moment. The boardroom here was much more formal than the charity's, and he found himself wishing it were more cozy. Even the one tree in the corner was scrawny, the soil dried out.

It wasn't truly employment insecurity that had been worrying at Nic lately. He'd just get transferred to another project if the board didn't go ahead with the system overhaul for the charity. But Kyle and the others would have to keep working on antiquated systems, and Nic's long nights of work to make it perfect would go to waste.

"Did they say what's happening with the timeline?"

"No. How far away are you from being ready for testing?"

"Days, at most," Nic told him. "I showed Kyle informally and he's approved everything."

"Good. Great!" Greg looked impressed. "Thank you for taking that initiative."

"Of course." Nic wasn't about to say that he'd hardly had to arrange a meeting... Kyle had curled up with him on the couch last night and he'd shown him the progress. Then, they'd made out for about an hour.

It was easy to arrange check-in dates with Greg: by next Tuesday, he expected to be finished, which was slightly ahead of the original schedule.

As they left the meeting room, Nic was almost buzzing from the renewed adrenaline. If he worked long hours today, he could maybe finish by the weekend...

His phone buzzed, and he looked down at it.

Going to be out for a while. Home late sorry. We'll talk soon. Miss you. xx

It was from Kyle, of course. Nic's heart sank at first, then rose. Raising a child was going to take a lot of time, and Nic couldn't share all of it. He composed a quick response.

Okay, good luck. Tell me if you need anything. xox

He almost didn't see Hank until he turned the corner for the lunch room and ran into him.

Nic was pretty tall, but Hank was still an inch or two taller and a solid wall to almost hit. He reeled backward to avoid touching the other guy and held up a hand. "Oh, sorry."

"Whoa. Got a lot on your mind, buddy?" Hank smirked at him. God, Nic wanted to slap the smarmy, patronizing tone out of him. He was every bit as good as Hank at his job.

"How's your little project for that... support group... going?"

"It's not a—" Nic decided not to finish his sentence and instead gritted out, "Fine."

"Oh yeah? It's still on?" That smile was goading.

Nic wasn't going to play that game. He smiled blandly. "As far as I know."

"Really." It wasn't a question.

Nic nodded once. "Mm." Even as he did, Hank leaned on the doorway of the lunch room, blocking the way in, but only casually. It was a casual non-threatening threat. Nic knew it well.

"I reckoned they wouldn't be needing a new fancy system what with the building burned down, huh?"

Nic's chest felt tight. Hank clearly didn't care that people had been in the building, that this was setting back their work... any of it. But if he jumped in to defend them, Hank would make even more snarky comments.

"You'd be surprised. Excuse me," Nic answered coolly and turned away. He didn't need coffee if it was going to come with some goading asshole.

He fumed all the way back to his office, but kept his face carefully blank. Every office had the guy who wanted to be a jerk just to get a rise.

How the fuck did Kyle put up with this? No wonder he'd wound up choosing a place like Plus to work, fighting the very kinds of people who judged him.

Greg would probably tell Hank to cool it, but that was a last resort. Running to the boss and whining about that one asshole? Yeah, not happening.

There *was* one way to channel his anger into something productive: get this project done even sooner, better, than Hank would believe. Impress Greg, set himself up for a good career here, maybe outpace Hank's career trajectory...

It was petty, but Nic could play this game.

He cracked his knuckles, typed in his computer password, and adjusted the neck rest on the back of his chair.

If Kyle was home late, Nic had extra time today.

He couldn't protect Kyle from homophobes and parenting stress, but he could cook him dinner, hold him close every night, give him a place to stay, and right now, make his work life so much easier.

And maybe Kyle would stop looking at him whenever he did something for him like he didn't deserve it and couldn't quite believe Nic thought he did.

Time to get to work.

38

KYLE

Kevin was bouncing his feet against the seat, looking around and out the window. "Are we gonna see Uncle Nic?"

"No, hon," Kyle answered automatically. "We're heading back to your mom's place." He had a key there, and it made more sense to bring him back to Evie's than Nic's place when they had things to talk about.

Kevin was quiet for a minute, then bounced in his seat again. "Can we go play?"

"No, we're going to head into the house and get you a snack and talk." Kyle wasn't going to lie to him until they got there, but he didn't want to instill dread into him, either.

Kevin was quiet for the rest of the drive, and Kyle's heart hurt. *I wish I could help him feel better.*

Even when he got peanut butter sandwich bites, Kevin didn't cheer up. He carried his own plastic bowl into the living room as Kyle steered him to the couch.

"Can we swing?" Kevin tried one more time. He was definitely trying to distract Kyle, which was adorably naïve.

"Not right now, pal."

Kyle settled on the couch and tucked Kevin into his side, looking around at the living room. Hopefully, being in a familiar place like this would put him at ease.

"So, I need to understand what's going on. Why did you want to fight?" Kyle asked, keeping his voice light. "What were you thinking?"

Kevin stared at the bowl in his lap, his hands tightly closed around it. "I don't know."

"Okay, how were you feeling?"

"Bad."

Okay, that was a start. Kyle kept his arm around Kevin's shoulders. "Okay. A sad or angry kind of bad?"

"I was mad," Kevin murmured, his shoulders slumping. He picked out a sandwich and ate it, then twisted apart the next one and ate it, too.

"Why?"

"I didn't want to share my blocks."

"You like sharing, don't you? This is something kind of new, huh? What's changed lately that made you not want to share?" Kyle asked.

Kevin sighed. "Mom doesn't like me anymore."

Kyle's chest tightened. *Uh oh.* "Why do you think that? Honey, I know she loves you, and I love you."

"Dana doesn't like me."

"Do you like her?"

"No!" Kevin exclaimed, his voice suddenly louder. "She's... I don't want to share Mom."

Aha. Kyle hugged him close. "Sharing is hard sometimes, isn't it, honey?"

"It's not fair. She just came back and... and... now Mom's with her all the time and I don't like it."

Despite what had happened today, Kyle was proud of his

son. He'd figured out what was making him mad so easily. He and Evie worked damn hard to make sure Kevin would grow up knowing himself.

"Well, Nic's taking some of my time," Kyle started.

"That's different."

Oooh. I shouldn't be so pleased about that. Kyle was thrilled, despite himself. He'd been hesitating for so long, certain that his son would hate whoever he picked, but Kevin *liked* Nic.

Then he put on his parenting mask again. *Right.*

"Your mom and I both love you a lot, and you just met Dana and Nic, right? They already like you, too. Right?"

Kevin nodded slowly. "Yeah."

"When you're feeling like this, that's called being lonely. You feel sad because you love someone and they aren't spending every moment with you, right?"

Kevin nodded.

"And there are different kinds of people. Some people don't feel lonely like that, but most of us do. It's hard to share people. But you wouldn't like it if you didn't have friends to play with, right? Javier? Ginny? Lionel? All your friends make you happy."

Kevin was still listening carefully. "Yeah. I like them."

God, I'm bullshitting all of this. Does he believe me? Kyle had to go for it. "Right. If you were just playing with me and your mom, you wouldn't like it. You love us, but you want to be around all kinds of people."

"Yeah."

"It's just like that for grownups. We love you a lot, but we want to play with all kinds of people. Loving someone else doesn't mean we love you any less. You can love all kinds of people. If you don't love Dana, that's okay. But your mom does, you know? So it's good to try to be nice to her, unless she's being mean to you."

Kevin kicked his heels and nodded, looking happier now. "Yeah. Thank you, Daddy." He promptly spilled his peanut butter sandwich cookies all over Kyle as he launched himself at Kyle to hug him around the waist.

Kyle laughed and hugged his son back, trying not to crush any of the cookies now scattered over the couch. *Thank you*s were rare in the parenting world, let alone right after the hardest conversation he'd had in some time with his son. "You're welcome. I love you, Kevin." He let go and sat back. "So when you have trouble sharing, no fighting, right?"

"Right." Kevin started to bounce again. "Can we swing now?"

Kyle didn't want to reward him for the early day home, but he did want Kevin to feel good about figuring out his emotions. That made the decision for him. "Yeah, darling. Let's head out."

The next couple hours were a lot easier than that first hour, and Kyle lost track of time while he played with Kevin.

"We're here!" It was Dana's voice coming into the room first when the front door opened, but despite that, Kevin sprinted off toward the front door.

"Hi Dana! I like your hair."

Kyle came around the corner and smiled at the moment of surprise that crossed both Evie's and Dana's faces.

"Thank you, hon." Dana crouched to hug Kevin. "I got it done up to look pretty when I was away. And your dress is so cute!"

"I got it done up when you were away," Kevin mirrored quite seriously, like he was conducting a formal adult conversation.

They hid their smiles, and Evie shot Kyle a grateful look as Dana took Kevin into the living room to talk about colors. "Thank you. How'd it go?"

"All fixed up," Kyle murmured, hugging her lightly. "He was jealous of Dana being around. I explained that we all need lots of friends and people to love, and I think he got it."

Evie nodded slowly. "Now we hope that sinks in."

"I hope so," Kyle agreed. Then, he cleared his throat. "And... he likes Nic. Speaking of whom, I should get hom—uh, to his place."

Evie's eyes sparkled. "When do we get to see him again?"

"Soon," Kyle promised, grabbing his jacket.

His goodbye hug from Kevin almost toppled him over, and his chest was still warm as he headed to the car.

I didn't fail as a parent today. Isn't every day like this, over and over? I think I can handle it. Especially if I'm not alone through it...

And no, he wasn't alone with Evie around, but just like he'd told Kevin, he couldn't rely just on her. He needed someone.

As for Nic? One of these days, he'd be brave enough to tell him that.

39

KYLE

Kyle was falling.

No, jolting—shuddering—someone was grabbing him, shaking him awake.

"Shit."

"You're awake now. Are you okay?" Nic's voice was warm and close to his ear, his hand still tight on Kyle's shoulder.

Kyle honestly wasn't sure. His brain was spinning over the events of just moments ago, which had seemed so real to him.

The flames were licking up the walls, the dull roar of oxygen being eaten by the ravenous wall of heat.

He couldn't get out. Couldn't see the door through the smoke.

Denver wasn't there, but now it wasn't just Denver.

It was Denver, but beyond lay Nic, and then Kevin.

He had to choose one.

"You were having a nightmare," Nic murmured.

Kyle closed his eyes for a second and rolled onto his side away from Nic, grabbing a tissue from the bedside table. He dabbed the sleep out of his eyes, then rubbed his cheeks briskly. He didn't want to fall asleep and straight back into that nightmare.

Coming home late from Evie's house, everything had seemed fine. They'd shared a delicious dinner cooked by Nic, and watched a made-for-TV movie, and gone to bed happy. And then... boom, his brain fucked everything up.

Nic cuddled into him, pressing his chest along Kyle's back and looping his arm over his side.

"I know," Kyle mumbled at last, when he couldn't put it off any longer. "I've been getting them ever since."

"The fire?"

Kyle flinched and nodded. The sight of Nic lying there, chest barely moving, between his boss and his son...

Yeah, he knew it was a psychological trick by his mind, a mirror of his worries, but holy crap. It had *felt* real. Who would he choose?

It had to be his son. That much was clear, but the cruelty of being forced to consider the near-impossible scenario...

"You need to talk?" Nic murmured, kissing bare skin. The warmth of his lips against the top vertebra of his spine, then the side of his neck, helped ground him.

"I'm still pretty upset over it," Kyle murmured, his voice quiet. This space didn't feel real—the gap between bedtime and morning. His emotions were unguarded, his thoughts shifting from moment to moment until his troubles seemed hard-edged and insurmountable.

"That's so normal. Hon, that was a near-death experience, right? Of course you're going to be worried about it, thinking about it, for a while," Nic murmured, his hold on Kyle tightening.

Kyle liked that. He felt... safe, in this little bubble of exhausted intimacy between them. "Yeah. I know."

"What would help?" Nic murmured. "Other than time?"

Kyle already knew the answer, and he knew Nic knew. "Going back there. I think... I should have picked up my car." Having Nic do it for him had been a coward's move. A fortunate one, since he'd had to pick Kevin up, but still...

"You weren't ready." Nic rubbed with his thumb along Kyle's breastbone.

"Still not sure I am." The thought was scary. Kyle had avoided all mention of the fire—the news articles or the TV coverage. He didn't want to see how bad it had been, how much was lost, and how damn close he'd come to dying in some stupid, random attack.

And he had this irrational fear, too.

"What if..." Kyle trailed off.

"Mm?"

Kyle swallowed hard. Nic wouldn't judge him—he reminded himself of that fact several times over. Finally, he drew a breath. "Was it me they were going after?"

Nic caught his breath—the regular warm tickle against Kyle's neck ceased. He made a quiet sound, then murmured, "Why?"

"I... it was this one-time thing, and since I stayed away, nothing else has happened to any of the board members. Or what if they're hanging around?" Even as he spoke, Kyle knew it was stupid, but it was like turning a tap. The words just didn't stop. "What if it's some, I don't know, homophobe who doesn't like the way I am?"

Nic was quiet for a minute, but he idly rubbed along Kyle's ribs, tracing along the skin slowly. The contact brought Kyle down again, and he raised a hand to rest on Nic's wrist. "You're worried you're too much again," Nic finally concluded.

Kyle winced. *I am. Crap.* "I... yeah."

"And it's understandable to be afraid of whoever did it. Still no word?"

"Nothing. Denver said the cops have told him they're still investigating. Interviewing people or whatever, I guess. Nobody knows anything useful."

"Whoever did it..." Nic trailed off, and Kyle felt the low vibration of a growl in his chest.

"You're sexy when you're protective," Kyle murmured, rubbing Nic's arm as he tensed up behind him.

Nic chuckled quietly and gradually relaxed. "Sorry. I just... wish I could do more."

"You've given me your damn home. You've done a lot."

"Well," Nic murmured, his voice playful, "I've been getting... benefits."

Kyle chuckled quietly, then raised Nic's hand to his lips to kiss the palm gently. "That's a plus for both of us."

There were a few moments of silence as Nic shifted his head against the pillow, seemingly contented to hold him like this while they drifted off again. He wasn't showing signs of moving. Kyle was already more relaxed.

"I'll bring you to the spot in the morning," Nic murmured. "If you want me to."

Kyle nodded as he closed his eyes. He wasn't sure he trusted himself to drive there, and he didn't want to go through that alone. "Yeah. Thanks, hon."

"Welcome. Get some sleep."

He couldn't remember anything else until dawn.

Two cups of coffee made their idea from the previous night feel less harebrained and terrifying, and more sensible.

It didn't stop Kyle's hands from shaking as he locked them together in his lap, leaning back in the passenger seat of Nic's car. But, because he was perfect, Nic didn't comment if he noticed. He just turned up the radio to danceable pop and shimmied along in his seat until Kyle couldn't resist joining in.

God, Nic was adorable, and Kyle so appreciated the distraction. It made him almost forget where they were going until they pulled around the final corner.

It was impossible to miss the scorched building, and it jarred him at first—like his brain expected to see the intact office and tried to superimpose it on the reality of what his eyes were showing him.

He reeled, reaching for the cupholder and hooking his fingers into it, just for something solid to grip.

Nic's hand covered his own and he cast him a quick sideways look as he drove up to the building, slowing to pull over by the side of the road.

Kyle's chest was tight as he shook his head quickly. "No, go to the parking lot."

Nic didn't question him, but he cast another quick look before rolling down the street to turn into the lot.

The building—or lack thereof—loomed into view, impossible to look away from. It wasn't leveled, but it was pretty damn close.

"Shit. Did the firefighters even turn the water on?"

"It was a bad day for it or something, apparently," Nic told him, unbuckling his seatbelt. "And it was set alight from multiple points. Someone was determined."

Prompted by the movement, Kyle did the same, then climbed out of the car for a closer look. There were steel fences around the place for the safety hazard, but it was easy to see everything through the fence.

Fuck. He could pick out, among the larger chunks, the burnt, twisted remains of lighting fixtures and furniture.

He cast a quick, sharp look around, but there was no movement from any of the nearby buildings. No firefighters hanging around being useless, and no spectators. Especially no victims.

We all made it. "Nobody was hurt, were they?"

"Nope." Nic came up behind him and wrapped his arms slowly around his waist. Though Nic's hold was light, Kyle pressed back into him to ask for more contact, and Nic obediently squeezed him.

It was a hell of a lot easier to wrap his head around the fire now that he saw the final consequences. It wasn't unmanageable. It was hard to see, hard to adjust to, and God knew he was probably going to keep having nightmares, but... he could overcome it.

"It's not *that* bad," Kyle murmured at last.

He felt Nic's breath of relief against his neck. Nic murmured, "Yeah. It's just a building. Stuff is stuff."

"And Denver said the insurance company's being great." Kyle tensed up again, then let a breath escape. He couldn't let himself obsess over who did it and why. For all they knew, it had been stupid teens on a dare, and not about *them* specifically. Or *him*.

Nic nodded slightly. "Mmhmm. And a little birdie tells me you're on track to get your new software installed from scratch on all your brand-new systems when the charity moves into their temporary office."

"Oh." Kyle's lips quirked into a smile. "Did they?"

"Mmm." Nic swayed with him slightly, and Kyle let himself close his eyes for a moment.

E. DAVIES

Yeah, he was going to see this image in his mind's eye for a while, but it wasn't *that* bad. Everyone had made it.

"It's like starting from scratch, I guess. No more old filing cabinets to worry about," Kyle chuckled quietly.

Nic breathed out a quick laugh. "Yeah. Right?"

"Right." Kyle patted Nic's arm. There was nothing to see here. If this was closure, he was glad he felt it now. "Come on. This is boring."

Nic kissed the back of his neck and let go, pulling Kyle's hand to lead him back to the car. "Okay. Let's get milkshakes and go for a drive."

"God, yes."

Kyle didn't notice how hard he was smiling until he checked his hair in the rearview mirror. When Nic pulled away and rested his hand on the gear shift, Kyle covered it with his own for a moment.

Nic rolled down the windows, turned up the music, and shot Kyle a bright smile as he started to drum on the wheel. "Excuse me."

"What?" Kyle laughed.

"Backup vocals, please."

40

NIC, TWO WEEKS LATER

Nic had never anticipated settling into a domestic routine so quickly, with a minimum of fuss.

Every time he'd pictured himself moving in with a boyfriend, Nic had imagined there would be some long, complicated process of negotiating who got which side of the bed, the first shower, or who had to cook.

And sure, they disagreed sometimes on those points, but they settled them easily. Nic had been out with Kyle and his friends a few more times now, and everyone was treating them like a couple.

They were still anticipating that Kyle would move out as soon as the police investigation had concluded, but that was dragging, and the longer it went on, the more Nic wanted to ask him to stay. Kyle had even mentioned that his lease was month-to-month, not yearly.

In the meantime, Kyle was back to working remotely—not that that term was strictly accurate, since they didn't have a temporary office set up yet to be remote *from*.

Also, Nic suspected that the charity hadn't asked or told

Kyle to start work again, but he'd been growing more antsy every day without something to do. Nic had explained that now that the database was complete, he could set it up before they even got into their temporary office, and Kyle had jumped on that idea.

Nic couldn't blame him. In Kyle's shoes, he'd be climbing the walls for something to do. And it gave Nic lots of opportunities to watch *him* at work as they settled on opposite sides of the couch or dining room table, both typing away at their laptops.

Honestly, this felt an awful lot like the kind of relationship he'd always wanted. Quiet, easy, cozy, sexy, sweet. *Right. Nothing like Jake.* In fact, he hadn't thought about him in weeks.

When Nic was with Kyle now, even around other people, he didn't feel like he was staring at the sun or vying for that attention all to himself. He wasn't trying to earn it. Instead, *he* was blossoming. He was more relaxed and happy by himself and in groups.

At the office, he was making friends quickly. People were treating him differently now that he wasn't hiding away in his office, coding all day. No doubt the pink shirts and floral ties Nic found himself wearing more often helped him seem more approachable. He was happy to blame Kyle for them.

"How was therapy today?" Kyle idly asked as he shut down his laptop and wandered to the kitchen.

"Great. Uh. Basically all dick talk."

Kyle swung his head around and looked at him, leaning on the counter while he waited for the tap water to cool off and fill up his glass. "Huh?"

"Yeah." Nic grinned. "Less awkward the more you do it, I

promise." Kyle reached for a second glass and raised his brows, so Nic nodded. "Yes, please."

"Is it? I should practice on you, then," Kyle smirked.

"Like you need help with your dick talk."

"I don't hear complaints." Kyle winked. He handed over a glass to Nic and they both drank deeply, as if anticipating what might be ahead.

The glass clinked against the counter as Nic pushed it aside, then shrugged. "Hard to talk dick when your mouth's full of it."

"You cocktease." Kyle shoved his glass away and leaned in to press his lips—cool and wet now—against Nic's. His breath was warm as he murmured against them, "You gonna follow up on that?"

"Why don't we find out?" Nic laced his fingers with Kyle's and pulled him toward his bedroom.

It was a familiar dance by now—they hit the bed, undressing each other without a second thought. Nic shrugged out of his clothes without a shred of the self-consciousness he'd felt at first, and Kyle looked as radiantly confident as ever sprawled naked on the bed beneath him, hands behind his head.

After a moment of admiring him, Kyle tried to reach toward his cheek to cup it, but Nic swatted his hand.

"No. Stay."

"Oooh. Bossy. I love it," Kyle groaned, tucking his hand behind his head again while Nic slid down the bed.

Kyle was sporting a semi already, his thickness against his thigh and rising. Nic idly wondered how long and much he could tease Kyle, how close he could get him to coming without even touching... but today wasn't the right time to find that out.

The velvety skin was stiffening in full view of Nic, blood flushing down the shaft and all the way to the head.

Nic couldn't help but compare. His cock would be as big as Kyle's one day, except he wouldn't get hard on his own like he did now or like Kyle did. But it would be bigger, and after he was healed, he could take his turn fucking Kyle sometimes...

God, that was a hot thought, but it was months or years away. Nic tried to push it out of his mind, leaning in to run the tip of his tongue from the base to the head of the shaft. He kept it light, teasing and breathing over the sensitive skin.

Against his shoulders, Kyle's thighs trembled and then tensed as he pushed his feet into the bed. "Fuck," he hissed.

Nic mouthed slow kisses along the shaft, pinching it between his lips. He was a little addicted to the taste and the warm weight in his mouth, so it was as much of a challenge to himself as Kyle to keep this slow.

Kyle was fully hard now, his dick throbbing with need for Nic, but Nic didn't indulge just yet. He kept licking in small circles around the shaft, kissing it, brushing his nose against it... When he looked up at Kyle, Kyle's mouth was open, his cheeks red and his stomach and arms visibly tight from the self-restraint.

"God, you're hot," Nic whispered. He kissed the head of Kyle's cock, pressing it against his lips and tightening them around the shaft as he slowly pushed his mouth down onto it.

"Hah... hnngh!" Kyle gave a breathless laugh that turned into a groan, his thighs shuddering and twitching. "Fuck. I was just... thinking the same thing. Christ, that's fucking good!"

Nic swiped his tongue slowly around the shaft and under the head, then over it as he bobbed his head once or twice, then pushed further down until Kyle's cock bumped the back of his throat. He sucked hard, not giving him a moment's rest.

"Fuck. Fuck, so—fuck, sensitive, fucking..." Kyle was fidgeting and squirming, barely restraining his instinct to thrash.

Nic didn't let up, though. He moaned but pulled up his head and pushed down again just as hard, in a silent demand that Kyle keep up with the pace. By the time he swallowed his shaft a few more times, Kyle's burst of sensitivity had given way to a need for more.

"Fuck. Nic, yes..." Kyle spread his legs wider, flinching and trembling. "Faster, please. Fuck. I wanna fuck your mouth. You're so fucking gorgeous... 'specially with my dick in your mouth..."

There's sweet talking for you. Nic managed not to laugh, and instead moaned hard, showing Kyle how fucking delicious he found that hot weight in his mouth.

"—Hah! Unnh, mmph, yes. God. Fuck. Hnnnh—"

In a steady, quick rhythm, the sounds of pleasure slipping from Kyle's lips gave Nic a rhythm to follow. He sped up to match it, squeezing his fingers around the base of Kyle's shaft and milk every fucking ounce of *need* from him.

"Gonna come, baby," Kyle moaned, not that Nic needed a clue. His balls were heavy and close, his abs as tight and tense as a brick wall, and every sound of need he gritted from clenched teeth was more breathless than the last.

Nic was so turned on he could barely breathe around that thick shaft. He reached down to jerk his own shaft between two fingers as gently as he could. He didn't want to come on his own yet, but Christ, he needed some attention.

He pulled his lips slowly up to the head, keeping the suction tight and swirling his tongue around it a few times. Kyle was really fucking fun to tease.

"Yes! *Yes*, fuck, yes, more, please..." Kyle pushed up off the bed, seemingly unable to help himself at last. One hand fell from where he'd been grasping the sheets by his head and grabbed the back of Nic's head.

Kyle thrust forward erratically and whimpered in pleasure, his cock sliding across Nic's tongue as his cum spilled over it, his hand tight in Nic's hair. "Yes... Jesus, Nic!"

Nic swallowed hard with each thrust of Kyle's hips and squirt from his throbbing dick, loving the bittersweet taste and the thick warmth. He kept his eyes up, trying to meet Kyle's gaze.

When Kyle's grip finally loosened and he did, Nic's cheeks flushed at the way Kyle was watching him—like the fucking center of his world.

"You're... baby. Jesus." Kyle was breathless and slack with pleasure, and as Nic's mouth finally slipped off his softening shaft, his hand came to rest on Nic's cheek instead. "Fucking incredible. Jesus, you're hot."

Nic was just about squirming from his own need, his cock throbbing in a quick, pulsing rhythm with his racing heart. He still had a hand on it, and he was positive that if he jerked himself off a couple times, he might just come on the spot.

It was hard to give Kyle even these few moments to recover when admiring his flushed, sweaty skin and gorgeous body made heat flush through Nic all over again.

"I'm gonna... just..." Kyle tried to catch his breath, then growled and flipped them over in one quick move.

"Jesus!" Nic grabbed for the bed, but they'd been nowhere near the edge. His adrenaline was still spiking, and the move made his cock grind against Kyle's hip.

God, he needed Kyle *now*.

"You're so fucking hard," Kyle whispered, his breath hot on Nic's needy shaft. Then, Kyle licked from base to tip in one quick move and wrapped his lips around it, sucking it into his mouth tightly.

The wave of heat that crashed through Nic nearly made him knee Kyle in the face as he pushed his hips up. "Fuck!" He couldn't keep his voice down for that one.

"Mmm," Kyle moaned around his dick, running his tongue up and down the shaft a few times before bobbing his head.

Nic was already so turned on that his toes curled hard into the bed, his muscles trembling with need. Kyle was giving him the exact same few seconds of overwhelmed sensitivity before his body kicked into gear and demanded more.

Kyle's mouth on him was hot and perfect. His couple of inches weren't going to hit the back of Kyle's throat or anything, but feeling himself rubbing between Kyle's bumpy palate and soft tongue was fucking heavenly.

"Fuck, I'm gonna come faster than—than anything," Nic whimpered.

Kyle slowly pulled his mouth off Nic and licked the shaft a few more times. His voice was deep and rough when he murmured, "Can you come from penetration?"

"Being fingered?" Nic wasn't opposed to that.

Kyle kissed the head a few times, which made Nic squirm and bite back a high-pitched whimper of need. "No, fucking me."

Oh, fuck. *That* was almost enough to make him come on the spot. Nic barely managed a nod, as hard as he could. "I won't get deep enough to hit—"

"Perfect. You don't need to. I already came," Kyle reminded him with a roguish wink.

"Oh my God. Yes, please, yes," Nic mumbled into his hand, then bit the side of it, trying to calm himself down for a second. *This* was worth the interruption.

Kyle was chuckling gently, kissing his thigh and squirming back up his body to lean over to the bedside table. "Hold on, then... what position works best? Do you know?"

"Let me spoon you."

Kyle's warm, slick fingers on his cock felt good, but nothing like his mouth or what Nic anticipated he'd feel next. He grabbed Kyle and rolled them onto their sides, his breathing already quick with need as he ground against his back, then scooted further down, getting his hips lined up just right so he could press against the entrance.

They'd done a lot in the last few weeks, but never this. Nic was nervous for a moment, his hand resting on Kyle's shoulder. "You want...?"

"Fuck me," Kyle whispered, twisting to look over his shoulder at him. "And kiss me, dammit."

Nic tightened his thighs around Kyle's and pushed close, then inside. It was shallow, but it was tight and slick and it felt *good.*

He thrust hard without needing to be told twice, focusing on keeping Kyle's hips pressed tightly against his, his knees drawn up so he could get deeper...

"Gonna... so close," Nic moaned. He'd already been close enough and the whole new kind of stimulation had pulled him back down for a moment, but he was revved up again. The bed shook as he thrust into Kyle, and Kyle moaned, rubbing his arm and thigh and anywhere he could reach.

"Come, baby," Kyle breathed out. "God, you're hard. I can feel you in me. That's so fucking hot!"

Nic dug his nails into Kyle's hip as his head spun. One or two more thrusts, and he was about to...

"Kyle!" Nic's body seized and tensed, his muscles quivering in involuntary shudders as he thrust as hard as he could into Kyle, wrapped around him and in him. *In* him! The thought was so goddamn hot, let alone the feeling of his manhood inside, tight and wet.

He couldn't breathe, but in the best way possible. At last, the tension drained out of his body when his muscles stopped quivering, his mind clearing up.

"Shit," Nic whispered with a breathless laugh. "I forgot to kiss you."

"I'll forgive you if you do it right now," Kyle murmured playfully, squirming out of his hold and rolling on his back.

Nic kept his arms and legs around Kyle as he kissed him hard, sucking Kyle's lower lip until Kyle was out of breath again.

Kyle groaned. "Fucking refractory periods."

"We'd be chafed raw if we didn't have them," Nic pointed out, a smile tugging at his lips as he kissed Kyle's neck.

"Fair point. God. That was awesome," Kyle whispered. "Did you like it?"

Nic nodded. The feeling of holding Kyle, thrusting into him... if he could get deep enough that he hit Kyle's prostate, he could only imagine how incredible that would feel. "That's why I want phallo. I'm going to make an appointment. That's what today's therapy was about."

"Oh," Kyle whispered, shifting until he could get a hand on Nic's shoulder and rub the back of his neck. "That's awesome."

"You think? I mean, it's a huge thing, and it'll take so long to recover..." Nic sighed. "And the money. Not that the money matters to me, but..."

Kyle shook his head. "You do what you need to. I just want to see you happy. Whether or not you can fuck me like a porn star, I don't care. This is the best sex of my life already."

Oh. Nic's jaw dropped. Hearing that from Kyle so plainly...? It was the truth.

"If you want phallo, I'll help you talk about it beforehand or recover afterward... whatever you need," Kyle told him, his voice gentle but firm. "That's what boyfriends are for."

The stress drained from Nic as he closed his eyes, then pressed his nose into Kyle's shoulder. "Fuck. Thank you. I love you."

He hadn't really meant to say it—more think it. He'd thought it enough times lately in little, everyday things. But he hadn't let it slip until now.

There was silence for a second or two before he caught his breath, his mood dropping.

Kyle wasn't saying it back. Nic couldn't look at him. He didn't want to know why.

"Refractory periods will have to wait... I gotta get to sleep," Nic murmured.

"Me, too," Kyle murmured. He was rubbing Nic's arm and hand gently, settling down against him. He wasn't pushing Nic away, then, so that was something. Kyle was squirming, finding the right way to lie with him.

Give him time. He just accepted the biggest news I could throw at him.

"Goodnight," Nic murmured, closing his eyes.

Kyle yawned and went still against the pillow, apparently finding just the right spot. "Night, Nic."

Nic's thoughts kept him awake for another minute, but his eyelids were too heavy to hold out much longer.

Wait for him. It's worked every time so far. Please let it work again.

41

KYLE

"I... love you. I love you, dammit. I'm sorry I didn't say it before."

The words echoed in the empty condo as Kyle paced back and forth like he was trying to wear a hole in the floor.

He didn't know how to say it.

Kyle cleared his throat and murmured, "I love you, Nic." Then, he sighed hard and threw his hands in the air. "Fuck. Fuck this."

It wasn't the words themselves that were the hard part. Words were easy—anyone could say them. It was finding the right moment, admitting it to himself, *believing* everything...

Nobody had told him that before and really meant it. Not like Nic meant it. Sure, boyfriends had idly thrown the word around, trying to get something out of him, and his family had lied about loving him for years...

It took time to process Nic's words, by which point, it had been much too late to answer. Things had been awkward for those minutes before sleep, and then again this morning, but they'd gotten through it.

Kyle wanted to keep things as normal between them as possible until he found the right moment to respond.

Normal now included picking Nic up from his office, and he checked the clock anxiously again. If he left now, he might get stuck in traffic more than if he waited another ten minutes. But if he waited, and miscalculated the driving distance to Nic's office...

Dammit, he knew where to find it. He'd picked Evie up before. This wasn't any different.

Except he was picking up his boyfriend, and then his son, so they could spend the night together. According to Evie, Kevin was looking forward to his night with Uncle Nic and Daddy, and Kyle already had his pancake shapes planned for tomorrow morning.

"Fuck it." Standing around telling the empty air he loved it wasn't his style. Kyle grabbed his keys and left, rubbing them like a lucky charm before he started up his car.

It worked, and the drive to the office was nearly traffic-free and painless.

Nic worked on the same floor as Evie, so Kyle already knew where to check in and how to get up there in the elevator.

He instantly remembered why he didn't like coming here. The office was so sterile, filled with boring people wearing boring suits. He was pretty damn out of place with his green hair, plaid blouse, and skinny jeans.

When he reached the floor and stepped out of the elevator, Kyle cast his eyes around, scanning the faces of the people there in search of Nic.

But before he could find him, his gaze landed on someone else altogether: a familiar face he couldn't place at first. That wasn't uncommon, between his many one-night stands and his work, but something bothered him, too. Where did he know him from?

"Oh, shit," he breathed out. The guy in the ill-fitting suit with the pushed-back hair leaning against a cubicle and looking around as if sensing eyes on him had been one of the men in the alley on the night of the fire.

Those hadn't been firefighters. Of course. He felt so fucking stupid.

This was one of the guys who'd knocked Denver out and dragged him into the lobby to keep him silent... one of the guys who'd lit the fire, smashed the board members' windows.

Don't give it away. Kyle tried to wipe the look of recognition off his face. *Get to Nic, get him out of here, then call the cops.*

He only got halfway to the corner with Nic's office before he cast another casual look at the other guy.

Their eyes met, and Kyle's heart sank. The game was up.

The other guy's eyes narrowed and he started to walk toward him.

There was no doubt in Kyle's mind that he was coming for *him*. He'd never been less thrilled about his distinctive look as when this man was approaching, hulking and aggressive, with *that* look in his eye.

He'd seen it before, in other people. It never meant something good.

Kyle refused to give the arsonist the satisfaction of looking afraid or shouting anything, but he was never going to make it to Nic's office before this guy intercepted him.

Fuck. Me.

42

NIC

It was a few minutes past six. Nic fidgeted with his mouse and looked at the clock again, but time didn't move any faster.

He was expecting Kyle any time now—he should have been here at six, in fact—but he was trying not to worry. If there was a traffic jam nearby, a few minutes was nothing.

Still, he'd just wrapped up this project and he didn't want to start another one when he was about to leave, so it made more sense to get out of here. Nic nodded to himself and shut down his computer, packing up his stuff to wait for his boyfriend in the lobby.

It was pure chance he heard it as he walked by—mumbling, muffled but distinctive, like someone was in trouble... or telling someone else off. He couldn't tell which.

Nic looked around at the board rooms and nearby cubicles, but nobody was in a meeting with their boss right now. No office doors closed, either. Just... the stock closet.

It was definitely coming from the stock closet.

Nic adjusted his coat and the laptop bag on his shoulder as he looked around again. Nobody nearby, and he wouldn't want to attract attention anyway, in case he was about to interrupt a... well, more passionate rendezvous.

It could be nothing—a couple coworkers finding a private space to argue about the bank system that was going wrong this week on one of the other teams.

Or it could be something serious.

Fine. Nic would investigate.

He set his laptop bag against the wall, then slowly approached the stock closet and turned the knob to open it.

"—you ever tell the cops you saw me there?"

Kyle—and what was Kyle doing there?!—was on the ground. Hank was crouched over him, his hand fisted in Kyle's blouse, his fist close to Kyle's face as he hissed in his face.

"That fire's the last thing you and your son will need to worry..." Hank's growled threat trailed off when he looked over and saw Nic in the doorway.

Kyle was frozen on the floor. He wasn't moving, his eyes wide as expressions crossed his face: fury, but paralyzing fear. Nic knew that fear. He'd been there, on the floor, the fist to his face.

Nic saw red. He would *kill* anyone who was trying to hurt Kyle, let alone threatening him.

And his son? No. Not Kevin. Nic was *not* letting him get away with using Kevin as a threat.

Nic snarled as he crossed the slick tile floor of the closet in two steps, grabbing Hank by the shoulders and pulling him away from Kyle. It only took one twist to slam him to the ground. "How *dare* you? How. Fucking. Dare. You. Touch. Him!" He shook Hank bodily with every punctuated word, crouching over him.

"It's not what you think." Hank sneered, pushing his hands

away and twisting, sitting up to try to get free. "I'm not some gross fag feeling up your boyfriend—"

Nic held onto Hank's shirt with all his strength and slammed him back down again, ignoring whatever Kyle was saying. "You're not distracting me. You set the fire. *You set it!*"

"I don't know what you're..." Hank drew back just enough to get the space, then tried to sucker-punch him.

"You goddamn tried to kill him!" His fist connected with the side of Hank's face. He hit twice more, for Kevin and Kyle and Denver, and how *dare* Hank try to use them?

Nic wanted to tear him apart for *daring* to lay a hand on Kyle.

There were people now, shouting, calling out to each other.

He heard words: *cops. Kyle. Hank. Fire.*

"He set the fire!" Nic shouted over it all, baring his teeth as he was pulled to his feet and off Hank.

Hank's eyes burned as he stared at Nic silently, not denying it any longer. "So what if I did?"

All this time, it was the guy two cubicles over. Nic felt sick.

He slumped into a rolling chair, people's hands still on his shoulders as they stepped between them, pulling Hank out of the closet.

Only one thing hit his mind then: where was Kyle? He had to see him.

"Kyle...?"

43

KYLE

I just froze. Why did I just freeze?

The guy—Hank—had pulled him into the closet without a word, and he'd gone along with it. Goddamn stupid. That shit could get him killed someday!

Kyle replayed it over and over—Hank growling threats about him, telling him he knew about his son, that if he told the cops a word, the fire would be the least of his worries...

And then Nic had come. But Kyle had frozen in the face of the hatred that twisted Hank's expression into icy indifference.

For a second, he'd seen what Denver had seen. It terrified him to the core. Being left to die in the smoky ashes of the office building? Hank had no shred of humanity in his soul, Kyle was certain of it.

"Hey." It was Nic, pulling him to the side. Kyle had just been standing, staring off into space while people moved, talked around him. The cops had taken the statement, and then he'd just been... standing here. "There you are. C'mon."

He stumbled and walked with Nic. *This* was the man he could trust. He'd follow Nic anywhere.

"The cops are taking Hank away. He was already a suspect, and he confessed to them, too, just now."

Kyle slowly relaxed. That meant they were safe, right? "He did?"

"Yeah." Nic's arm slid around his waist. "You all right?"

Kyle caught his breath and shook his head slowly. "But I will be now." He followed Nic's gesture and spotted Evie on the periphery of the action, talking to a police officer. "Shit. Kevin."

Nic shook his head. "I already said we need a little more time, and we'll take Kevin tomorrow."

Kyle couldn't find it in himself to disagree. Nic was right, again, about what he needed. He nodded slowly. "Thanks for... finding me."

"Of course." Nic squeezed him harder, his expression steely.

Kyle pressed his hand to his face and pulled away, rubbing as if the world would seem more real. So much had happened in a few short minutes and he wasn't fully over it.

Hank, this coworker, had set the fire? But why? Kyle didn't know him. Did he hate Nic?

The questions will come out later. He was in the cops' hands now.

"Let me drive you home," Nic murmured. "To my home. Our home."

"My car's... pretty picky." Kyle didn't miss the implication. He was going to follow up on that tomorrow. He trailed off when he remembered that Nic had picked up his car from the fire site. He knew it all already. "Yeah."

Nic squeezed him around the shoulders and took him by the hand, leading him toward the elevator.

They had it to themselves, which gave him a minute to decompress before they reached the street outside.

There were a few cop cars, but Nic led him away from them and to Kyle's car.

"I thought you were gonna kick his ass," Kyle smiled weakly once they were driving. He closed his eyes, envisioning once more the way Nic had stormed in there, hauled Hank off him, and floored him in one quick move.

He'd never had someone protect him before. Nobody ever spoke up—nobody ever wanted to put their neck on the line for someone like him.

Nic had been about ready to slam Hank through the wall. God, that was kind of hot.

"I wanted to," Nic admitted. "If I hadn't been thinking more, I would have. But it doesn't look good to kick the shit out of a guy in a closet before you call the cops."

"Shame," Kyle chuckled bitterly. "I would have done it myself."

Nic nodded. "I know. You were just in shock at first."

"Yeah. Yeah, I was," Kyle murmured, his gaze dropping to his lap.

"It happens." Nic reached out to squeeze Kyle's knee, and that was all he said about it. Then, he started to chat about his day, telling Kyle about the programming work he'd done.

It was good conversation and Kyle didn't have to answer, just nodded a lot.

His body was still tense, his thoughts racing from one thing to the next as he replayed those few minutes.

As he waited for Nic to unlock the front door, Kyle's breath caught in his throat. He was going to be safe to go home now. The cops had Hank in custody, and no doubt they could find the other guy or guys who had been involved.

Everything's going to be better.

So why the fuck did he still feel so tense?

Kyle barely waited until their shoes were off when they were in Nic's apartment before he grabbed Nic by the waist, steering him for the bedroom.

"God, yes," Nic moaned, but when he reached out for Kyle's shirt, Kyle pushed his hands away.

Instead, Kyle pushed Nic onto the bed and undressed him first, taking only as much time as he absolutely needed not to rip his shirt off.

When Nic was naked, Kyle stripped himself in quick, brusque movements, tossing his clothes aside and grabbing lube. "I really need—"

"Yes. Please." Nic was breathless, his hands running up Kyle's sides to his shoulders.

That angular, strong body under his, the delicate thickness of his manhood between his thighs, already flushed and angling slowly upward, the rough texture of his hair when it was all pushed out of place... Kyle's gaze dragged slowly up and down Nic's body to take in every goddamn detail that he loved.

"As long as I can kiss you," Nic added in a breathless whisper, which drew Kyle's gaze again.

Their eyes locked, and he couldn't look away.

Kyle braced a forearm next to Nic's head and leaned down for a long, hard kiss. Their teeth and tongues and lips clashed, vying for control, or maybe in their desperation to each show each other how fucking much he needed him.

"Mmmph," Nic moaned, rutting up against him so their cocks slid together, trapped between their bodies.

Fuck. As tempting as it was to get off with frotting again, sliding their manhoods together until they were hot and sticky and shaking with exhaustion, Kyle wanted—needed—to be inside Nic.

And Nic was already fumbling for the lube, his fingers sliding between his thighs. Kyle let him finger himself, casting an appreciative glance down.

"God, that's hot. I should watch you get yourself off more often," Kyle murmured.

Nic squirmed under his gaze and Kyle only stared harder. He felt so fucking possessive tonight. Nic was his, and his alone.

His protector, and his rock, and his dream, all in one. Here, under him, squirming and pulling his fingers out, giving him desperate eyes, waiting to be fucked.

Kyle bit back his whimper and kissed Nic hard, sucking on first the top lip and then the bottom, then running his tongue along it before pressing an open-mouthed kiss against his lips. All the while, he shifted until he was straddling Nic, their legs tangled and hands entwined.

How had that happened? Nic's fingers slotted perfectly between his, his palms pressing against his as he pushed their hands into the bed on either side of Nic's head.

"Nah!" Nic moaned sharply against his lips as he pushed against him, then inside. It took a thrust or two to get his hips angled right, but he was so fucking hard already—just one look at Nic was enough to have that effect on Kyle—that it was easy.

Everything was easy with Nic. And so damn *right*.

Kyle grunted in pleasure at the tight heat that wrapped around him, the friction as he pushed deep inside Nic's body. He wanted Nic to forget everything except his name.

"Kyle," Nic breathed out, his lips parting as he rolled his head back.

Kyle kissed up along his throat, savoring the burn of

stubble on his lips as he worked along his jaw to his ear, then licked and nibbled the earlobe as firmly as he dared.

Mine.

Kyle pulled back slowly and pushed in again, keeping his first few thrusts slow and shallow to open him up and get him ready for him.

"Yes" and "fuck" were Nic's most frequent refrains. He kept shuddering under Kyle with each thrust, especially since his cock bumped and ground Kyle's stomach.

And how fucking hot was that? He'd felt it inside him, shallow but exactly what he wanted, the head just deep enough to tease his prostate but not grind it during his post-orgasm sensitivity.

Even better: Nic's body wrapped around him as Nic's muscles strained to pull them so tight together their skin burned; Nic's desperate panting breaths in his ears; Nic's tiny sounds of need and pleasure as he came hard; Nic erratically, quickly, wetly thrusting inside Kyle... every goddamn detail was burned into Kyle's brain.

And Nic had trusted him enough to talk about what he wanted. Fuck, Kyle would be there for whatever the hell he had to do, and he'd love every inch of Nic along the way. The couple he had now, the couple more he was going to add... it was all part of him, and Kyle loved the package.

Love.

The word rang in his own ears, but he swallowed it and pushed hard into Nic, the bed shaking. It was fucking, screwing until he couldn't think straight, but it was more than that.

He couldn't stop kissing Nic, and though Nic's eyes were half-closed, they weren't breaking their gaze. They studied every second of each other's pleasure, and Nic's hands were tight against Kyle's.

This was making love, hard and fast and *raw*.

Raw not because they'd foregone condoms lately after agreeing they weren't fucking anyone else anyway, but because of something else.

Kyle felt like every inch of his soul was on display to Nic's piercing gaze, and he *liked* it.

"Oh, God. I'm gonna come," Nic moaned. The angle, his knees pushed up, was perfect for him to grind against Kyle, and that was exactly what he'd been doing with every thrust. "Hard, baby...!"

Kyle swallowed Nic's moan with another hard, open-mouthed kiss as he slammed their hips together, sweat beading between their chests as their skin pressed and stuck to skin.

Nic caught his breath and choked for a moment, squeezing his eyes closed at last, and Kyle kept kissing his neck and shoulder and ear to give him every little extra bit of sensation he could.

"*Fuck!*" Nic's hands shuddered in Kyle's, his fingers trembling and arms jerking, and the rest of him was pushing up into Kyle, seizing up tightly, clenching around Kyle...

Kyle hit the edge of pleasure at the same moment, the hard squeezes around his sensitive shaft impossible to ignore. He couldn't hold back.

"Yes...!" he moaned against Nic's lips, gasping as heat rushed through him and into Nic's tight, perfect ass. He kept their stomachs pressed together hard, grinding against Nic as they came. "Nic!"

Nic was whimpering his name, trembling under and around him, and all Kyle wanted to do was wrap himself around him and stay exactly like this forever—in him, their bodies locked together and burning with need for each other.

Forever.

Kyle barely remembered hitting the bed afterward, but Nic curled into him and wrapped all his limbs around him, and they didn't need to say another word.

44

KYLE

Yesterday—the fight, Hank's arrest, everything but the mind-blowing sex—was a hazy bad dream in comparison to the day Kyle was enjoying now.

He, Nic, and Kevin were all out together, and they were going to see Uncle River, whom Kevin both idolized and adored. No matter what had happened less than twenty-four hours ago, life felt peaceful and basically perfect.

It helped that he and Nic had talked that morning. It hadn't been the big conversation he'd pictured—it had been the simplest, easiest chat in the world.

Yes, Kyle wanted to move in with Nic.

Yes, they were officially boyfriends. They had been, informally, for a while, but they both wanted to make sure the other was okay with the word.

And most of all...

Yes, he wanted Nic to coparent, now that he was certain Nic wanted that, too.

His cellphone rang just as they made it to River's house, so

Kyle waved his boyfriend and son ahead. "I'll be inside in a minute. I gotta take this."

It was Denver, after all, and Kyle couldn't miss that call.

He leaned against his car as he answered, watching River open the door and sweep Kevin off his feet while Kevin giggled, then kiss Nic's cheeks.

"Hey, Kyle. How are you?"

"Doing okay. You? Is there news?"

Denver chuckled. "Yeah, lots of news. Are you sitting down?"

Kyle squinted at the car hood, which would be too hot for sitting. Leaning would have to do. "Pretty much. Why?"

"First, the bad news. We've finalized the arrangements for our temporary office, so you'll need to come back to work."

"Oh, thank God."

"Only you would be glad for that," Denver teased. "Nerd. Or workaholic. Or both..."

Kyle snorted. "Nah, I just miss the pizza."

Denver laughed. "I should also say, the board was so impressed with your presentation, and your quick thinking during the fire, and your overtime you've been trying to sneakily get away with since then... You're effectively getting a promotion to a job title that reflects the work you actually do, and we're working on a pay raise effective as soon as possible, and retroactively."

Kyle's jaw dropped, and he suddenly lost the ability to talk for a moment. The job title was good for his resume, but more money would make a big difference to his quality of life.

And if he moved in with Nic, like they'd loosely discussed that morning before leaving to pick up Kevin... well, that would help, too.

"Thanks," was all he managed.

Denver's voice was warm. "Of course. Finally, I have news on Hank. He rolled on the other guys who were responsible for the events of that night. They're all going to be punished—the cops are assuring us of that. No way will they get a slap on the wrist."

"Thank God," Kyle breathed out. "So we're all safe?"

"You're safe... and you can move back home. That is, if you still want to," Denver said, his voice light and teasing.

Kyle blushed as he wandered closer to the house and pulled open the door for a peek.

His best friend, his son, and his boyfriend were all laughing inside. Kevin was on the floor telling a story while Nic and River looked at eyeshadow palettes. Everyone was getting along like... well... like a house on fire.

Kyle snorted at his choice of metaphor, but his heart was warm.

"I don't think I do, actually. More on that soon," Kyle told Denver, keeping his voice down so he didn't disturb them.

"I can't wait to hear. I'm happy for you, Kyle. You deserve this."

Kyle blinked back the tears. "Thanks. Talk to you soon, Denver."

He hung up and slipped inside, closing the door quietly behind him. Nic was standing in the bathroom doorway now, no doubt watching River apply some kind of makeup.

Kyle came up behind him and slid his arm around his waist. As Nic leaned back into him and smiled, Kyle murmured, "I love you."

Nic stiffened and drew a quick breath of surprise, turning toward him. His eyes told the whole story. Kyle knew him well enough for that by now.

You do? Are you sure? Are you ready? All the questions Nic wanted to ask, but no words would satisfy him.

In answer, Kyle just kissed Nic gently until their knees went weak, ignoring River's teasing groan and his son's laughter.

It was the truth, and that was all they needed together.

Forever.

EPILOGUE

NIC, TWO MONTHS LATER

The party was in full swing, and so was Nic. Every time Kyle spun him across the makeshift dance floor in the middle of the new office, Nic's kilt flared out and they both laughed.

The charity had rebounded quickly once the insurance money came through, and they'd gotten several offers from landlords who *wanted* them there.

Their new building wasn't much fancier than the old one, but it was more secure, and more importantly, they were in the same building as several other LGBT organizations. The pizza parties were going to be awesome.

Nic grinned as Kyle spun him toward him again. "I'm beginning to think you just want to get an up-kilt peek."

"Guilty," Kyle teased, wrapping his arm around Nic's waist. "Can you blame a man?"

"You have a lifetime to get an up-kilt peek," Nic reminded him.

"I know. But I want one tonight. Will this help?" Kyle held out another glass of punch.

"Maybe." Nic held up his finger to Kyle, then waved River

over to them. "How long-lasting is this lipstick supposed to be?"

River winked playfully at him. "Ben or Ash could wear it and probably have some left at the end of the night. You two? I dunno. It'll be a challenge."

"Are you saying we're making out too much?" Nic grinned, leaning into Kyle. "Even more than they do? Impossible."

"Never," River snickered. "Just that Kyle's wearing about as much of it now as you are."

Nic pretended to gasp, then shrugged and took the cup of punch. "No harm, then." He was more outgoing now, unbuttoned in public, and it showed in the way people reacted to him. "So, you didn't bring *your* boy toy?"

River looked sheepish now and cleared his throat. "Er, no. Scheduling thing. And he's not *my* boy toy..."

"I'm starting to think he can dish it but he can't take it." Kyle shook his head at his best friend. "And he still won't tell us anything. We need to redouble our investigation."

"This isn't about me." River clicked his tongue. "This is a celebration of your office, and the two of you. You've come so far!" He beamed at them both, and Nic was totally willing to let him change the subject.

Nic flushed with pleasure. River was right. His phallo surgery was scheduled, and they'd talked about parenting. Since Kyle had learned that Nic would officially adopt Kevin if they ever *did* happen to get married, he'd started dropping hints about proposing. For his part, Nic would have been ready to say yes months ago.

Denver clapped his hands for the shortest-ever speech about the future of the charity, thanking Nic for his work on the software and database that made their work lives so much easier now and Kyle for being the best right-hand man he could ask for.

The whole time, Nic glowed as brightly as Kyle. He could feel eyes on them both, and he didn't mind one bit.

For the first time in his life, he had a future that he couldn't wait to see.

All was well.

FREAK (F-WORD #2)

Five years ago, Zeph met River. The timing couldn't have been worse. An orphan with something to prove and the ghosts of his past breathing down his neck, Zeph took the offer from a pro MMA gym to live and train in the Midwest. River let him go easily. If it was a convenient excuse to escape emotional intimacy, neither of them had to admit it. Until now.

Drag queen and makeup artist River isn't easily fazed, but meeting Zeph on his home turf throws him for a loop. Something about Zeph still gets under his skin. And River's next job, a drag show in L.A. and Vegas, will require a security guy to look after the performers. Who better than a tattooed mixed martial artist who still gives him smoldering looks?

It doesn't take long for them to fall together. They're opposite as can be, but dating for ten days wasn't long enough the first time around. Another ten days could get it out of their systems... but are they fighting for or with each other? It's easy to get hard. It's hard to be easy. Vulnerability is off the table, until the table turns. How long do you have to have known a guy to put your life into his hands?

AUTHOR BIOGRAPHY

E. Davies grew up moving constantly, which taught him what people have in common, the ways relationships are formed, and the dangers of "miscellaneous" boxes. As a young gay author, Ed prefers to tell feel-good stories that are brimming with hope.

He writes full-time, goes on long nature walks, tries to fill his passport, drinks piña coladas on the beach, flees from cute guys, coos over fuzzy animals (especially bees), and is liable to tilt his head and click his tongue if you don't use your turn signal.

facebook.com/edaviesbooks

twitter.com/edaviesauthor

instagram.com/thisboyisstrange

bookbub.com/authors/e-davies

Brooklyn Boys

Electric Sunshine

Live Wire

Boiling Point

F-Word

Flaunt

Freak

Faux

Forever

After

Afterburn

Afterglow

Aftermath

Men of Hidden Creek

Shelter

Adore

Miracle

Redemption

Audiobooks

You can see all my books available in audio here:
edaviesbooks.com/audiobooks